Lost & Found

Brooke Davis grew up in Bellbrae, Australia, and now lives in Perth, where she works as a bookseller. She is a graduate of the University of Canberra and Curtin University. *Lost & Found* is her first novel and has been published in over twenty-five countries. It was a number one bestseller in Australia and won Fiction Book of the Year at the Australian Book Industry Awards 2015.

Praise for *Lost & Found*

'Uproarious and affecting . . . eccentric and sympathetic . . . *Lost & Found* could be ginormous.'

Independent

'[An] eccentric road-trip debut . . . There is no doubting Davis's talent for characterisation or her gifts of description.'

Sunday Times

'Both hilarious and devastating. This is a story of loss and hope with one of the most vivid casts of characters I've come across. In particular, it is red wellied, seven-year-old Millie our heart weeps and soars for. A great read with ballsy, brilliant writing. A joy.'

Matt Haig, author of *The Humans*

‘A poignant debut … the emotion threaded through Davis’ story of loss and grief and hope is real.’

New York Times

‘Here is a mercurial talent . . . completely authentic and real . . . Seven-year-old Millie doesn’t just tug at the heart strings, she rips them right out . . . A rich and distinctive debut.’

We Love This Book

‘Thought-provoking and eloquent . . . A very special book that will stay in your heart long after reading.’

Heat

‘An unexpectedly uplifting book about death, grief and growing old . . . *Lost & Found* is an off-kilter glimpse of Australia that builds to a life-affirming climax.’

Sunday Express

‘A *Wizard of Oz*-esque journey . . . there’s a lot of warmth, wisdom and humour.’

Daily Mail

‘A novel that dances on the wire between heartache and joy.’

West Australian

‘Offbeat and funny . . . painfully, tenderly observant . . . [as] three lonely grief-stricken misfits find one another.’

The Times

'An exuberant and cheering tale that will stay with you long after the last page.'

The Lady

'Brilliantly written . . . This is a special, unique story; a novel to cheer you up, make you laugh and even make you tear up at the end. Already a bestseller abroad, *Lost & Found* deserves to fly off the shelves in the UK too.'

Running in Heels

'[An] enchanting debut.'

Vanity Fair

'A charmingly quirky story . . . Hugely funny.'

Image

'A fantastic debut, which was hard to put down. The author has managed to write a touching and heart-warming tale, which will melt even the hardest of hearts.'

Novelicious

'Extraordinary, moving and laced with *Amélie*-style wonderment.'

Sainsbury's Magazine

'The whimsical writing and surprising storyline hooked us immediately . . . A candid look at life, death and everything in between.'

Woman's Day

'Everything about the characters and the writing feels right, and the result is a book that's heartbreaking, funny and brilliant.'

Courier Mail

'The book has been compared to *The Unlikely Pilgrimage of Harold Fry*, and like that much-discussed novel, it pulls back the veil on the inner lives of older people in a way that is both amusing and moving.'

Women24

Lost & Found

Brooke Davis

WINDMILL BOOKS

1 3 5 7 9 10 8 6 4 2

Windmill Books
20 Vauxhall Bridge Road
London SW1V 2SA

Windmill Books is part of the Penguin Random House group of companies whose addresses can be found at global.penguinrandomhouse.com.

Penguin Random House UK

First published in Australia and New Zealand by Hachette Australia in 2014

First published in Great Britain by Hutchinson in 2015
First published in paperback by Windmill Books in 2015

www.windmill-books.co.uk

A CIP catalogue record for this book is available from the British Library.

ISBN 9780099592297

Typeset by Bookhouse, Sydney
Designed by Lindsay Nash

Printed and bound by CPI Group (UK) Ltd, Croydon, CR0 4YY

FSC www.fsc.org MIX Paper from responsible sources FSC® C018179

Penguin Random House is committed to a sustainable future for our business, our readers and our planet. This book is made from Forest Stewardship Council® certified paper.

For Mum and Dad

I don't know how else to thank you for making me

part one

millie bird

Millie's dog, Rambo, was her Very First Dead Thing. She found him by the side of the road on a morning when the sky seemed to be falling, fog circling his broken shape like a ghost. His jaw and eyes were wide open, as if mid-bark. His left hind leg pointed in a direction it normally didn't. The fog lifted around them, the clouds gathered in the sky, and she wondered if he was turning into rain.

It was only when she dragged Rambo up to the house in her schoolbag that her mother thought to tell her how the world worked.

He's gone to a better place, her mother shouted at her while vacuuming the lounge room.

A better place?

What? Yes, heaven, love, haven't you heard of it? Don't they teach you anything in that bloody school? Lift your legs! It's doggy heaven, where there's eternal dog biscuits and they can poop wherever they please. Okay, legs down. I said, legs down! And they poop, I don't know, dog biscuits, so all they do is poop and eat dog biscuits, and run around and eat the other dogs' poop. Which are actually dog biscuits.

Millie took a moment. *Why would they waste time here, then?*

What? Well, they, um, have to earn it. They have to stay here until they get voted over to a better place. Like doggy Survivor.

So, is Rambo on another planet?

Well, yes. Sort of. I mean – you really haven't heard of heaven? How God sits up in the clouds and Satan's all underground and everything?

Can I get to Rambo's new planet?

Her mother switched off the vacuum cleaner and looked squarely at Millie. *Only if you have a spaceship. Do you have a spaceship?*

Millie looked at her feet. *No.*

Well, you can't get to Rambo's new planet then.

Days later, Millie discovered that Rambo was most definitely not on a new planet and was, in fact, in their backyard, buried halfheartedly under the *Sunday Times*. Millie carefully lifted the newspaper and saw Rambo but not-Rambo; a Rambo shrunken and eaten and wasting away. She snuck out every night from then on, to be with him while his body went from something into nothing.

The old man crossing the road had been her Second Dead

Thing. After the car hit him, she watched him fly through the air and thought she saw him smile. His hat landed on top of the yield sign and his walking stick danced around the lamppost. And then it had been his body, cracking against the curb. She pushed her way through all the legs and exclamation marks to kneel beside his face. She looked deeply into his eyes. He looked back at her like he was only a drawing. She ran her fingers over his wrinkles and wondered what he'd used each one for.

She was then lifted away from him and told to cover her eyes, because she was *just a child.* And as she wandered home the long way, she thought it might be time to ask her dad about people heaven.

You see, Squirt, there's heaven, and then there's hell. Hell is where they send all the bad people, like criminals and con artists and parking inspectors. And heaven is where they send all the good people, like you and me and that nice blonde from MasterChef.

What happens when you get there?

In heaven, you hang out with God and Jimi Hendrix, and you get to eat doughnuts whenever you want. In hell, you have to, uh . . . do the Macarena. Forever. To that "Grease Megamix."

Where do you go if you're good and bad?

What? I don't know. IKEA?

Will you help me make a spaceship?

Hang on, Squirt. Can we finish this next ad break?

She soon noticed that everything was dying around her.

Bugs and oranges and Christmas trees and houses and mailboxes and train rides and markers and candles and old people and young people and people in between. She wasn't to know that after she had recorded twenty-seven assorted creatures in her Book Of Dead Things – Spider, The Bird, Grandma, next door's cat Gertrude, among others – her dad would be a Dead Thing too. That she'd write it next to the number twenty-eight in letters so big they took up two pages: *MY DAD*. That, for a while, it was hard to know what to do other than stare at the letters until she couldn't remember what they meant. That she would do this, by flashlight, sitting in the hallway outside her parents' bedroom, listening to her mum pretending she was asleep.

the first day of waiting

When playing connect the dots, Millie was always Dot One, her mum Dot Two, and her dad Dot Three. The line came from deep inside Dot One's belly, wrapped itself around Dot Two and Dot Three – usually watching the telly – and back again, to make a triangle. Millie would run around the house, her red hair bouncing about her head, the triangle between them spiraling around the furniture. When her mum said, *Would you stop that, Millicent?*, the triangle roared into an enormous dinosaur. When her dad said, *Come sit beside me, Squirt*, the triangle curled into a big, beating heart. *Ba-boom. Ba-boom,* she whispered, skipping awkwardly to its rhythm. She nestled in between Dots Two and Three on the couch. Dot Three grabbed Dot One's hand and winked. The flashing pictures from the telly lit up his face in the dark. *Ba-boom. Ba-boom. Ba-boom.*

On The First Day Of Waiting, Millie stands exactly where her mum points to. Right near the Ginormous Women's Underwear and across from the mannequin wearing the Hawaiian shirt. *I'll be right back,* her mum says, and Millie believes her. Dot Two wears her gold shoes, the ones that make her footsteps like explosions. She walks toward the perfumes – *Kaboom!* – past the menswear – *Kablammo!* – and out of sight: *Kapow!* The line between Dot One and Dot Two tugs and pulls, and Millie watches it getting thinner and thinner, until it is just a tiny scratch on the air.

Ba-boom. Ba-boom. Ba-boom.

Millie will carry this around with her from now on, this picture of her mum getting smaller and smaller and smaller. It will reappear behind her eyes at different times throughout the course of her life. When movie characters say, *I'll be right back.* When, in her forties, she looks at her hands and doesn't recognise them as her own. When she has a stupid question and can't think of anyone in the world to ask. When she cries. When she laughs. When she hopes for something. Every time she watches the sun disappear into the water she will feel a little panicked and not know why. The automatic doors of shopping centres will always make her anxious. When a boy touches her properly for the first time, she will imagine him shrinking into the horizon, far, far, far out of her reach.

But she doesn't know any of this yet.

What she does know, right now, is that her legs ache from standing. She takes off her backpack and crawls underneath the Ginormous Women's Underwear clothing rack. Her mum said there are women who can't see their privates because they eat entire buckets of chicken. Maybe these undies are for them. Millie has never seen chicken come in a bucket. *But I hope to,* she says out loud, touching the undies softly. *One day.*

It's nice in there, under the giant undies. They hang low around her head, so close to her face that she breathes on them.

She unzips her backpack and pulls out one of the frozen juice boxes her mum has packed for her. She sucks at it through the straw. In the cracks between the undies, she watches feet going for walks. Some going somewhere, others going nowhere, some dancing, others skipping, shuffling, squeaking. Tiny feet, big feet, in-between feet. Sneakers, high heels, sandals. Red shoes, black shoes, green shoes. But no gold shoes. No explosion footsteps.

A pair of bright-blue gumboots plods past. She looks down at hers. *I know you're jealous,* she says to them. *But we need to stay here. Mum said.* She cranes her neck to watch the gumboots jump down the aisle and off into the toy section. *Well,* she says. She pulls out her Book Of Dead Things from her backpack, rips out a sheet of paper, writes *To Mum, I'll Be Right Back,* folds it in half, and props it up on the ground exactly where her mum had pointed to.

She takes her gumboots for a walk. Up and down the escalators, walking at first, then jumping, hopping, and waving like the queen. She sits at the top and watches the steps swallow themselves. *What happens if the stairs don't flatten themselves in time?* she asks her gumboots. She imagines the stairs spilling out over the escalator and into the aisles. She tries to connect eyes with every single person who walks past her, and each time she does, the air jumps in front of her like the old movies her mum watches. She plays hide-and-seek with a boy who doesn't know he's playing. When Millie informs him that he is *found,* he responds by asking her why her hair is *like that,* and makes spirals with his index finger.

They're ballerinas, she says. *They jump off my head at night and do shows for me.*

Pff, he says, and smashes a Barbie headlong into a Transformer, making a spitty blowing-up sound with his mouth at the same time. *They do not.*

Millie sits on the floor of the women's changing room. *I know where you can get some undies,* she says to one woman who's turning around and around in front of a mirror like she's trying to drill herself into the ground. *Sorry, who are you?* the woman says. Millie shrugs. Two ladies talk behind the door of one of the cubicles. Millie can see their feet in the gap between the door and the floor. Bare feet and sparkly UGG boots. *Don't take this the wrong way,* the UGG boots seem to say. *But do you really think coral is your colour?* The toes on the bare feet curl under themselves. *I thought this was pink,* they seem to say back.

Millie waits with the waiting men, who wait in chairs outside the changing rooms, waiting for women, peering from behind purses and shopping bags like frightened animals. The walls nearby are covered with huge pictures of girls laughing and hugging each other in their underwear. The waiting men sneak glances at them. It occurs to Millie that the giant undies could be for these giant girls.

She sits on a chair next to a bald man biting his fingernails.

Have you ever seen chicken come in a bucket? she asks.

He rests his hand on his knee and looks at her out of the corner of his eye. *I'm just waiting for my wife, kid,* he says.

She stands under the hand dryers in the toilets, because she likes the feeling of the wind whooshing through her hair, as though she's leaning her head out of a car window on the highway, or like she's Superman, circling the Earth. How does the hand dryer know to start as soon as you stick your hands out? It is amazing, this, but the women in the toilets don't notice, and just stare, panicked, into the mirror, trying to work out what's wrong with them before anyone else does.

Sitting behind the plants on the edge of the department-store café, she watches steam rising from coffee mugs. The man who looks like Santa and the lady with the very, very red cheeks lean over their coffees toward each other. They don't say anything but the steam from their coffee kisses and dances around their faces and above their heads. Another man eats while not looking at his wife and has coffee steam that makes the most beautiful shapes in the air. Millie has never seen shapes like this. Are there any more shapes left to make up? The woman with the shouty kids has a coffee that breathes in and out, letting out long, tired sighs.

There's a man in the corner with a tree-bark face. He's wearing red braces and a purple suit, holding on to his coffee cup with both hands, as if he's stopping it from flying away. A fly lands on the plant in front of her. *What if everything could fly?* she whispers to her gumboots, watching the fly bounce from leaf to leaf. Your dinner could fly into your mouth and the sky could be covered with trees and the streets might switch places, though some people would get seasick and planes wouldn't be that special anymore.

The tree-bark-face man blows on his coffee so hard that the liquid spills over the edge and the steam splits in half. Some shoots forward and some upward. He stares deep into the cup for a few minutes, then blows on it again.

He stands up. He has to plant both of his hands on the table and push himself up with everything he has. He walks straight past her, and Millie tries to connect eyes with him but he doesn't look up. The fly follows him, buzzing around his body. He reaches out a hand and slaps it against his thigh. The fly falls to the ground.

Millie crawls on her hands and knees toward the fly and scoops it into her palm. She holds it up to her face, squeezes her palm shut, and stands to watch the back of the tree-bark-face man as he shuffles away from the café and out the main entrance.

Millie finds her backpack underneath the Ginormous Women's Underwear. She takes out her Just In Case glass jar, puts it between her knees, unscrews the lid, and lowers the fly into the jar. She screws the lid back on and pulls out her Book Of Dead Things, as well as her markers. *Number 29,* she writes. *Fly in department store.* She can see *DAD* backward in big letters through the paper. She taps the marker on her gumboots. Picks up the jar and holds it to her face. In the crack between the undies the mannequin looks down at her from across the aisle. His shirt is bright blue and has yellow palm trees on it. His eyes seem huge through the glass, like they're centimetres from her face. She moves a pair of underwear so she can see only his knees.

Millie grips the jar while she watches for gold shoes all afternoon. And when afternoon becomes night, and the last door is clicked shut, and everything goes black – the air, the sound, the earth – it feels like the whole world is closing. She presses her face against the window, cups her hands around her eyes, and watches people walk back to their cars with other people, with husbands and wives and girlfriends and boyfriends and children and grandmothers and daughters and fathers and mothers. And they all drive off, every single one of them, until the parking lot is so empty it makes her eyes hurt.

She crawls back under the Ginormous Women's Underwear and takes a sandwich out of her backpack. As she eats it, she watches the mannequin through the gap in the undies. He watches back. *Hello,* she whispers. The only other sound, a humming from the lights in the display cabinets.

the second day of waiting

Millie once thought that no matter where you fell asleep, you would always wake up in your own bed. She fell asleep at the table, on the neighbor's floor, on a ride at the show, and when she woke she was under her own covers, looking up at the ceiling of her own bedroom. But one night she woke when she was being carried from the car into the house. She looked at her dad through half-closed eyes. *It's been you all this time,* she whispered into his shoulder.

On The Second Day Of Waiting, Millie wakes to the sound of high heels clacking toward her. She has spread herself out during the night, and her feet poke from underneath the clothing rack. She pulls her knees into her chest, hugs them, holds her breath, and watches the high heels clack past. *Click-clack, click-clack, click-clack.* They're black and shiny, and red-painted toes stick out at the ends like ladybugs trying to crawl in.

Why would her mum leave her under the undies all night? Millie holds on to her stomach and peers through the gap in the undies. She knows why her mum might leave her there but she doesn't want to think about it, so she doesn't. The mannequin is still looking at her. She waves at him. It's a careful wave, her fingers folding down one after the other until she holds them all in a fist. She's not sure if she wants to be his friend yet. She pulls on her gumboots, crawls out from under the undies, and looks up at the sign she stuck on the rack last night.

In Here Mum.

She tears it down, folds it up, and slides it into her back-pack. The man with the tree-bark face walks toward her. He shuffles down the aisle, straight past, and toward the café. Millie follows, and watches him from behind the pot plants. He sits down like it hurts, and stares at his coffee. Millie walks over to him and puts her hand on his.

Have you seen chicken come in a bucket? she asks.

The man looks at her hand and then up at her. *Yes,* he replies, pulling his hand away from hers and tapping his fingers on the table.

Well? Millie says, sitting down in the chair opposite him. *What's it like?*

Exactly how it sounds, he says.

Millie bites her bottom lip. *Do you know many people who are dead?* she asks.

Everyone, he says, looking into his coffee.

Everyone?

Yes. Do you? he asks, still tapping his fingers on the table.

Yes. Twenty-nine Dead Things, she says.

That's a lot.

Yep.

He leans forward in his chair. *How old are you?* he asks.

Millie crosses her arms. *How old are you?*

I asked first.

Let's say it at the same time.

Eighty-seven.

Seven.

He sits back in his chair. *Seven?*

Millie nods. *And a half. Almost eight, really.*

You're young.

You're old.

The dimples on his cheeks are waking up. *Your boots match my braces,* he says, tapping his fingers on his braces.

Your braces match my boots. Millie looks at his hands. *Why do you tap your fingers when you talk?*

I'm not tapping, he says, tapping. *I'm typing.*

Typing what?

Everything I say.

Everything you say?

Everything I say.

What about what I say?

I don't do that.

Are you gonna eat that? she says, pointing to a muffin. He pushes the plate toward her.

Millie shoves the muffin into her mouth. *Why won't you drink your coffee?* she says, mouth full, pushing his coffee toward him.

I don't want it. He pushes it back.

Millie wraps her hands around it and leans over it, feeling the steam rising beneath her chin. *Why did you get it?*

It's nice to have somewhere to put my hands.

Millie smiles. *Oh*. She pulls her feet up onto the chair and rests her chin on her knees. Spread out on the table is a long line of small plastic squares, each one about the size of her fingertip. *What are those?*

He shrugs.

You don't know?

He shrugs again.

Millie leans over the table. *They're computer keys,* she says. *Like the ones on the keyboards from school*. She folds her arms. *But they're not on a keyboard.*

Yes, he says.

So you do know, she says.

They're all dashes. From different keyboards. He leans forward in his chair. *Do you know what a dash is?*

Maybe.

You put them between two words to make one word.

Like what?

Like . . . He thinks for a moment.

Happy-sad? Millie says.

Not really.

Hungry-sleepy?

No, he says. *Like, action-packed. Or blue-eyed.*

But not happy-sad.

No.

Or hungry-sleepy?

No.

Why have you got so many? There's lots of them lined up against each other in a long, straight line.

I collect them.

Why?

Got to collect something.

Millie thinks about her Book Of Dead Things. *I collect Dead Things,* she says.

He nods.

She holds his gaze as she nudges an index finger forward, moving one of the keys out of line. It hangs above the rest of them on an angle like it's mid-backflip. Tree-Bark-Face doesn't move. *They go between numbers, too,* she says. *Not just words.* She flicks another key and it skids along the table, stopping at the edge. He sucks in a breath and watches as it teeters and then falls into his lap.

Don't do that, he says, picking it up and putting it back in line.

Where did you get them all from?

Borrowed them.

From who? Millie spots a screwdriver sticking out of his jacket pocket.

He puts a hand over the screwdriver, shielding it from Millie's gaze. *No one ever suspects an old person,* he says, smiling a half smile. *We're kind of invisible.*

What's your name?

Karl the Touch Typist. What's yours?

Just Millie.

Where's your mum, Just Millie?

She's coming. She has gold shoes. It is when she says *gold shoes* that Millie feels Dot Two pulling and she holds her stomach. She shifts in her seat and puts the fly's glass jar on the table. *You made a Dead Thing yesterday.*

Karl picks up the glass jar and studies it. *I did?* he says, tapping the glass.

Millie nods. *I'm giving her a funeral.*

The first funeral Millie ever held was for a spider her dad squished with his shoe. Her mum had jumped from one foot to the other and said, *If you don't squash that spider, Harry, I'll squash you.* Her dad stood up from his chair, wrenched off his shoe, and slammed it against the wall.

One.

Two.

Three.

Four.

The spider slid down the wall and landed on the floor. Her dad picked it up by a leg, threw it out the front door, sat down, and continued watching television. He winked at Millie from across the room. Millie couldn't bring herself to wink back.

She watched her dad watch three whole shows before she said anything.

Can we give the spider a funeral? she said as the credits rolled. *Like we did for Nan.*

Funerals are for people, Mills, he said, flicking through the channels. *And maybe dogs.*

What about horses?

Horses, too, he said as a cricketer tried to sell him some vitamins.

Cats?

Yes.

Snakes?

No.

Why?

Because. On the screen a car wound its way along a beautiful mountainside. The whole family smiled at each other. They all had shiny teeth.

Trees?

No.

Why?

Because.

Centipedes? Planets? Fridges?

Millie! he said. *People. Maybe big animals. That's it.*

Why?

You'd be having funerals all day, every day. And we can't do that.

Why?

There's other stuff to do, he said as a man on the screen looked her in the eye and yelled at her about mobile phones.

That night, she packed a backpack with everything she needed, grabbed her flashlight from under the bed, and snuck out the front door. She found the spider on the grass near the driveway and picked it up with both hands. It looked different now, smaller and lighter and dried up by the sun. The night breeze circled around her hands and made the spider tickle her palms.

A huge *whoosh* of wind lifted the spider right out of her hands. Millie ran after it, watching it high above her head. It flew through the air against the stars, over her front yard, out into the street, across the road, down the street, and into an empty lot. The moonlight illuminated its edges. The whole night seemed to be covered with moonlit spiders far, far away, pinned to the black sky.

Then, just as quickly as it began, the wind stopped, and the spider dropped to the ground like a falling star.

A tree rose out of the centre of the empty lot. It was the biggest tree she had ever seen, much bigger than even her dad. She put the spider into her backpack and climbed to the very top. The moon felt so close she could almost spin it around in circles. She straddled the branch, leaned her back into the trunk and, from her backpack, pulled out the spider, an old Vegemite jar, a ball of string, a tealight candle, matches, and a piece of cardboard.

Millie gave the spider one last look before placing him in the Vegemite jar on top of some tissues. She lit the tealight candle and put it in there with him, then wrapped a piece of string around the top of the jar, tied a knot at one end, and threaded the other end through the hole in the cardboard sign. She tied the string around the branch of the tree. The jar hung from the branch like a lantern, swinging a little as the tree moved. The small cardboard sign said *Spider ?–2011* in her best writing.

Millie ran her fingers over the line in between the question mark and Spider's death-year. Back and forth, back and forth. It was strange, she thought, that this line – this long, straight line – was all there was to show of his whole life.

karl the touch typist

here's what karl knows about funerals

Karl had never talked to Evie about her funeral. Why would he? It was too hard to get the words out. They were like a weight in his mouth. He just wanted her to live while he was living and that's all he knew.

So his son organized it for him, while Karl was busy remembering how to get up, brush his teeth, part his hair, chew. The funeral itself had been long, slow, repetitive. Before the service began, he was hugged, endlessly, by people he barely knew. He made sure their cheeks didn't touch. It didn't feel right to rest his palms on the back of someone who wasn't his wife.

Karl sat in the front pew, eyeing the coffin, scarcely breathing. It felt strange to breathe when she couldn't. Flowers exploded from the coffin lid. He willed the coffin to open, Evie to jump out: *Surprise!* She would have to high-jump the flowers.

If this is a practical joke, he whispered, *I won't be mad.*

He remembers standing during one of the eulogies. It was by the only friend from Evie's old work still alive. They kept dying, all their friends, as though they were on a battlefield: dropping dead in supermarkets, on bowling greens; fading out in nursing homes and hospitals. But this woman was still alive, standing at the lectern like God's gift, and Karl thought, *I wish you were dead.*

He walked toward the coffin. *Evie,* he whispered, circling it and running his fingers along the edges. People were murmuring around him, but they sounded miles away. He pushed his face into the pine lid. Closed his eyes. Breathed in. *Evie,* he whispered again, his lips against the pine. He had to know. He grabbed at the lid. And flung the coffin open.

She was dead in there, that was for sure, stone-faced in a way he had never seen, but he couldn't take his hands away from the edge of her coffin. Not when the priest tugged at his elbow; not when a gust of wind blew in through the doorway; not when the coffin lid slammed shut with such drama and force that it squashed his fingers. He didn't feel the pain because there was pain everywhere already.

And he wanted to type it but they wouldn't let him because they were holding his hands to stop the blood so he just yelled it, he yelled it as loud as he could.

I AM HERE, EVIE. I WILL ALWAYS BE HERE.

millie bird

The tops of some of your fingers are missing, Millie says, grabbing Karl's hand as they walk out of the café.

Yes, he replies, tapping on her hand. *They are.*

His mouth makes that line that adults make when they are most absolutely not going to talk about this one thing right now, and maybe not ever. So she keeps her questions inside herself and puts them in the part that remembers things for later. She rubs the stubs of his fingers as she holds his hand. Did he bite his nails so much that he bit his fingers right off? Did a family of mice eat them in his sleep? Or did someone chop them off because he didn't do what he was told? Millie's mum threatened her with that once, Millie remembers, when she was tapping her fingers on her dinner plate during *Dancing with the Stars. I'll rip those things right off,* her mum said, without turning around to face her. *Don't try me.* And Millie didn't try her – she hadn't meant to try her – and sat on her fingers so they wouldn't try anyone without her knowing.

Millie leads Karl to the Ginormous Women's Underwear, shakes off his hand, and crawls underneath. She slides the undies down the rack so Karl can see in.

What are you up to down there, Just Millie? he says.

I told you, she says, unscrewing the lid of the glass jar. Millie unzips her backpack and pulls out her Funeral Pencil Case. She removes a tealight candle and some matches and places them on the floor. She stares at them. After a moment, she holds them up to Karl. *Could you? Please?*

He glances around him. *Should we be lighting fires?*

Yes, she says.

Karl seems to consider this answer, then nods. Millie watches the wick catch fire and holds her stomach. She clenches her teeth and tries not to remember The Night Before The First Day Of Waiting. She tries to put it in the part of her head that never remembers anything. She hands Karl the jar. *In there, please,* she says.

Karl carefully lowers the candle into the jar and hands it back to Millie. She ties the jar to the rack, and the fly dangles behind a row of flesh-coloured undies.

You need to say something, she says to Karl.

Me? Karl says, pointing to himself.

Yes, you, Millie says, pointing at him pointing to himself. *You did it. You made a Dead Thing. Aren't you sorry?* Her head detaches itself and she's watching her dad squish the spider with his shoe. Was he sorry?

Of course, Karl says, putting his hands on his hips. *Of course*, he repeats. *But*, he says, taking a big breath, *it's a fly*.

Yes. Millie nods. *You're right. It is a fly*.

Karl looks down at Millie. Millie looks up at Karl.

Karl sighs. *What should I say?*

What would you like someone to say at your funeral?

Karl stares at his feet. *I doubt anyone will say anything*.

Well, Millie says, crossing her arms, *you need to say something*.

Why do you know so much about these things?

Why don't you? she says.

a fact about the world millie knows for sure

Everyone knows everything about being born, and no one knows anything about being dead.

This has always surprised Millie. There are books at school with pictures of mums with see-through stomachs, and she has always wanted to lift up the shirt of a pregnant lady, just to see if it really is true that your stomach goes see-through when you are pregnant. This makes sense, she thinks, to give the baby a chance to get used to the world before it is in it, like a glass-bottomed boat; otherwise, what a shock! How scary the world would be if you didn't know it was coming. Millie has also seen the books with the cartoon people who love each other so much that the man gives the lady a fish and the fish gets inside the lady and lays eggs, and those eggs turn into a human baby. She knows the baby comes out from the place you pee, but she has not seen pictures of this. After Millie goes swimming in the ocean, she always watches her pee carefully for babies. Just. In. Case.

Adults want her to know these things, otherwise they wouldn't have given her these books. But no one has ever, ever given her a book about Dead Things. What is the big secret?

Okay, Karl says. *The Fly, loved by many, forgotten by none.* He clears his throat. *God save our gracious queen,* he sings, so softly that Millie can barely hear him.

Louder, Millie says, and he does: *Long live our noble queen, God save the queen.* Millie watches the feet walk past through the gap in the undies as he sings. Some of them speed up as they get closer, some of them slow down. One pair of shoes stops completely. *Send her victorious* – he's really belting it out now, and his dimples are waking up again – *happy and glorious, long to reign over us.* Karl raises his arms with a flourish, his fingers typing in the air. *God save the queen.* He takes a bow. The shoes – wide, black, clumpy – are still there in the aisle, and one foot is tapping. Millie brings her knees to her chest.

Are you quite done, sir? a woman's voice says.

Karl looks in the general direction of the shoes. His eyes widen. *Yes, thank you, sir. I mean, ma'am.*

Arms grab at Karl, push him down the aisle, and the woman says, *Let's go,* and Karl says, *I'm terribly sorry, I really didn't mean to say that. I'm not intimating that you in any way resemble a man!*

Millie leans her body into the pole in the centre of the rack. Karl says, *You're very ladylikc, honestly.* And then, *Excuse me,* over and over again until she can't hear him anymore.

A lady nearby says, *What's all the hoopla about?* Millie mouths, *Hoopla,* as she packs up her Funeral Equipment. She pulls her backpack in close and makes her body as small as it can be, like the babies do when they're stuck in their mums' tummies. She presses her face against the metal pole. It's cold on her cheek. The fly's jar swings in some imaginary breeze, the candlelight making trails that disappear and reappear. She runs her fingers through the air, and it feels like nothing, but it's keeping everyone alive.

How can that feel like nothing?

Through the gap in the undies, the mannequin's still looking at her, and she looks back. She likes the way he is always looking at her. It makes her feel like he won't let the clumpy shoes take Millie away too.

Millie sits in this position until it's night in the department store again. Her feet sweat in her gumboots. Her knees stick together. The light in the jar is still burning, but only just, and the flickering shadows make the undies look like they're joining together at the edges, becoming one super-enormous-ginormous-pair-of-women's-undies, and The Super Pair Of Undies circles around her head, getting closer and closer, and Millie is sure it is going to wrap itself around her and suffocate her, and then the light in the jar goes out, and Millie is breathing in too much air, and her cheeks are wet with tears. She buries her face in her knees and squeezes her eyes shut.

She hears footsteps and thinks, *Gold shoes, gold shoes, gold shoes,* and her breath is so quivery, like the old people who breathe loudly just to let you know they still can, but it isn't her mum at all, because the footsteps are sliding along the floor, and Mum doesn't walk like that. The footsteps move toward her, and there's a flashlight shining everywhere, and now the flashlight is on the fly's jar, and the footsteps are so close to her, and the flashlight is still on the jar, and the footsteps have stopped altogether, and the flashlight is like a spotlight on the fly, like an alien spaceship trying to pull it up with a space beam, and Millie has to hold her quivery breath so that the alien beam doesn't get her as well.

But then there's something in the corner of her eye, a sparkle of something beyond the undies, and the mannequin looks at her, and his eyes seem wider for some reason, and there's something in her stomach, something pulling, and it feels like Dot Three, but that can't be right, and then the mannequin falls forward somehow, and the sliding feet yell, *Ow!*, and the flashlight clatters to the ground, and the mannequin is on the ground too, and he is still looking at her, and the flashlight lights him up, like he's onstage, and Millie feels a smile on her face just appear there, and she touches it with her fingers. She wants to touch the mannequin's face too, because he's smiling at her in the flashlight.

another fact about the world millie knows for sure

It's important to have your mum.

Mums bring you jackets and turn on your electric blanket before you get into bed and always know what you want better than you do. And they sometimes let you sit on their lap and play with the rings on their fingers while *Deal or No Deal* is on.

Millie's mum is a wind through the house. She is always washing overalls or ironing undies or wiping lamps or talking on the phone or sweeping the driveway or putting sheets on things. Her hair is always sweaty and kind of crooked, her voice is like a violin, like she is trying to lift something really heavy all the time. Millie is always getting in her way no matter how much she tries not to, so she has learned to sit against the walls and in corners, to stay outside, hide in bushes and up trees.

Sometimes, before she Goes Out, Millie's mum disappears into the bathroom for not very long at all. Millie listens at the door, and it sounds like a factory in there with all the clanging and spraying and squirting. Her mum always reappears with coloured-in skin and magazine hair. A sweet smell follows her like a smell-shadow.

One day when her mum went next door to talk to the neighbours, Millie kneeled on the bathroom floor and opened the cupboard under the sink. There were things that squeezed and things that poured. They were all so patient in there. She lined them up in a row on the cold tiles, from smallest to biggest. She looked at this audience of cosmetics for a long time. *Ahem,* she said to them.

She picked up a lipstick and painted her earlobes and sprayed perfume into the air over and over again, just to watch the mist of it, and brushed mascara on her cheeks, and rubbed blush on her fingernails. Her mum suddenly appeared in the doorway, and Millie tried to sit against the wall, out of her mum's way, but she grabbed Millie under the armpits, plonked her on the bench, and wiped her face clean with a cloth. She brushed her hair straight, put lipstick on her lips, something on her eyelashes and something on her cheeks. Her mum was so close to her, and her voice was smiling when she swiveled Millie around to look at herself in the mirror. *See?* And Millie did see, she saw that she could be a different person if she wanted. New and Improved.

Now, on her Second Night Of Waiting, Millie decides to make herself New and Improved. She wants her mum to walk up to her and say, *Excuse me, madam, but I'm looking for a small child. Have you seen her?* And Millie will take off her hat and wipe her lipstick on the back of her hand and say, *Mum! It's me! Millie Bird!* And her mum will laugh and scoop her up and carry her out to the car, and Millie will wave good-bye to the department store. *Bye, café; bye, giant undies; bye, pot plants; bye, Karl; bye, mannequin,* and her mum will drive her back home and Millie will get to sit on the kitchen counter while they cut up vegetables for dinner.

So she finds the nicest dress she can – it's yellow and feels like a cloud should – and puts it on over the top of her clothes. She goes to the wall of makeup, where small, black plastic cases hang from metal hooks like they're bait. She picks the ones that are within reach, and carefully applies lipstick, eye shadow, and blush the way her mum showed her. She has to stand on a pile of books to see in the mirror, but she does it without once falling over. *See?* she says to the mannequin. She finds a floppy red hat. Puts on green nail polish. Looks at the shoes, and knows her gumboots will probably give her identity away, but she's not taking them off, not ever. She duct-tapes four Matchbox cars to the bottom of each gumboot and skates around the shop.

She skates past the racks of bras, so many of them hanging there. Lined up like soldiers waiting to be called into action. Millie's head detaches itself and sees her mum after the shower, her hair dripping and limp around her head, steam rising off her skin. Her boobs hang off her body like water balloons, and they try to hit each other when she walks from the shower to the wardrobe. She catches Millie watching her as she slides the bra loops over her shoulders. *You'll have them one day,* her mum says.

Millie does not want them. Not ever. She found some magazines once in her dad's bedside table. The boobs jutted out of the women's bodies as if you could unscrew the back like a brooch. They looked unpredictable. Demanding. And then there was The Naked Woman Who Wasn't Her Mum who hid in their bathroom one afternoon. *You didn't see me, kid,* she said. Millie's eyes were drawn to her nipples like they were magnets. And Millie thought, *Yes, I did.*

She skates to the games section and, one by one, pulls board games off the shelf and lines them up in front of the mannequin. There's Twister and Monopoly and Guess Who? and Mouse Trap and checkers and backgammon and Battleship and Operation and Scrabble and Hungry Hungry Hippos and Connect Four. She doesn't really know how to play any of them, so she just rolls the dice once for the mannequin and once for her, and moves all the pieces around, and the battleships are trying to sink Park Lane, the Guess Who? people are an audience for Mouse Trap, and the hippos are eating the checkers.

After you hit the man with the flashlight on the head, I followed him, she says to the mannequin, putting a bra cup over her mouth and tying the loops behind her head. *For hygiene,* she explains, a bit muffled now, thinking of the hospital shows her mum watches. *He went in there,* she says, pointing to an office toward the back of the store. She puts Scrabble letters into the Operation man. *He got a pack of peas for his head.* She delicately removes the letter *M* from the Operation man's stomach. *And he fell asleep. He left the key in the door.* She holds up the key and grins. *I locked it.* Pats the mannequin on the head. *I owe you,* she whispers into his ear.

For dinner, Millie invites the Guess Who? people, the mannequin, a hobby horse – the Guess Who? people might be less self-conscious if there is someone else there with just a face – and a toy dog who looks exactly like Rambo. She seats them at the biggest dining table in the furniture section. It is at least double the size of their dining table at home and doesn't have any coffee-mug rings or candle wax or Millie's name written on one of the legs. The napkins and place mats and plates and bowls are all white and the same as each other.

She hoists the mannequin onto the chair at the head of the table and sits Rambo on a placemat. The Guess Who? people and the hobby horse stare at her from across the table. She likes how they look at her as if they expect her to do something. *Okay,* she says, and skates away, returning with an armful of streamers. She throws them across the table and wraps them around the chairs and ties bows around the forks.

She sets a place for her mum next to the mannequin.

Just.

In.

Case.

She pulls up a chair for herself between the mannequin and Rambo, pats down her dress, and adjusts her hat. She feels the mannequin's eyes on her. *What?* she says. *She's just caught up.* She clears her throat. *Dear God,* she says, her hands in prayer, squinting at the mannequin through half-closed eyes. *Tonight we will be serving Fanta soup for entrée, snakes and dinosaurs for main, a side salad of mint leaves, and banana sundae for dessert. I hope this is okay with you.* She fills her glass with grape juice. *But first, some toast.* She stands and clinks glasses with all her guests. She does it again, because there's music to it, she does it faster and faster, and skates around the table, *clink-clink-clink-clink-clink,* and then skates around the other way, *clink-clink-clink-clink-clink.*

She sits on top of the table instead of in her chair, because she's The Boss, and they all eat, and talk about how the dog from next door keeps making big poops on their lawn and how Mrs. Pucker always gets fancy makeup in the mail but it doesn't help her and how Ablett must be very sorry that he switched clubs because his new team plays like a bunch of girls. And the whole time, the mannequin watches her, without blinking, without saying a thing.

another fact about the world millie knows for sure

She doesn't know where her dad's body is.

When they visited her dad in the cemetery he was in a tiny box in the wall. *Dad's too big for that,* she said.

It's a magic box, Millie's mum replied.

What kind of magic?

Just magic. Okay?

Can I see inside it?

The magic won't work if you do that.

Like Santa?

Yes. Exactly like Santa.

She gave a box of raisins to Perry Lake, one of the big kids at school who knew everything about everything. *What happens to dead bodies after they die?*

He shoved a fistful of raisins into his mouth and chewed.

Depends, he said.

On what?

On how many boxes of these you got.

The next day, Millie upended her schoolbag at his feet. A pile of raisin boxes poured out. He opened one and emptied the contents into his mouth. *They go hard.*

Hard?

Yeah. And cold.

Cold?

Yeah.

Like plastic?

He shrugged. *Maybe.*

Do they shrink?

Shrink?

Yeah.

He threw a raisin up in the air and caught it in his mouth.

Dead bodies do not shrink.

Millie's smothering a heaped bowl of banana lollies with chocolate topping when the thought occurs to her. She puts a hand on the mannequin's. *Don't take this the wrong way,* she says, his hand cold and hard underneath hers. *But.* She leans into his face. His eyes look back at her like he is only a drawing. *Are you a Dead Thing?*

the third day of waiting

Millie sits in the office in the back of the department store. It looks different in the daylight. There is a desk with pens and paper and paper clips positioned neatly side by side, and an in tray and an out tray that don't have anything in or out of them. Millie picks up a paper clip and a pen, and puts one in the in tray and one in the out tray. The yellow dress she wore last night is folded in the centre of the desk. There's a big television screen attached to the side wall. She flicks at the Matchbox-car wheels on the bottom of her gumboots.

She opens her Book Of Dead Things, laying it flat on the desk and smoothing down the pages. She stares at the picture she drew of her dad's magic box. The dash pulses at her. Like it has a heartbeat. She knows about dashes now. That you can carry lots of them around in your pocket. *Harry Bird,* the picture says. *1968–2012. Loved.* She says the word out loud. *Loved.*

By who? Millie had said to her mum. They were standing hand in hand, looking at her dad's magic box like it was a painting.

You, her mum replied.

And you?

Her mum cleared her throat. *Of course.* Millie watched her twist her wedding ring around and around her finger. She had started wearing it again that week.

And everyone else?

Yes, Millie.

Why doesn't the sign say that then?

Millie! She shook Millie's hand loose, kneeled on the ground, and put her head in her hands.

Millie didn't move. *Mum?*

Because nothing's free, Millie, her mum said. *Not even this shit.* Her mum didn't look at her as she stood and walked off toward the car. *Come on,* she said. Millie took one last look at her dad's magic box before following.

When The Ladies From Tennis dropped by their house that night, one of them hugged Millie and said, *His body is gone, but his soul is still with us.*

Is that what's in the magic box? Millie asked.

It's in you, the lady said, placing a flat palm on Millie's chest.

Millie looked down at the lady's hand. *How did it get there?*

It's always been there.

What?

Proper girls don't say, "What."

What?

Proper girls say, "Pardon me."

Pardon me?

Good girl.

The Lady From Tennis stood to hug Millie's mother.

Pardon me? Millie said again, but the women didn't hear her.

The next day Millie went to the milk bar. While the girl who worked there giggled with a boy who didn't work there, she filled up her schoolbag with raisins and walked out.

What's a soul? she said to Perry Lake, after showing him the raisins.

It's like a heart, but it's in your stomach, he replied.

What's it look like?

Like a really big raisin. He eyed her schoolbag.

She zipped up her bag and held it behind her back. *What happens to it when you die?*

Falls out.

It falls out?

Yeah, like a placebo.

What's a placebo?

They fall out of women. After they have a baby or whatever.

What do they do with it?

They put it in the freezer and eat it.

Your soul?

No, the placebo. They keep your soul.

Where?

Some other freezer.

Where's that?

The school bell rang in the distance. Kids ran past them, yelling and laughing in packs. *Somewhere,* Perry said, rolling his eyes. *I don't know. I don't know EVERYTHING.*

Could I have it without knowing?

Perry put out a hand. It was long and thin and bony. *Just gimme the raisins,* he said.

The door to the office bursts open. Millie feels the draft from the movement of the door, and it sucks at her clothes like a vacuum. Millie sits up straight in the chair, snaps her book shut and slides it behind her back. A lady stands in the doorway, mid-conversation with someone out of sight.

What about dinner at mine tonight? the lady says quietly.

No, Helen. It's a man's voice.

No? I'm making Mexican?

I'm busy.

Tomorrow?

Busy.

You'll just get back to me, then.

Helen, I'm busy for the rest of my life.

Okay then, Stan, she says brightly, louder now. *I'll bring over that bruise-dispersing cream for you. We can rub that thing right out.*

Millie sees the back of the man as he walks off. *You're not touching my face, Helen,* he says.

Righto, then, she says to his retreating back. *You just let me know, won't you, Stan?* She turns to face Millie.

Helen's small for a grown-up, but wide, as if all her height has gone outward. The buttons cling to her blouse, like people hanging from a cliff. Millie looks down at the lady's shoes. Small, black, clumpy.

Well! the lady says, as if she can't believe how exciting the word is to say. She plonks herself into the chair on the other side of the desk. Her cheeks are pink and round. *Haven't you got yourself into a pickle?* She picks up a remote from the desk and points it at the wall. The television comes alive.

Millie appears on the screen. It's hard to make out and it's in black and white with no sound, but it's definitely Millie. TV Millie is outside of this office. She walks up to the window, peers through it. Pokes her tongue out. Grabs the keys out of the door handle, and walks away.

Helen presses Pause on the remote. Real-Life Millie looks at TV Millie. It's so strange to look at herself doing something she's already done, and that she can't undo.

Real-Life Millie looks defiantly at Helen. Helen raises both eyebrows. Real-Life Millie raises both eyebrows back.

what millie did last night

Millie knew the way home but believed her mum was making sure Millie knew how to Do What She Was Told, that she knew how to be Good. So, after a talk with the mannequin at dinner, Millie decided to make things easier for her mum to find her. Using paints from the hardware section, she painted *IN HERE MUM* as tall as she could on the glass of the automatic doors. Backward, of course, so her mum could read it from the outside. She arranged the Connect Four pieces so they formed a right-turning arrow and placed the stand near the entrance. All the mannequins lining the aisles had their arms positioned so they were pointing in the direction Millie's mum should follow. Some of them held signs. *Hi Mum!* one said. *Keep going!* said another. *Stop here for a snack!* said the next mannequin, and Millie placed one of her Roll-Ups in its upturned hand. The Guess Who? people were arranged in an arrow, the houses from Monopoly indicated a left turn, the Twister spinner gestured forward. The nine mannequins closest to the undies each held a letter on a piece of paper to spell *IN HERE MUM*. The mannequin with the Hawaiian shirt held the final *M*. She hooked some bras together and strung them from the mannequin's hand across the aisle, tying them to the top of the Ginormous Women's Underwear rack like a finish line. Millie decorated the trail with Christmas lights she found in a bargain bin, and then – letting her red boots poke out just a little bit – lay under the giant undies to wait.

But when the shoes came they weren't gold.

Are you with that man? Helen is saying. *The singing one?* She opens the desk drawer and begins lining up its contents in a neat row on the desk. A Toblerone wrapper. *He seemed lovely.* An empty juice box. *But is he a little bit.* Fly's glass jar. *A little bit.* Two hands full of lolly wrappers. She sprinkles them all over the desk, dropping them from high above her head as if she's showing Millie how rain works. *Soft? In the head? No? Of course not. I'm sorry.* A Roll-Up. *But is he. Slow? A bit?* She leans across the desk and whispers, *Retarded?* She clasps a hand over her mouth. *Oh. Of course not. I'm sorry. I can't believe I just said that. I didn't want to remove him from the shop, it's just that. Stan has very high standards for this place.*

Helen runs her fingers thoughtfully over the Roll-Up. She leans toward the doorway. *He's very particular,* she says loudly. She sits back in her chair. *Does that man, the singing one. Does he. Have a dungeon or anything?* She disappears under the desk, emerges with a pile of board games and places them on the desk in a teetering pile. Connect Four, Battleship, Twister, Monopoly. She rests an elbow on the top of the pile. *Whips and things? Chains? He doesn't chain anyone up, does he?*

We're friends since yesterday, Millie says.

He's just an old man, she continues. *You can be an old, lonely man, hanging around girl-children, and be completely normal. Right?* She ducks under the desk again and comes to stand, holding Millie's backpack in one hand and an open bucket of paint in the other. *Ta-da!* The paint slops over the side and drips onto the floor. *It's society, you know?* Helen pauses, puts the backpack and paint on the table, moves the pile of board games aside, and sits on the desk. *Is all this,* she wiggles her index finger at Millie's face, *for him? The makeup?*

Millie wipes a hand across her lips. There's a smudge of bright red on the top of her hand, like war paint. *I'm hungry,* she says.

Oh, darling, I'm sorry. I had cookies. But Stan, she says loudly out the doorway again, *Stan ate them. He'll eat my cookies. When it suits him.* She waits, her ear cocked toward the door.

Stan appears in the doorway and Helen jumps. Millie sucks in a breath. It's the security guard from last night. He has a black eye. He's on his mobile phone but he stares at Millie, unblinking, pushing the pads of his fingers into the swelling on his cheekbone. *Well, I'd finished* The Cosby Show *on DVD and wanted to get something else, didn't I,* he says to the phone. *Didn't know I was gonna get attacked.* He's still staring at Millie.

Helen let me out this morning. Millie's whole body feels like it's clenching. *Listen, Ma, can you hang on a tick?* He puts his hand over the mouthpiece. *You better get her something to eat, Helen,* Stan says. *Before they come.*

Helen jumps off the desk. *Of course,* she says, and opens another drawer. She's flushed red in the face. *Mentos? They're surprisingly satiating.*

Before who comes? Millie says.

I'm on a diet, Helen says. *The Atkins one? Is it Atkins? Or Paleo? You get to smell all the food you want. It's fantastic.* She looks sideways at Stan. *Not that I need to.* She rips the packet of Mentos, pops two in her mouth and two on the desk for Millie. Millie picks them up and chews them greedily. *Go on a diet, I mean. I'm not one of those women who worries about those sorts of things. It's more about treating myself like I deserve. It's very empowering.*

Stan rolls his eyes. *Helen,* he says. *Just get her something proper, okay? They'll be here soon. They got a ways to travel so she needs to be fed.* He gives Millie a last look, turns, and leaves. *Huh?* Millie hears him say into the phone as he walks away. *No, it was a little kid. I'm not suing her, Ma. Mum! I'm not. Well, they left her here, didn't they? They can't have much.*

He's lovely, isn't he? Stan? She looks out the door and spits the Mentos into a tissue.

Who's coming? Millie says. She is sick in the stomach. *Mum will be here,* she adds. *She's just. Lost.*

Oh, darling, Helen says, throwing the tissue into the rubbish bin by her feet and wiping her hands on her trousers. *I'm sure she is.*

My dad died. But my mum will be here.

Oh, darling. She walks around to Millie's side of the desk and kneels on the ground in front of her. She grabs one of Millie's hands and holds it with both of hers. *How did he pass? Oh, don't answer that.* Helen talks like she is surprised by the words that come out of her own mouth, as if someone else is saying them. *Don't. If you don't want. But if you want. How? Was it? That he passed? Was he into. Gambling? A little bit? Did he get mixed up in something?*

Mixed up?

Drugs? Helen whispers.

They gave him drugs at the hospital.

Was it. A mental hospital?

He had cancer.

Oh, sweetheart. I had cancer once. Well, I thought I did. Terrible time. Terrible. Turns out it was just a very big boil.

My mum will be here.

Right on my neck. Right here. Terrible time. What? Of course. Sweetheart. Of course she will.

A phone rings in Helen's pocket. Helen jumps to her feet and answers it. *Yes. Yes. She's right here. Of course, yes.* She hangs up. *Oh, darling. They're coming for you.*

Who?

Child Services. They're so fantastic with abandoned children.

Abandoned?

They'll give you another mum and dad for a little while. Until they find yours. Through the doorway, Helen watches Stan laugh with a young female staff member.

But Mum said to wait here.

I know, darling. I know. But. She sighs and walks to the door, putting her hand on the doorframe and watching Stan. *Some people don't always say what they mean.*

Millie grips her Book Of Dead Things tightly behind her back. Helen whips around to face Millie. Her body wobbles under her shirt. The button people claw desperately at the cliff edge. *Oh, don't worry, darling. They'll love you. You're adorable. Now, darling, just wait right here. Yes? Promise? Yes?* She pauses and they stare at each other. *I'll bring back juice. And cookies. Yes?* Without waiting for an answer, she walks out the door.

Millie watches Helen walk away and out of sight. She wants to throw up. A kid walks by the open office door with his mum and screams, *But I wanted the blue one!* Millie wants to scream in his face, *But I want my mum!*

Millie rips off the Matchbox cars from the bottom of her gumboots and climbs down from the chair. She grabs her bag and puts the toy cars inside. She takes a quick look out the door. No Helen. No Stan. She takes a deep breath and runs as fast as she can in the direction of the café. Her bag slides up and down her back. Down the aisle with the brooms and cloths and mops in bright colours. Past the photo lab, people flicking through photos on bright screens. Past the CDs and phones and electrical gadgets. Millie hides behind a cardboard cutout of a famous singer when she sees Stan coming. He flicks through the DVDs and mumbles to himself. *Got it, got it, don't want it, got it,* he says. His phone rings. *Yeah? Yeah, yeah, I'll be right there.* He walks past her and doesn't see her.

At the café, Karl is in his usual spot. Millie hides behind her usual pot plant. She spies Helen at the counter.

Ba-boom. Ba-boom. Ba-boom.

Just a small bit of cake, please, Helen's saying to the girl behind the counter. *The carrot cake, please. Yes, just two pieces, please. Yes, please, that one. Great, thank you, just the three pieces, that'll be fine.*

Karl, Millie whispers.

Karl sits up and turns toward the pot plant. *Um,* he says. *Yes?*

It's Millie. She pokes her head around the fern leaves.

Just Millie? Where have you been?

From the cover of the pot plant, Millie gives him a rundown of events since she last saw him. *First the mannequin saved my life. Then I stole a key. Then the security guard was locked in. Then we had dinner. Rambo was there. And the hobby horse. And the Guess Who? people. And the mannequin. I'll introduce you later. And then I asked the mannequin if he was a Dead Thing.*

And then I tried to help Mum. And then Helen offered me juice and cookies, but I didn't get either. And then my new mum and dad were coming. And then I escaped. And then I found you. Are you going to eat that?

Karl hands her his muffin. *That's all?*

That's all, she says, her mouth full.

Escaped from who?

Her. Millie points and ducks as Helen, no more than twenty metres away from them, talks to a customer.

They're not for me, Helen says. *I'm on a diet. The North Beach one? Kate Moss uses it. You can hold all the food you like.*

Karl looks the other way as Helen walks past them and back toward the office. *An escape, you say?* He stands. *Okay.*

Okay? Millie says.

We're getting you out of here. Right now, he says loudly. The girl looks up at him from behind the coffee machine.

Shh, Millie whispers.

Karl sits. *Yes. Sorry about that*. He waves at the girl.

But we should go.

Yes, he says, and stands again.

They make their way to the giant undies, sticking to the aisles in between the main ones. The mannequin in the Hawaiian shirt looks down at her. Millie can't look away. *Grab him*, Millie says.

What?

Proper men say, "Pardon me."

Pardon me?

We're taking him.

Him?

Yes.

Why?

He saved my life.

Karl looks at Millie, then at the mannequin, then back at Millie. *I will do that,* he says, too loudly again. *Any friend of yours is a friend of mine.*

Shh, Millie says.

Oh, yes. Right. Karl picks up the mannequin and holds him so they're dancing cheek to cheek.

Ready? Millie says.

Ready, Karl answers.

They snake their way past the appliances, the cookware, the colouring books, the towels. A woman tries to spray perfume on Karl as he walks by. He giggles. The entrance is metres in front of them – it shines blindingly in the middle of everything. They're running and causing a scene but no one seems to notice and they're going to make it.

We're invisible, says Millie.

Yes, says Karl.

They look at each other and smile. They're actually going to make it.

But then Millie sees the Guess Who? people looking up at them, and it's too late to say anything, and Karl's foot catches on their faces, and he falls headfirst into the bargain bin full of Christmas lights in the middle of the aisle. Millie falls at the same time, hitting her head on the side of the bin. Karl drops the mannequin on top of her, and a leg comes loose and skids across the floor.

Then the three words she doesn't want to hear. *There she is.* Helen and Stan and a man and a woman wearing fancy uncomfortable clothes coming toward them. Her New Mum. Her New Dad.

C'mon, Karl, Millie says, standing, rubbing her head and pulling at his arm. But he's managed to get himself all twisted up in the Christmas lights, and his thrashing about is only making matters worse.

Grab him, Stan, says Helen, running toward them behind the security guard. *I think he's. I mean. I don't want to jump to any conclusions. But. Everybody. Based on what I've seen. He's probably. Most definitely. I think.*

Karl's arms and legs are still flailing all over the place when Stan catches up with them. He helps Karl out of the bin and holds on to his arm. *Okay, you dirty old bastard.* Stan says. *Show's over.*

Oh, Stan, Helen says, running up to them, breathless. *You did it.* She puts a hand on his upper arm and her eyes widen. *You're so strong.*

Karl doesn't look at Millie but says, *Go, Millie, go. I'll find you,* out the side of his mouth, and the Guess Who? people look at her like they expect her to do something, so Millie grabs the mannequin's leg and she *does something*; she weaves through the forest of people, around and under and through. *GoMilliego*, she sings as she runs as fast as she can out the door and through the parking lot. As she's running, she looks back, and it's still there, painted in big letters that slide over each other as the doors open and close: *IN HERE MUM*.

Millie walks up the pathway to her house, places the mannequin's leg on the step, and tries to open the door. It's locked. She grabs the spare key from under the mat, unlocks the door, checks the street for the police car that's been looking for her, and then walks in. It's cold and dark. She's tired from running all the way from the department store. From the doorway, she says, *Mum?*

Millie walks into the kitchen. *Mum?* The word echoes off the walls. Dishes are piled high in the sink and there's something in the rubbish that stinks. She walks into the lounge room. *Mum?* The couch is huge in its emptiness, and the television is a big black hole in the centre of their lounge room. Why has she never noticed how big and black it is, how it looks like you could press a button and it would suck up your whole house?

Her dad's beer cozy is on the coffee table. Millie holds it up to the light streaming through the window. Dust particles dance around it in the sunlight. She rubs the material with her fingertips. It's black, with a yellow map of Australia on one side and a very big-boobed woman in a bikini on the other. Millie slides it onto her forearm and rubs it against her cheek.

She walks into her mum and dad's room. Her mum's side of the bed is all rumpled up. She lies under the covers for a bit, pulling them over her head. It's cold and dark in there, too. She reaches her hand across to her dad's side, then peels back the covers, stands, and presses the palm of her hand on the wardrobe door, like she's trying to make a handprint on it. She closes her eyes and slides the door across. When she opens her eyes, there is nothing there but wire coat hangers. Like the shoulders of skeletons.

She sits on the bed and drags her fingers through the air and it feels like nothing and she wants to say, *Sorry, Mum, I am so sorry, Mum, I am sorry for doing the things I did.*

a fact about the world millie knows for sure

Sorry is sometimes the only thing left to say.

What should you say when someone dies? she whispered to her dad as her mum watched *Deal or No Deal.* The sister of a girl at school had died and her teacher had told Millie to make a card.

Mills, baby, her dad whispered back. He hoisted her up onto his lap. *No one's going to die.*

She furrowed her brow. *Everyone's going to die.*

Well, he said, and stopped. He put his hands under her armpits and twisted her around to face him. *Well. Yes. But no one you know.*

Everyone I know.

But not anytime soon.

How do you know?

I just know.

What on Earth are you two talking about? her mum said as the ads blared out of the television.

Mum, Millie said, looking at the back of her mum's head. *What do you say to your friends when people they love die?*

Her mum turned around and flashed her dad A Look. She grabbed Millie by both hands and leaned into her face. *You don't need to know any of this stuff, Millie*, she said. *You're just a child. A little girl. You should be, I don't know, playing dollies. Offices. Shops.*

Millie shrugged.

Her mum sat back in her chair and eyed her. *Who was it?*

Bec's sister. From school.

Deal or No Deal came back on the telly. *Send them a card*, her mum said, turning back toward the television. *Say something nice on it.*

Like what?

Like . . . deal! Are you kidding me? Take the money!

Millie's dad put his hand on Millie's head. It felt so gigantic on there. *Say, I'm sorry for your loss.*

It's not my fault.

Of course not. He put his arms around her and pushed her head into his chest. *Just be kind,* he said. *That's all.*

Later, when Millie's dad was dead, her mum sat in front of the telly, all day every day, and Millie put her hand on her mum's arm and said, *I'm sorry for your loss.* And her mum hugged her, so tight Millie could hardly breathe, and said, *I'm sorry for your loss too, Millie.*

And now, as she looks out the window from her mum and dad's bedroom, scanning the street for the police car, she locks eyes with the old lady across the road. She, too, is looking out the window from her house. She, too, Millie can tell, has lost someone. Millie doesn't know how she can tell, but she just can. *I'm sorry for your loss,* Millie mouths at her, slowly and deliberately, her forehead on the glass of the window. The old lady stares at her. And then pulls the curtains shut.

agatha pantha

Agatha Pantha had tried to avoid her husband's naked body as much as possible throughout their marriage. It was too grass-hoppery; all bent-over and thin. His bones appeared surprised to be there, jutting out of his skin as though they were trying to find the exit. On their wedding night, when he unzipped her dress in that damp way that would soon become unbearably familiar, she caught sight of his penis, glinting in the moonlight like an unsheathed sword. She finally understood why he always walked as if he were being pushed from behind. It seemed abnormally large for his body. During the sex he unfurled his body and presented himself to her like a magic trick. She looked at him with blurred eyes, trying to melt his body into the walls. He assumed they were her Sex Eyes, the eyes you practice in the mirror from the moment you guess that something like sex exists.

When the deed was done and he scampered to the

bathroom, Agatha pulled the blanket up under her chin and imagined his penis swaying from one leg to the other as he walked, like an orangutan swinging through the jungle. As she lay there, waiting for his return, it was not surprise, shock, or even rage that she felt; it was disappointment. Disappointment that having a man flounder about on top of her like a piece of cooked spinach was the best humankind could come up with.

She remembered learning that all men had these monstrosities dangling between their legs. She couldn't look at a man for a number of months afterward. Just the knowledge that there were so many hidden penises around unnerved her. She didn't know how other women could live in a world like this. She felt surrounded, trapped. Men walked past her in the street and said *hello* with such smugness, and all Agatha could do was look at the ground and think, *He has a penis he has a penis he has a penis.*

Later, though, as she watched her husband's penis sadden and age, as all creatures do eventually, she was able to look men in the eye as they walked past her in the street. *Hello,* she would answer back, her eyes clear, her lips calm. But she would think, *I pity you and your dying penis.*

Ron's saddening penis was Agatha's first clue that her husband was aging. The second came when she saw the hair in his ears, waving in the wind like the hands of drowning men. She watched on helplessly as hair began to disappear from one place on his body and reappear in others. Third was a stroke that made him lose feeling in his left leg. He had to hold on to his thigh and pull it alongside him when he walked.

Hop, draaaag. Hop, draaaag. Hop, draaaag.

Fourth was the plastic bedpan he took to keeping on his bedside table at nighttime. Consequently, Agatha's mornings began with the soft splash of her husband's urine against the sides of it as he dragged himself to the toilet.

Hop, splash, draaaag, splash. Hop, splash, draaaag, splash.

One morning she realised the orange juice made the same noise as she carried it to the breakfast table. She never bought it again.

Fifth was the development of a fat deposit that reached from his chin to the bottom of his neck like a pelican gullet. Every word he uttered was punctuated by this soundless tremble of flesh, crescendoing out from his face the louder he spoke. It wobbled at her, day and night, as permanent a fixture in her life as the sun. And, like the sun, she could only just bear to look at it.

It was around this point that she stopped talking to her husband. She grunted, sighed, nodded, pointed, elbowed, but never spoke. It wasn't malicious. She just had nothing left to say. They had covered their likes, dislikes, differences, similarities, height, weight, shoe size. They had spent forty-five years having arguments, sharing opinions, discussing just how one might go about winning *The Price Is Right*. She could now, with startling accuracy, predict what he would say, think, do, wear, and eat. What she did have left to say – like *Get it yourself* – was easily achieved by gesture. So they ate together, slept together, sat together, breathed together – but had never been further apart.

When her husband died, neighbours suddenly dropped by unannounced, appearing on her doorstep from behind huge, hulking casseroles full of dead animals, and pity. Their children carried slabs of coconut slice and looked put out. They all set up camp in her kitchen, as though they were running a political campaign. They materialized in her hallway, her bedroom, and her bathroom, as if they could walk through walls, cocking their head to one side and clawing at her. They talked with their faces only centimetres away from hers. *I understand,* they all said, because Susie/Fido/Henry died last year/last week/ten years ago because she/it/he had lung cancer/was hit by a car/wasn't really dead but was dead to her because he was living with a twenty-six-year-old on the Gold Coast.

Why are there nineteen bunches of flowers in my sunroom? she asked on one of her frequent wanderings from room to room. No one answered. The flowers were elaborate explosions of things, like bouquets of fireworks, frozen in time.

Phillip Stone from Number 6 gave her a cup of tea she didn't want and placed a hand on her shoulder. He had never touched her before.

Let it out, Agatha, he said.

The heat of his palm made her skin prickle unpleasantly

beneath the fabric of her blouse. *I don't have a cat, if that's what you're getting at,* she replied, stepping out of his reach.

You're in denial, said Kim Lim from Number 32. Their noses almost touched. *Don't be afraid to express your sadness,* she added. Agatha smelled coconut slice on her breath.

She caught Frances Pollop from Number 12 in her wardrobe, wielding a tape gun in the air like a chainsaw. Ron's clothes were in boxes all over the floor. Agatha and Frances looked at each other. The tape gun wobbled a little above Frances's head. After a good minute, Agatha turned and walked out, closing the bedroom door behind her.

And then, just as suddenly, they all vanished. They left behind Crock-Pots, foreign smells, and the loudness of silence. Through the window, Agatha watched them walk out of her gate and down the road to their houses. The lights in their windows were like pupils. Their letter boxes like periscopes. Even the flowers in their front yards seemed to be gathered around in a circle, whispering to one another.

She left the lights off. The boxes of her husband's clothes had been pushed against the wall in the hallway. Even in the darkness, she could see *SALVOS* written on each one in black marker. The letters had been traced and retraced over and over. Sticky tape was wrapped ferociously around the centre of each box.

The phone rang in the kitchen. Her answering machine clicked on. *You've reached Agatha Pantha,* it said, in someone else's voice. *Please leave a message*. The absence of his name felt like vertigo.

Agatha? another voice said. *Are you there?*

She didn't know the answer to that.

Agatha stood in her bedroom and stared at her husband's slippers. It was what she did now, just walked around and stood in rooms. She felt it then, something trying to clamber its way out of her throat. Agatha held on to the bedpost and swallowed over and over again until it went away. *It's all this talk*, she said to her husband's slippers. *They're talking me into it*.

She sat on the bed and cupped her knees with her hands. *How do you get old without letting sadness become everything?* Her mother had been young once, with her easy limbs and pretty fingers, but then she had saddened, and shrunk. The ends of her sentences began to tremble, and she seemed to be always holding her breath.

Agatha's relatives had called this *grief*. They didn't say the word out loud, but mouthed it, as if it were blasphemy. Agatha, a fully grown and married woman at this point, opinions of her own beginning to gather steam in her head, thought the word vague. Cartoonish. Most of all, she thought her mother's state was something you could avoid, like sidestepping a puddle on the street.

At the time, Agatha hadn't realised she was looking into the future. That her mother was her, that soon Agatha would be her. Wasn't evolution about being better than your mother?

Agatha did not feel better than her mother. She could see her mother in her now, in her spotted hands, in the Death Lines that marked her face, in the varicose veins running up her legs like tree roots. She felt the sickening inevitability of the whole thing. Like becoming her mother was the point of it all.

So Agatha stood in the kitchen and opened the fridge. Light flooded the room. She peered into it, her eyes adjusting. Arms of meatloaf and finger sandwiches and pink cupcakes topped with nipple cherries lined the shelves. One by one, she removed all the casseroles. She whisked them out of her house and upturned them on the footpath. Chicken stock and carrot and gravy and onion and hunks of beef splashed satisfyingly on her shins. She gathered a load of lamingtons in her arms and launched them from the doorway. They landed in her rose-bushes, on the windshields of parked cars, at the foot of nearby letter boxes. She hurled a three-tiered sponge cake over her head like a soccer throw-in. It separated in the air, and red jam splattered thick on her driveway. She lined the sandwiches up along the top of her small brick fence. With both arms held out, she walked the length of it, feeling the sandwiches squish under her feet. Slices of cucumber squirted out the sides. She balanced two pink-frosted cupcakes on top of her letter box. She wrapped both hands around a hunk of meatloaf, drew it back behind her head, and followed through. The meatloaf fell apart in her hands. The cupcakes tumbled onto the footpath. A cherry landed next to her foot, and she kicked it.

She washed the Tupperware, the casserole dishes, and the old ice-cream buckets, the water in the sink rising high up the sides as she thrashed her hands about. She dried them all with violent flourishes. And then she stacked them, one on top of the other, in her driveway. Like a totem pole from some forgotten ancient culture. There was a sadness to the soft sway of it that Agatha tried to ignore.

She wrote a cardboard sign to place beside it. *THANK YOU FOR YOUR KINDNESS*, it read, in big, dark letters. She traced and retraced the letters. *BUT I DO NOT REQUIRE IT.*

She added, in smaller letters: *Also, I Don't Care For Coconut.*

She stood on her doorstep and blinked through the sweat on her eyelids. She ate a potato bake straight from the Pyrex dish with her fingers, and surveyed what she had done. Was it art? Or was it war? She had never understood either, but as she watched the river of food in the gutter flow down the street, she thought perhaps it might be both.

The lights from the homes around her flicked on and off, like warning signals. She pushed a fistful of potato and cheese into her mouth. She sensed the street tensing. *I'm expressing my sadness, Kim Lim!* she yelled into the night, flecks of potato bake flying. She stepped inside, slammed the front door behind her, and locked it. She locked the back door. She locked the windows. She closed all the curtains. *I'm turning the television on now!* she yelled, and she did, shadows skittering all over the walls. She turned the volume up as high as it could go. White noise filled the room. She dragged a chair to the front window and sat down, leaning forward. She pulled back the curtain so she could see out into the street. *Ksssshhh*, said the television in the background. The sun was coming up. *I can't wait to see their faces!* she yelled. Yelling seemed to help.

Seven years have passed and Agatha has not left her house since that night. Not to water the garden, or catch a bus, or sweep the driveway. She has not opened her front door or her curtains; she has not listened to the radio or read the newspapers. She has not turned the television off, and the *ksssshhh* sound is the only truth of which Agatha is sure. Seven years of unopened mail floods her hallway. She wades through the letters when walking from her bedroom to the lounge room. *Just because you know my name*, she yells at them, *doesn't mean I owe you anything!* They seem to snap at her heels.

Every Monday, a woman from the supermarket leaves a box of food under her window. A man from the post office collects her bill money from the doorstep and feeds mail through the slot in her door every second Tuesday. She pays them in envelopes marked *HERE, TAKE IT* that she slides under the front door. The grass on the front lawn lies flat and brown amid the dust. The weeds grow tall. Ivy covers the house. Agatha has opened the front window and put her hand through to cut a hole out of the ivy with her sewing scissors. She does not know what is going on in the world, but she knows what is going on in her street.

She has acquired that blob body synonymous with old women, where it becomes difficult to tell where anything begins or ends. Her chin sprouts long, meandering hairs. She always plucks them, but they always return, as if they're part of God's plan. She has taken to wearing brown-tinted sunglasses from the moment she wakes until the moment she goes to sleep. For Agatha, the brown shield around her eyes acts like corn flour, thickening and slowing the world around her.

a day in the life of agatha pantha

6:00 a.m.: Wakes without an alarm. Doesn't open her eyes until she's wearing her brown glasses. Notes the time on the clock on the wall in front of her. Nods approvingly. Walks to the bathroom to the beat of the ticking clock. Is careful not to trip over her husband's slippers, which have not been moved since the last time he wore them.

6:05 to 6:45: Sits in the Chair of Disbelief and measures Cheek Elasticity, Distance From Nipples To Waist, Foreign Hair Growth, Wrinkle Count, Projected Wrinkle Trajectory, and Arm Wobblage. Notes the data in an exercise book titled *Age*. Narrates the entire event while looking at herself in the mirror. *I'm measuring Arm Wobblage now!* she yells at herself while she bats a hand at the underside of her upper arm. *It's up from yesterday!* she yells after checking the data. *It's always up from yesterday!*

6:46: Allows herself one deep, dark sigh.

6:47: Showers. *I'm washing myself now!* she yells. She never yells anything too specific in the shower.

7:06: Dresses in one of her four brown skirt suits. *Stockings!* she yells as she pulls them over her belly button. *Skirt! Blouse! Shoes!*

7:13: Cooks a breakfast of two fried eggs, one rasher of bacon, and a piece of whole-wheat toast.

7:21: Sits in the Chair of Degustation, cuts her breakfast into small squares, and eats it, one square at a time. *I'm eating bacon now!* she yells in between mouthfuls.

7:43: Sits on the Chair of Discernment. She watches the street through the hole in the ivy, her body leaning forward, her hands gripping her knees. *Too freckly!* she might shriek at a passerby, jumping out of her chair and pointing her finger in the air, as if playing bingo. *Too Asian! Too bald! Pull your trousers up! Stupid shoes! Too many hairclips! Thin lips! Suit too purple! Pointy nose! Asymmetrical face! Knobbly knees!* Sometimes the insults extend to the neighbours' yards. *Cut your hedges! Too many flowers! Letter box is slanty!* Or even the birds. *Too chirpy! Not enough legs!* The words rebound off the walls of the room, and her voice becomes louder and louder, culminating in one final, all-encompassing insult that never seems to have the effect she wants. *Humanity is doomed!*

12:15: Collapses in a heaving lump on her chair.

12:16: Allows herself to be sweaty and relieved.

12:18: Lunch. A whole-wheat Vegemite sandwich. Does not cut it into squares like her breakfast; instead cuts it into long, thin strips. *Variety is important! If you want to keep your wits about you!* she yells as she dangles a sandwich strip above her mouth.

12:47: Afternoon tea. A pot of tea and an Anzac biscuit. Sits in the hallway on the Chair of Resentment. Looks at the brown wall and yells things like, *Loud lawnmowers!* and, *Nosy neighbours!* Sometimes she can't think of anything, and just says, *Brown walls!* Being resentful makes her face feel more pointed than usual, and, for reasons she can't quite put into words, she gleans satisfaction from this feeling. *I like this feeling!* she confirms to the wall.

1:32: Cleans the house, yelling, *I'm scrubbing the coat hangers!* or, *I'm polishing the light globes!*

3:27: Sits in the Chair of Disagreement in the sitting room and writes complaint letters, keeping them in a box marked *FOR DISTRIBUTION AFTER ALL OF THIS*. She underlines *THIS* but is not specific about what *THIS* is.

4:29: One of two things happens. Sits in the Chair of Disappearing, closes her eyes, and listens to the *kssssshhh* sound from the television. Or, very, very occasionally, sits in the Chair of Disappointment and stares at her husband's slippers.

5:03: Dinner. A roast, usually. Covers the meat, potatoes, and broccoli with gravy.

6:16: Sits in the Chair of Disengagement. Drinks a mug of Bonox and watches television static.

8:00: Removes all her clothes – *Shoes! Blouse! Stockings!* – and hangs them up.

8:06: Sits in the Chair of Disbelief and stares at herself in the mirror.

8:12: Puts on her nightgown and turns off the light. It is only in the dark of night that Agatha removes her brown sunglasses. But even then it's only in her bed, when she pulls the blanket up over her face, squeezing her eyes tightly closed. And even then the world feels too close, hovering above her, only centimetres away. And in the soft seconds between asleep and awake – that tiny gap in consciousness where you are just awake enough to know and just asleep enough to not know, at around 9:23 p.m. – Agatha Pantha allows herself to be lonely.

but today, at 10:36 a.m., everything changes

6:00 a.m.: Wakes. Fumbles for her brown glasses.

6:05 to 6:45: Sits in the Chair of Disbelief and yells, *I'm counting wrinkles now! I don't think I've seen this one on my knee before!* She writes, *New Kninkle* under *Wrinkle Count*.

6:47: *I'm turning on the water now!* she yells, standing in the shower.

7:06: *Stockings! Skirt! Blouse! Shoes!*

7:22: *I'm eating eggs now!*

7:56: Sits in the Chair of Discernment. *Parking too far away from the gutter!*

8:30: *Flowers aren't growing!*

9:16: *Footpath is dirty!*

10:12: *Helmets aren't fashion accessories!*

10:36: A police car drives slowly past. *This is different!* she yells.

10:42: The same police car drives down the street from the other direction. *That, too!*

10:47: A small girl with curly red hair runs down the street, opens Agatha's front gate, runs into Agatha's front yard, and hides behind Agatha's fence. *What?* Agatha yells.

10:48: The police car drives past again. The girl sinks into the weeds, her back against the fence. She looks at Agatha. *What?* Agatha yells.

10:49: The little girl peeks over the fence. Looks up and down the street. Looks back at Agatha. Stands, walks out of Agatha's front yard, across the street, and up the pathway of the opposite house. She tries the door, finds a key under the mat, turns back to look up and down the street. And disappears inside the house.

10:50: *What?* Agatha yells.

Agatha has been watching this house. Three months ago, she saw the ambulance arrive with the lights off. She saw the white sheet over the stretcher, the vague lines of a body. She saw the street rally around them, carrying their thank-God-it-was-you-and-not-me food. She saw the florist vans parked down the street in a long line. She saw the mother shrinking down to bones. *You should eat some of the food they keep bringing you!* she yelled at her once, tapping on the window. She saw the child. She was just a child.

I'll leave you alone! she had yelled. *It'll be the best thing for you!* She leaned back in her chair and folded her arms. *Trust me!*

So when Agatha sees the little girl disappear into the house on the other side of the road, she knows that the little girl's father is dead and that her mother isn't home. The mother had looked at Agatha two days ago. Right through the hole in the ivy, right through the glass of the window, right in the eyes. She'd put a suitcase in the boot of her car and her eyes said something to Agatha, something like an apology, something like screaming, something like pleading, something like this: *How do you get old without letting sadness become everything?*

And Agatha's body had vibrated a little.

Agatha hadn't understood what was happening, but she could tell something was happening. *Something's happening here! Something's awry!* she yelled, standing up and pressing the side of her face against the glass, watching the mum and the little girl drive off down the street. Agatha could feel it. There was something happening.

11:37: Agatha tries to forget all about the little girl's return. She tries to forget the mother's face and the fact that there is no car in the driveway. She tries to focus on all the houses that she can see except for the one opposite. *Lawn is patchy!* she yells. *I can see a weed just there! Your dog's ugly! Too many kids! They're ugly too!*

But then the door across the road opens. The little girl appears. Agatha watches her cross the road, open Agatha's gate, and walk up her driveway. *What?* Agatha yells. The little girl knocks on Agatha's front door. She's holding a piece of paper. *No, thanks!* Agatha yells through the window. *I've got enough!* The little girl disappears and then returns brandishing a plastic crate. She manoeuvres it in front of Agatha's window and stands on it so she is face-to-face with Agatha through the glass.

The little girl holds up the piece of paper. *What's this?* she asks.

Agatha squints at it. *If I tell you, will you go away?*

The little girl nods.

It's a travel itinerary.

What's that?

It's a piece of paper that says where someone's going. Is that your mother's name?

The little girl nods again.

She went to Melbourne. Two days ago. Agatha pauses. *And*

she's going to the United States in six days. They stare at each other through the glass. *Now, go away.*

the next day

7:43 a.m.: The little girl stands at the window of the house across the road, watching Agatha. They stare at each other. The little girl's eyes say something like: *How do you get old?*

8:07: Agatha hangs a pillowcase over the window so she can't see through the hole in the ivy.

9:13: There's a knock on the window. Agatha jumps. *I'm hungry,* a small voice says. Agatha turns the volume up full bore on the television. *Kssshhhh.*

12:15: Agatha removes the pillowcase. The little girl is still watching her from the window across the road, but now she sits in a chair.

3:27: Agatha tries to write complaint letters, but all she can think of to write is, *Dear Little Girl's Mum, Who do you think you are?*

4:16: The child is still looking at her through the window. Agatha can't concentrate. All she can think about is the mother's face, the carless driveway. Before she knows what she's doing, she has waded through the letters and opened the door. She's holding some Anzacs and a cup of tea. The air is so fresh on her face, on her whole body. She hasn't felt fresh air on her whole body like this, since . . . since. She can feel it blowing on her legs, feel it through her stockings. Her skin prickles. Her breath catches. *This is different!*

The weeds around her front door are at head height, and they greet her like a group of malnourished people. *You're not getting anything from me!* she yells, swinging her elbows at them as she storms past. She stands at her front gate and faces the street. *Too many cracks in the footpath!* she yells. *I'm crossing the road now! Hedge is too fancy! Look out, car, I'm not stopping for you! This is not that hard at all! It's just walking, after all! I've done it a million times! As long as I have legs that can walk, I should probably use them!*

Agatha walks up the pathway to the little girl's house and knocks on the door. The little girl answers it.

Hello, the little girl says.

Agatha hands her the plate of biscuits and the cup of tea. The little girl stares at the offerings. *Well?* Agatha says. The little girl takes the plate but ignores the tea. *Have you rung your mother?*

The little girl places the plate on a nearby table and starts eating a biscuit. She won't meet Agatha's eyes. *Her phone's off.*

Relatives, then. Agatha looks at the cup of tea, then sips it. *Any of those?*

My aunty lives out east, the little girl says. *Melbourne.* Agatha feels like a giant looming over her. Was she ever this small? *But Mum says we don't need anyone else.*

Oh, she did, did she! Tried your aunty?

I don't know her number.

Don't you have an address book?

Mum had it in her phone.

Look it up in the White Pages!

What are White Pages?

What's her name?

Judy.

Judy what?

Aunty Judy.

Aunty Judy! From Melbourne! Agatha turns and walks back down the pathway. *What am I supposed to do with that!* She throws one arm up in the air, the tea splashing over the edges of the cup.

The little girl runs after her. *My dad died.*

Yeah, well! Agatha turns around to face the girl. *So did mine!* She sips her tea forcefully.

When did he die?

Sixty years ago!

Mine died three months ago.

This isn't a competition! But if it was! I've lived without mine for longer than you! So!

What happened at his funeral?

What kind of question is that!

Mum didn't let me go to Dad's funeral.

Well, that was probably the best thing for you!

Why are you yelling?

Why are you whispering!

I'm not.

Neither am I! Agatha turns to cross the street but stops short. She stares at the house across from them. She takes another forceful sip of tea. *I live there?*

The little girl nods.

But it's . . . Agatha can't finish the sentence. It's the house in the street that children would be frightened of, that adults would have scorn or pity for. She turns back to the girl. *You're sure I live there?*

The girl nods again. *Can you help me find my mum?* she says.

Of course not! Agatha says. *I have things to do! I'm very busy! Go to the police!*

I can't. They want to give me a new mum and a new dad.

Go back inside! Agatha yells, striding toward her house. *Keep trying your mother!*

6:16: Sits in the Chair of Disengagement. Drinks a mug of Bonox and watches television static.

6:24: The television static begins to look like the little girl's face.

6:25: Pours the remainder of her Bonox down the sink.

6:26: Removes all her clothes. *Shoes. Blouse. Stockings.* And hangs them up.

6:31: Sits in the Chair of Disbelief and stares at herself in the mirror.

6:33: Her face becomes the little girl's face. She accidentally knocks the portable clock off the bathroom bench and it smashes on the tiles.

6:33 to 6:45: Stares at the smashed clock.

6:46: Puts on her nightgown and turns off the light.

and the next day

5:36 p.m.: Agatha knocks on the little girl's front door and hands her a plate piled with roast meat, potatoes, broccoli, and gravy.

Thank you, the little girl says, and begins to eat from the plate with her fingers while standing.

What are you doing!

What do you mean? the little girl says, face already covered in gravy.

You should be outside! Playing! You're just a child! Don't sit at the window!

You do that.

But I'm old! I'm allowed to do that! I'm allowed to do whatever I want! That's what happens when you get old! Write that down! It's important!

I'm hiding.

From who?

Helen. Stan. My new mum and dad. The police.

Agatha stares at her. *What did you do?*

I don't know, the little girl says, and starts to cry.

8:12: Agatha puts on her nightgown and turns off the light. As she's climbing into bed, she trips over something soft. She turns on the light.

8:13: She has kicked her husband's slippers across the room.

8:14: Agatha turns on the bathroom light and looks at herself in the mirror. She starts feeling it again. That thing rising up her throat. *She's talking me into it!* she yells.

and the day after that

6:00 a.m.: Agatha has had enough.

7:43: She packs her large handbag with everything she needs. Her Age Book. Two watches and a small battery-run clock from the cupboard. Spare underwear. Two blouses. Some Anzac biscuits. Her jar of Bonox. Her notepad for writing complaint letters.

8:12: Agatha knocks on the little girl's front door. She grips her handbag tightly and has her suit jacket buttoned up.

Have you tried your mother again? Agatha says when the little girl opens the door.

The little girl looks at her feet. *Her phone's still off.*

The first sign of one of those telephone machines, you're ringing her!

The little girl notices Agatha's handbag. *Where are you going?*

And you'll be ringing her the entire way! She can't get away with it that easily!

Are you taking me somewhere?

If you think I'm getting on one of those jet planes, you can think again!

Pardon me?

And I can't take you to the police! I know what they do to women like me! Who live in places like that! She gestures toward her house. *They'll lock me up! Put me in some home with all the dribbling people!*

The little girl looks unsure and doesn't move.

Don't just stand there! Pack your bags! We're going to Melbourne!

The little girl disappears for a moment and returns with a backpack.

Is that it?

She picks up a long plastic object that lies on the ground beside the door and nods.

What on Earth is that? Agatha says.

The little girl hugs it to her chest. *It's a leg.*

karl the touch typist

Karl did not own a computer, typewriter, or even a keyboard. He touch-typed on garbage-bin lids, on air, on the heads of small children, on his legs. He typed questions out with his fingertips before he asked them, just to make sure he wanted to. In the privacy of his own home, before he moved in with his son, Karl drew keyboards on coffee tables, on walls, on his shower curtains. He loved the way typing made hands move, the way fingers square-danced around one another, doing the do-si-do. He had watched his mother's fingers, then eventually Evie's, bouncing off the keys like drops of water on hot asphalt, and found the crooked typing finger of a woman to be as elegant and arousing as the arch of her foot or the nape of her neck.

When Karl's son said good-bye in the nursing home, he said, *We'll see you soon, Dad,* and kissed him on the cheek. Karl felt his son's scratchy face against his, and it was suddenly unfathomable to him that his own son had to shave. Life had been one blink and one breath and one piss, and now he was here, sitting on a bed in a room full of old men who couldn't keep their shit to themselves. He stood at the window and watched his son cross the parking lot. He walked so deliberately, that boy, from heel to toe always, and Karl thought, *When did he decide to walk like that?* Evie's footsteps had been so light and unpredictable, like salt falling from a saltshaker. His son seemed conscious that each step was bringing him closer to something of which he was unsure. Heel to toe, heel to toe.

It was his daughter-in-law Amy's idea. *I walk into my own house and brace myself to see a dead man in the recliner,* he heard her say one night through the papery walls that separated their bedrooms. She was a pointy little woman, one whose perfume always arrived before she did.

He's my father, his son, Scott, replied.

I'm your wife! She paused. *You know what the doctor said about my blood pressure.*

There was a long silence, and Karl lay in his bed with his arms straight at his sides, as though he were waiting to be shot out of a cannon.

Okay, his son said finally. Karl squeezed his fingers together. *I'll talk to him.*

Karl turned his head to one side and felt the pillow on his cheek. He squinted into the darkness. *Evie*, he whispered, and held out his hand like a peace offering. He traced her body in the air with an open palm. He tried to feel her nose on his, her breath on his face, her hand across his back.

Evie, he said again, because it was the only word that came to mind. He put his palm on the pillow by his head and closed his eyes.

When Scott and Amy rose for work the next morning, Karl was already sitting at the dining table with his bag packed at his feet. He wore his hat and the gloves he'd once used for driving.

Dad, Scott said, stopping in the kitchen doorway.

Karl cleared his throat. *I think I'm ready to move on*, he said, fingers tapping on the table.

Scott pulled out the chair beside him and sat down. Karl laced his fingers together. Scott placed a careful hand on top of Karl's. As he ran a gloved thumb over his son's knuckle, Karl thought, *I made this hand*.

Karl sat on the edge of his bed. He was in a room with four other men. The pallid colour of their skin seemed to match the pallid colour of the walls. They all lay in their beds with a kind of stunned boredom, their mouths open, their eyes blinking as if they had to remind themselves to do it.

So, Karl said out loud. *This is it.*

A nurse stopped in the doorway and eyed him. *You gonna unpack, love?*

Of course, he replied. *Just getting my sea legs.*

The nurse smiled. She had a pretty smile. *Take your time,* she said, leaning into the doorframe. *But we're serving dinner in an hour.* She winked at him and turned on her heel, her ponytail flicking at the air. Her bum jiggled beneath her uniform as she walked away.

It was still light outside when Karl walked down the hallway to the dining hall for dinner. The clock on the wall said 4:30, and as a plateful of unidentifiable foodstuffs was pushed in front of him, Karl thought, *So this is it.* He sat at a long table, like the sort he'd seen in movies about prison. He still wore his driving gloves and hat.

The jiggly bummed nurse pulled up a chair beside him. She grabbed his hand and looked into his eyes. *Okay, love?* she asked.

He couldn't remember the last time someone had looked at him like they meant it. He closed his eyes and allowed himself this moment. She had dark hair, dark eyes, pale skin. She was so clean. He thought, *Another time, another place, I would kiss her.* Being able to rest his nose in her cleavage would make this place bearable.

Instead, he just looked back at her with his old-man eyes. He said, typing into her palm, *Yes, thank you.*

His body felt pathetic in comparison to hers, so old and shrunken, but she looked at him with a type of kindness that made him forget that. And then she stood up and jiggled away, and he sat there, looking at what might have been mashed peas, thinking about how much he wanted her to jiggle on top of him, right in this chair, in front of everybody. No one would even notice. And as he surrendered to the peas, spooning them into his mouth, feeling them sink down his throat, he thought, *I never do what I want to do.*

these are the things karl knows about

TOUCH TYPING

When Karl was a tiny boy thinking enormous thoughts, he would sometimes pretend he was sick so he could accompany his mother to work. She worked in a big room full of typing women, and Karl would sit underneath her, the top of his head touching the bottom of her chair, the perfect line of her legs in front of him, pushed together with such tenacity you would need a crowbar to pry them open. But there was still a sweetness about them, somewhere in the roundness of her calves. He only remembers his mother in bits and pieces now. In legs, and fingers, and reflections in mirrors.

The women had seemed otherworldly to him, like something

that might be kept in a glass case or on a wall. He closed his eyes underneath his mother's chair and listened. The typing was loud and unforgiving. All these pretty women, their bodies perfectly still, their fingers warring against typewriters.

Things began to advance for Karl when he learned the term *touch typing*. He realised that the women didn't have to look at their fingers to make them move in such dramatic ways. This made him feel something he didn't understand. He wouldn't know it was all about his own skin until he met Evie.

Years later, after his first day at typing school, Karl sat at the kitchen table and plunged the tips of his fingers into a bowl of ice. They were red and throbbing. But it was nice to see pain on his fingertips, and feel it running up his forearms, like something trying to get inside him. It felt nice to have something trying to get inside him.

For the first time in his life he felt in a position of power, in the decisive way he was forced to use his fingers. The keys flew at the page – *thwap, thwap, thwap* – like he was throwing punches. He loved the potential of those white pages. That they would start off as nothing and become something. It made him feel as if he, too, could become something.

By day he filled pages with meaningless sentences about cats and dogs, and Jack and Jill and Jane. He typed them as though they were the most important things anyone ever had to say. By night he dreamed in typing exercises. In the morning, he sang the exercises into the showerhead, closing his eyes and letting the water run down his face. His mind lit up in letters as he spoke.

He loved watching his fingers skidding across the keys. He could see that perhaps he was beautiful, because he was creating something. It wasn't music they played in concert halls or art they hung on walls, but to Karl it was both of those things, and more.

EVIE

Karl had met Evie at typing school. Eventually he would come to like the way she clutched at her chest when she talked, as if she were trying to stop her heart from falling out. When they first met, however, he simply thought her name would be good to say during sex. There was something excitingly sacrilegious in the way he could tie Original Sin and sex together. He had, of course, known her as Eve back then; Evie would come later, when he knew her knees and elbows and belly button better than he knew his own. Her name had, from the very beginning, felt incomplete without the ie, kind of hanging there with a drama that seemed unnecessary.

After two months, there had been three conversations, the eyes, the touches, that walk she did with those hips he couldn't blink out of his mind. If she was in the room, he couldn't think of anything else but her presence. Her heat and energy were so noticeable to him. It wasn't just his mind, running through the various things that would happen once she gave him permission to know her, it was also his body; he felt it needing to be near her, as though his skin was going to burst into flames if they didn't touch.

One night, she pirouetted out the door after class, her eyes resting on him. Karl sat in front of his typewriter thinking, *Eve'sfingers-Eve'shands-Eve'ssmile-Eve'shair.* When the last straggler had filed out, he removed, with great difficulty, the letters *M, A, R, Y,* and *E* from his typewriter. He calmly walked to Eve's desk and removed the *R* and *M* from hers. He glued the letters to the tips of his fingers, MARRY on his right hand, ME on his left, and appeared on her doorstep in the fading light. He held his hands up on either side of his face, wiggling his fingers a little. She put her hands on his forearm and typed, *Yes, thank you.*

Their wedding day was simple. Nothing too grand, nothing too quiet. Nothing went wrong, really, unless you count the organist fainting at his post, mid–"Here Comes the Bride." But even that was okay, because when his head fell onto the keys, and that terrible sound of discordant notes crunched together, echoing throughout the church like a moment of suspense in a film, it made Karl feel as though his life was worthy of suspense, and worthy of film.

Karl stood at the front of the church, feeling the sweat gather in the lines on his palms, feeling the eyes of the typing women seated across two pews, looking like birds on a wire.

Their legs were all crossed identically, and everything about them seemed so conscious of the angle of their tilted heads, and he thought, *Have these women always been like this?* There was something about them that made him uneasy.

And then Evie stood opposite him, looking at him so warmly from her plain, unremarkable face. He loved that plain, unremarkable face. The smattering of freckles, the uninteresting nose, the thin lips, the ordinary eyes. When quizzed about Evie's appearance, Karl had trouble describing it. He knew the derogatory implications of the word *plain*, so instead he lied and said she was pretty.

Women were funny, he knew. Not hilarious, but strange and unpredictable. They saw every possible implication of a word, like a prism refracting the light, making too many patterns on the wall. He had learned from an early age to say little and pretend he was slow. When you don't say much, Karl discovered, women assume you're deep and mysterious; they don't, for whatever reason, assume you're stupid.

Her dress was a dull white, and there were no patterns on it, like the reams of paper he threaded through the typewriters, day in, day out. The wedding ring he gave her was customized, a plain silver band with an ampersand typewriter key attached to it in place of a stone. Later that night, as he removed her dress in the glow of moonlight and lay it on the bed as though it were her, he typed on the fabric, *I am so glad I met you, Evie.* But he didn't type like he was warring with the fabric, or throwing punches. He typed delicately, as if he were typing into liquid and trying not to make any splashes.

And when he typed, *I am here, Evie*, across her collarbone, so softly he was barely touching her, she put her lips on his ear and whispered, *Me too*.

LOVE

In their life together, Karl and Evie didn't go anywhere, ever. They were each other's foreign countries.

Only unhappy people leave home, Evie declared.

And we don't need to leave, he said, typing on her forearm.

Yes, she said, resting her forehead on his chin. *We don't need to leave*.

They lived such a small life. Trees and flowers and ocean and neighbours. They never scaled mountains, or braved rapids, or went on telly. They never ate strange animals in Asian countries. They never starved themselves or set themselves on fire for the greater good. They never delivered a rousing speech, sang in a musical, or fought in a boxing ring. Their names wouldn't be in textbooks for children, their faces wouldn't be on banknotes. They would not get their own statue. And when they died, their names would disappear like their last breath, a curiosity for cemetery-goers and nothing more.

But they had loved. They grew plants, drank tea in the

afternoon light, waved at neighbours. They watched *Sale of the Century* every night and, together, were reasonably accomplished at it. They exchanged Christmas gifts with their butcher, their fruiterer, and their baker. Karl gave an old typewriter to the young highly literate boy working at the newsagent. Evie made mittens for the girls working the morning shift at the supermarket. Karl was a guest in the local grade-six class, talking about the history of their town. Evie was a guest in the local year-seven class, demonstrating how to make a pavlova. Karl fiddled about in his shed. Evie fiddled about in the kitchen. They went for looping walks in the morning and evening, through local bush land, through the town, along the shoreline. Their life was a twenty-kilometre radius around their house.

DEATH

He remembers not being able to talk to her as she lay there at the mercy of machinery and starchy sheets. His words in the air, without hers, were horrifying. She was sleeping, she was always sleeping. She would open her eyes occasionally, but they reeled like a newborn's.

So he had stood up and pulled back the sheet that had been so tightly enclosed around her, as though someone wanted to trap her there, pin her to this bed like a specimen of the Almost Dead. He rested his hands on her arm, just bone really, nothing much more, and he typed, softer than breath, *I am here Evie*, and then walked around to the other side of the bed, and rested his palms on her other arm, and her skin was not her skin, there were bruises up this arm, so purple, with such definite edges, like maps of little-known countries, and he thought, *You are my foreign country*, but he typed, *I am here Evie*, and then he lifted up her hospital gown to just above her knees, and her thighs were just nothing, they were just nothing, and he rested his open palms on one, and felt so much nothingness, and he was crying now, he couldn't help it, he was so weak, he was so weak, there was just so much nothingness, and he thought about making nothing into something, and he typed with force and flair this time, watching his fingers, the way they moved on her skin, he so desperately wanted her to feel the beauty of what his fingers were doing, and he typed, *I am here Evie I am here Evie I am here Evie*, over and over again, all the way down her thigh, over her knee, down her shin, like a line of ants marching down her leg, and he leaned over the bed and typed down her other leg, *I am here Evie*, and then moved to the bottom of the bed, and held her feet, her very, very cold feet, in his fists, as small children hold crayons, and he was holding them so hard, as hard as he'd ever held anything, but she didn't move, she didn't notice, she didn't even stir.

I am here Evie

I am here Evie

I am here Evie

In the days following Evie's death, Karl whispered the words *My wife's dead* in the mirror, preparing for some sort of audience. He pictured the woman from the post office, the next-door neighbor, his brother. He loved the feel of their imagined discomfort. The power it gave him. It somehow made all that had happened worthwhile, as though he had gained some sort of secret power through the death of his wife.

He slept in their wardrobe, looking up at her clothes like he was gazing at the stars. They hung over him like apparitions, the lack of her so obvious in the thinness of these clothes. It felt as though he were lying under a guillotine; long, thin strands of cloth that would surely kill him, somehow.

He dreamed of her, of course he did, and woke up thinking, *That is the only time I'll see her now.* He stood up in the darkness and leaned into her clothes, with his arms out like he was flying. Her clothes were so cold.

He had remembered, every morning, since she died. Woken up, and the shock of remembering. He didn't want to sleep anymore, because he didn't want to forget, because the remembering was harder. It was so physical.

He sat on the toilet seat and stared at her bathroom things. The things she once spread on her skin or sprayed in the air or massaged into her hair. He brought the big saucepan in from the kitchen. He emptied all of her bottles into it. Her perfumes, moisturizers, hand creams, body balms, pill bottles. He mixed them together with his hands. The smell was awful, like something out of a department store. But the feeling between his fingers thrilled him.

He dug his hands in, deep, up to his elbows, mixed all her creams and smells together. Her empty bottles were strewn all over the bathroom tiles like carcasses. He squelched his hands together, making fart sounds. He did it over and over again, and let the brown mixture spurt out of the pan and onto the mirror, onto his face, onto the walls. He picked up the pan and sat it on their bed.

My bed, he thought.

He hovered his hand over her pillow, as though he could draw her out from the bed with his hand magnets. Light-brown goo dripped on the pillowcase. He took his clothes off and threw them on the ground. He hoisted himself up on the bed, and stood, teetering a little on the mattress, careful not to bump his head on the overhead light. He lifted the pan up to his belly. Breathed in. Closed his eyes. His mouth. And then raised the pan higher and poured the entire contents onto his head. He gasped. It felt like he'd jumped into a river in the depths of winter. He opened his eyes. The goo ran down his face and neck, and he shivered. He threw the pan against the wall, and it made a satisfying crash.

His son had found him hours later in the backyard, lying on his back on the concrete, basking in the sun. Completely naked except for dollops of brown goo all over his body. Hardening like a crust on his skin.

After dinner on his first night at the nursing home, he sat in the TV room with some of the other guests and watched *That Was Wack!* – a movie set in an American high school. He'd never seen an exclamation mark in a movie title before, and the title didn't make any sense to him, but he certainly found the film compelling. The main character was a young man named Branson Spike. He was not conventionally handsome; however, once you looked at him for long enough, you found a sweetness to the way he behaved that wasn't offensive – that was, in fact, endearing. Branson Spike didn't understand the way his peers behaved or his position in the world, but he tried and this seemed to be the point. Life in *That Was Wack!* was pool parties and midterms and how Veronica believed you fared on Vee's Body Aptitudinal Test, where the body parts of fellow students were scrutinized in agonizing detail and marked – often ungraciously – out of ten. Branson Spike just wanted to fit in, just wanted to find a girl, just wanted to be cool enough. Just wanted. With hilarious and sometimes regrettable results.

During an ad break, Karl looked around him. The room smelled of cleaning products and vomit. A woman sat in an armchair doing her knitting, which was a reasonable and comforting-enough scenario had she been one of those soft, rounded women with pink cheeks, a gaggle of grandchildren at her feet to knit for, a sparkle in her eye, some scones in the oven. But she seemed to Karl to be knitting her own umbilical cord to the living; knitting so she wouldn't die. She looked at the television blankly, hunched over the tangled mess of knitting like an animal crouched at a river.

The man seated next to him on the couch made a gurgling sound in his throat every few minutes. He turned to Karl and stared. There had been an attempt to shave his face, but it wasn't a very good one. Clean, tight stubble was interspersed with surprising spikes of hair.

Gurgle, the man said.

Indeed, Karl said.

Two other men were seated at a nearby table attempting to play cards. One of them had fallen asleep in his chair, his head lolling back. The other one hadn't noticed, or didn't care, and shifted cards around in his hands, mumbling listlessly to himself.

Karl turned back to the television. An ad for a footy game, a reality-television show, face cream, cream cheese, a fast-food restaurant. United in their central message: You are not enough.

It all made Karl feel small, heavy, colourless.

Who were you? he thought, looking at the knitter, the gurgler, the card sharks. *Weren't you someone once?* He felt a vortex of past tense sucking him in.

He avoided eye contact. He didn't introduce himself. He

didn't want to make friends. He felt as far away from them as he did from the young Americans on the telly.

And yet, as Karl watched the exploits of Branson Spike and his peers thrillingly unfold, he felt an overwhelming closeness to the boy. As Branson Spike pined after Veronica Hodges, the most popular girl in school, Karl felt his body tensing. He found himself unable to relax. He so desperately wanted Branson Spike to be loved.

He could see that hope in Branson Spike's eyes. That hope for the one woman. Karl knew that all it took was one, just one, who you could grab on to like a buoy in the sea, who could help you float, stop you from drowning. You were still in the sea, but it didn't matter, because you could hold her, lie on your back and float, look up at the sky and marvel at the things you may have missed. The day, the night, the clouds, the stars, the feeling of the ocean lapping beneath you. And he thought, *C'mon, Branson Spike.*

The beautiful Veronica Hodges was not that woman, as it turned out. Turned out the woman was his best friend, Joan Peters, who had been there all along. Cute, mousey, reliable. There. And Karl had found Evie, and Branson Spike had found Joan Peters.

But what would happen to Branson Spike when she left him? For a job offer, for someone else, to die? What happened to Karl? As the credits rolled, he caught his reflection in the black of the television screen.

What will happen to Karl? he thought.

Later, Karl sat upright in his bed in the darkness. The lights had been turned off hours ago, but he couldn't bring himself to lie down. He felt like if he did he would never wake up, or that he would become one of them. There seemed a depressing choreography to the smacking lips and whistling noses and rasping breaths that surrounded him. He thought, *I don't matter anymore.*

And then, with stinging clarity, *Have I ever mattered?*

He had become blank, but there was not the expectation of something blank, like a page or a canvas; there was not the hope and fear and wonder that blankness can sometimes create. There was just nothing. In the world of punctuation, he might have been a dash – floating, in between, not necessarily required.

Karl wanted to feel again. He wanted to walk onto a crowded bus and make eye contact with a woman with brown hair, blond hair, blue hair – just hair would be enough – and feel that flip in his stomach, that nice hurt. He wanted to laugh loudly, to lean over his knees with it, to throw grapes at someone, to sit in a mud puddle, to yell things, any-things, it didn't matter. He wanted to pull down a woman's skirt, to sit on the bonnet of a moving car, to wear shorts, to eat with his mouth open. He wanted to write love letters to women, tons of them. He wanted to see some lesbians. He wanted to swear loudly. In public. He wanted an unattainable woman to break his heart. He wanted a foreigner to touch him on the arm. Man or woman, it didn't matter. He wanted biceps. He wanted to give someone something big. Not meaningful, just huge. He wanted to jump and try to touch something way out of his reach. He wanted to pick a flower, to pick his nose. He wanted to hit something. Really, very hard. And he thought, *When did I stop doing things and start remembering them instead?*

And so Karl the Touch Typist pushed back the covers. He manoeuvered himself to the edge of the bed and kicked off his slippers, one, then the other, kicking them off like a child would upon reaching the homestead after a day at school, no care for where they might land. One slipper went straight up into the air, flipping like a gymnast, and the other clear across the room, landing on the end of a roommate's bed. No one stirred. He slid off the bed, pulled down his pyjama pants and stomped on them, leaving them to cower on the ground. He ripped off his pyjama top, the buttons pinging away to different corners of the room, and stood there for a few moments, reveling in the glorious feeling of being mostly naked. He dressed himself by the streetlamp light coming through the window.

He put on his shoes. His skin tingled with decision. He ripped a marker off the clipboard that sat at the end of his bed and wrote, *Karl The Touch Typist Wuz 'Ere*, in shaky letters, hugely, on the wall above his bed. He threw the marker up in the air and it clattered to the ground. After a moment's reflection, he picked up the marker and pocketed it. He placed his hat and gloves on the foot of the bed and waved to the four sleeping men. He peeked around the doorway and tiptoed down the hall. He opened the front door and stepped out into the night. And as he walked down the path and out the gate, he thought, *This is the bravest thing I've done by far.*

part two

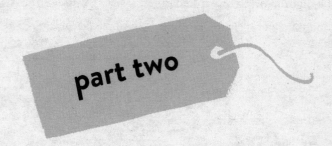

karl the touch typist

Karl sits at a desk in the police station, waiting for a police officer to attend to him. The station is not that different from typing school: rows of desks topped with computers, piles of paper and silent phones. There are no criminals being led past him in cuffs, no shots being fired, no dramatic exchanges between the staff. It's just like any other government office, and Karl can't help feeling a little disappointed by this.

He drums his hands on the desk. *Go, Millie, go!* he had said, and caused a distraction so she could get away. He is proud of himself for his quick thinking. But where will she go? What will she do? She is just a child and he has sent her off into the suburban wilderness.

He looks out the window. A mother walks past pushing a pram. *I'll find you,* Karl whispers. The woman turns toward the window. *Not you,* he says quickly, feeling his face burn red. He shakes his head at himself when he realises she could not have possibly heard. The woman disappears from view.

He looks at the mannequin, whom he has named Manny, and who is propped up against the desk next to him. *We'll find Millie, won't we, Manny?* Karl is glad that Manny is here, that he isn't outnumbered, that he has someone on his side.

Karl straightens Manny's shirt. He flicks Manny's trouser leg, where his leg should be. He looks down at his own hands. His left index finger and both ring fingers end just above the knuckle. When he types with them now, they just stab at the air, reaching out for something they'll never find. He has taught himself to type with the stumps, by dipping his wrist to make contact with the keys. He rubs his thumbs over them.

The police officer who brought him here leans over the reception desk in the corner, talking in low tones to the receptionist. Gary is the officer's name. A full, thick body, movements like a bulldog if it could stand upright. The receptionist is young, beautiful. She has long blond hair, pink nails, and cool blue eyes with heavy black around the rims of them, like she has circled them with black marker the way a teacher might circle an oft-repeated mistake. Gary flexes a bicep for her, pretending he's not doing it on purpose, but Karl knows he is doing it on purpose. As if he's bracing himself for an impact, about to be hip-and-shouldered from a running start. She trails her eyes up Gary's forearm, his bicep, his neck, and then finally to meet his eyes. Gary notices and grins triumphantly, as if he's won a race, a bet, at life.

Karl turns away from them, pulls a pouch out of his pocket, and empties it on the table. He found it in her bedside table drawer when he worked up the guts to start going through her things. A tag on it; *Karl,* it said. Inside the pouch are seven typewriter letters.

F, I, G, T, R, O, O.

She was trying to tell him something, he knows that much. He spends most of his days trying to work out what it is. He pushes the letters around in every configuration he can think of.

Root if G.

Fig root.

Grit of O.

Foot irg.

I forgot.

I forgot.

He always ends up here.

Forgot what? Forgot to turn off the stove? Forgot to tell you that I had an affair with a very good-looking footballer once? Forgot that I have a huge gambling debt to pay off? Forgot to tell you I'm not in love with you? Not at all? That I never was?

So, Gary says, sitting down behind his desk. *What's that, then?*

Karl sits up straight in his chair and sweeps the keys into his pockets. *So,* he says. *Nothing.*

Gary fiddles with some papers on his desk, gathering them together in piles. *Karl, is it?*

Yes, sir, Karl says, his hands in his pockets tapping on his thighs.

Why do you think you're here, Karl?

I've been arrested, sir.

And why have you been arrested, Karl?

I'm not sure. Gary.

I don't believe that at all, Karl. I think you're very sure as to why you've been arrested. Gary sits back in his chair. *I think you'd have to be a bloody idiot to be unsure. And I don't think you're a bloody idiot.*

Karl pauses. *I wouldn't be so sure about that, Gary. I'm quite often an idiot.*

Look, Karl. Look. Gary leans forward, resting his elbows on the desk. *There's been some pretty serious allegations made against you.*

Allegations?

Gary stretches forward to look over the desk. *What are you up to down there?*

Karl's hands are still in his pockets, tapping away as he speaks. His fingers move up and down underneath the fabric. Bugger. He knows how this looks. He pulls his hands out of his pockets. Rests them on his thighs. And then thinks better of it, but doesn't know where to put them. He holds his arms out from his side, like a child mimicking a rocket.

Gary nods toward Manny. *What's he for, then? He part of it?*

It?

Yeah, it. Gary writes something on a sheet of paper that sits atop one of his piles. *We'll need to swab the doll. And you, too,* he says offhandedly.

Mannequin, Karl corrects. He checks himself. *I'm sorry. What?*

The receptionist approaches the desk with two glasses of water. Gary's eyes light up. *Perfect timing, sweetheart,* he says as he takes a glass from her and sips from it. *Can you get the swab kit?*

The girl plonks the other glass in front of Karl. *Cool, yeah, sure,* she says, giving Gary a brilliant smile, then turning around with a generous flick of her hair against her back. Gary watches her walk away for a good five seconds.

And that's when Karl sees it, on the wall behind Gary's desk. A wall filled with posters of faces peering back at him. Some quite obviously their best faces, some quite obviously their worst. *Wanted*, some of them say. *Missing*, others say.

One of them is, unmistakably, his own face.

Missing, he is. Not *Wanted*. *Missing*. He understands that, and agrees.

Gary holds up a piece of paper in Karl's line of sight. Karl tries to focus. He feels the drumming of his heart. He wipes his palms on his trousers.

What do you know about Warwickvale Aged Care Facility? Gary's saying.

Karl recognises the logo on the sheet of paper and his jaw tightens. *Oh, yes.*

Yes what?

It's an aged-care facility.

Have you ever been there before, Karl?

No.

No?

I mean yes.

You mean yes?

Well, yes. And no.

Gary puts the piece of paper on the desk between them. He slides his elbows onto the desk and links his hands together. *What the hell are you talking about, Karl?*

Karl laughs. It's a high-pitched laugh. It doesn't sound like his laugh at all. *I, uh*. He clears his throat. *I've visited there. You get to my age, everyone you know is in there!* The same high-pitched laugh that isn't his.

Gary nods. *Right*. He stands. *Well. Wait here, would you?*

Karl nods, smiling, as Gary disappears into another room and closes the door behind him. Karl swivels his chair around and watches him through the window. Gary picks up a phone and dials. He notices Karl watching him. Karl waves and winks. Gary shuts the blinds.

Uh-oh, Manny, Karl says under his breath.

The receptionist click-clacks away on the computer.

Hi there, Karl calls from across the room.

She looks up. *Hi,* she says bluntly. Not friendly. A snarl on her lips.

What would Branson Spike do? *Nice place to work?* he asks.

She ignores him.

How's the pay? All right?

She puts headphones in her ears and continues to type.

Plan B, Manny, Karl says, casting a quick glance at the receptionist to make sure she's not looking his way. He picks up the glass of water and pours it on the crotch of his trousers.

Um, he says, standing and walking toward her.

Ugh! she says, jumping out of her chair. *Stop right there! What have you done?*

Karl stops. *I seem to have had an accident,* he says lifting his arms up so as to draw attention to the wet patch on his crotch.

Gross, she says, screwing up her face. *Old people are so gross.*

Karl shrugs. *Do you mind if I . . . ?* He points his thumb in the direction of the sign for the toilets.

Just go.

I'll swap trousers with him, he says, scooping Manny up under one arm.

I don't care, she says, taking deep breaths and sitting back in her chair. *Just get away from me.*

I'll be right back, Karl says. The sign for the toilets points down the hall to the right. The entrance is to the left. Karl glances back at the receptionist. She has her earphones in and her back turned. He smiles down at Manny, who looks up at Karl appreciatively. *We're coming, Millie,* Karl whispers. And heads toward the entrance.

agatha pantha

7:43 a.m.: Picks up little girl. Walks to bus station with little girl.

7:53: A teenage boy walks past them on the street. He has braces and pimples and wears his hat sideways. *Probably thinking about masturbating,* she says as they brush shoulders. *What?* he says back to her. He clutches a mobile phone to his ear like a life preserver. *What are you saying on that thing?* she says. *What do children have to say to other children? "Fred, I didn't wet myself last night?"* The boy shakes his head. *You're crazy, lady,* he says as he turns and keeps walking. *In my day, teenagers didn't exist!* she announces to his retreating back. *You were a child until you were two and then you were an adult!* She turns to the little girl and confirms, *He's the crazy one.*

8:06: Arrives at bus station. *What's masturbating?* the little girl asks. *It's what boys do to keep busy!* Agatha says. *What about girls?* the little girl says. *What about girls! Boys touch themselves, girls get themselves ready to be touched by boys. That's it, that's life! You should be writing this down!*

8:07: Finds pay phone in the station. Little girl rings mum. *Phone's still off,* she says.

8:09: Purchases bus tickets. *Two to Kalgoorlie!* she says to the lady behind the counter. *That'll be sixty-four dollars,* the lady says. *What?* Agatha says. *Sixty-four dollars,* the lady repeats. *How much?* Agatha says. *Sixty. Four. Dollars,* the lady says. *You're paying me back,* Agatha says to the little girl. *I don't have any money,* says the little girl. *You'll get a job,* Agatha says. *I'm seven,* the little girl says. *Exactly!* Agatha says. *My dad died,* the little girl says. *We've been through this,* Agatha says. *So did mine.*

8:13: Looks around bus depot. *Why are there so many drinks?* she says to the little girl. There are four refrigerators pushed flush against the wall filled with drinks ready to be purchased. *In my day, there was a pint of milk, or two types of SodaStream, yellow or black. Who knew what was in them. Black was a flavour and that was good enough. Why are there fifteen different types of water?* She squints at the fridge. *What on Earth is Vitamin Water?* The little girl shrugs. *In my day, you were lucky to get a glass of water that didn't have sewage in it!*

8:24: A blond boy sits on the other side of Agatha and stares at her. *What are you staring at?* The blond child is unmoved. *Humans don't like to be stared at. Cats, too. I found that out early. You should really be writing this down. Cats and humans don't like to be stared at. Get a pen!*

8:36: There's an advertisement on the wall, a photo of a lady holding a sign that reads *Old Can Wait*. Agatha stands in front of it as though they're facing off in a western. The blond boy is still staring at Agatha. *Old is not a choice!* she yells at him. The boy begins to cry and his mother glares at Agatha. *There's no point keeping it from him*, Agatha says, and sits down again. *Isn't that our bus?* the little girl says. Through the window, Agatha can see a line of people filing onto a bus. *Kalgoorlie*, it says on the front. *Oh*, Agatha says. She allows herself one deep, dark sigh.

millie bird

Sometimes, when Millie takes her gumboots for a walk through the park near her house, around the shops and down by the beach, she makes Walking Poems. She hears two words from the muscly couple running side by side (*He said*) and three words from the mum talking to her baby in the pram (*Want your dummy?*) and a word from the elderly couple holding hands like they're holding each other up (*specifically*) and then the silence from the girl not wearing much at all (. . .) but her sunglasses are the biggest thing on her body and she has music shoved in her ears and she's concentrating on moving the fat on her thighs to her boobs and the expression on her face, that concentration, is part of the poem too.

He said
Want your dummy?
specifically
. . .

So now, as she walks through the bus, up and down the aisle, running her fingers along the seats, sliding her feet along the floor, she makes a poem.

you like
only twenty
married in a church?
oh my God!

She likes how the words hit against each other sometimes, and other times slide in next to each other, so easily. The surprise of that. And she likes that it's a secret poem, even to her, because she won't remember it. And it will only exist for this moment.

The bus is flying, trees and scrub and houses hurtling past them. The road ahead is long and straight, and the end of it looks as if you might fly off a cliff, into the sky, into space, into the universe, into nothing, or something, or both.

The sun flashes on the grass, making a colour across the sky like fire, and suddenly her stomach hurts, everything hurts, because she thinks of The Night Before The First Day Of Waiting, so she sits down next to Agatha and tries to send her mum messages with her head. If she can detach her head to go into the past, why can't she detach her head so it will go to other places, too? She says, *SORRYMUMSORRYMUM-SORRYMUM* in her head.

The mum in the seat across from them breastfeeds her baby. The dad fusses over them. Millie's stomach pulls.

She looks at Agatha. *Have you got a family, Agatha Pantha?*

Well, that's certainly none of your business!

Who is in charge of families? Millie asks.

What? Agatha says. *The government, I guess!*

Can you start one if you lose yours? Just. In. Case.

You can't just start a family! You're four years old!

Seven.

You have to get pregnant first! And four-year-olds—

Seven.

Same thing. You can't get pregnant!

Why not?

You have to get your! Your! Agatha gulps. *Your monthly womanly visitor!*

Are they from the government?

Good God, no!

Where from, then?

They're not from anywhere!

Why are they called visitors, then?

That's just what we say!

Who?

Agatha sighs loudly. *Okay, I give up! Someone from the government comes to your house and makes you a woman!*

Millie eyes the breastfeeding mum and leans in close to

Agatha. *Will they bring me my boobs, too?* she whispers. *Because I'm not going to take them.*

That's what you say now! You don't want them, then you'll want them, and when you get to my age, when they're much longer than they are wide, you'll just wish you were dead!

The dad opposite them leans over his wife. *Would you keep it down, please?* he says, pointing to the baby and putting a finger to his lips.

No! Agatha yells.

Oi! the bus driver says from the front of the bus. *Pipe down back there!*

Agatha sits back in her seat and crosses her arms. Millie drums her fingers on the armrest.

What did you want to be when you grew up? Millie whispers to Agatha.

It doesn't matter! Agatha whispers back, loudly.

Can I know?

Okay! I wanted to be taller! I wanted to be happier! I wanted to be a nurse! I wanted to have my own set of very good sherry glasses! Not the kind the queen would use, but something very good! That's it! It wasn't much to wish for! But none of it happened! Life decides what happens, not you!

Did you want to get married?

Marriage is never something you want! It's something you do!

Millie fidgets in her seat. The bus driver keeps looking back at them in the mirror.

Did you and your husband love each other very much? Millie whispers.

What is this, a talk show?

Will you be my Dot Four? she asks.

What?

Shh! says the dad.

Okay, okay, Agatha says. *She's the crazy one,* she adds, pointing to Millie. *Just for the record.*

another fact millie knows for sure

Even though there were all these words that existed, it didn't mean you could use them. But there wasn't a book on it, you were just supposed to know this somehow. Everyone else seemed to know but her. You could say some words, and you couldn't say other words, and that's the way life was.

Examples of things you weren't allowed to say, to anyone, at any time:

How fat are you?

Do you have a vagina or a penis?

What kind of funeral do you want when you die?

One night, while her mum was on her hands and knees

scrubbing the bathroom tiles, Millie said, *What kind of funeral would you like, Mum? When you die.*

Her mum sat up like someone had yanked the back of her neck.

Millie took a step back. *A balloon popped today at school and George cried, and Claire laughed, but everyone was surprised and I want there to be a surprise like that at my funeral, one that makes everyone's heart go fast, so they remember their heart is still going, so I want you to have a balloon, and Dad to have a balloon, and I want you to pop them at different times.*

Okay? Millie said when her mum didn't answer.

Go to your room, her mum said eventually.

Millie did as she was told, and sat on the carpet next to her bed. She made patterns in the carpet with her fingers, and watched the world upside down through her window by lying on her back with her head hanging off the side of the bed. The ground was the sky, the sky was the ground, and the trees grew downward. Everything seemed a little freer in that upside-down world.

When her dad came into her room, Millie was looking down at the patterns she'd made in the carpet with her fingertips, tiny roads for tiny people. *Why, Dad?* she said.

Her dad picked her up and sat her on his waist, like he used to do when she was the littlest she remembered being. *It's just a rule,* he said. *You can't talk about it.*

Yes, but who said?

He shrugged. *God?*

But God kills people all the time. That's what Mum said.

So maybe it was someone else. The same guy who made the rule that you can't point at people and laugh, or walk into the post office without any trousers on. There's some guy making rules that we all need to stick to. Got it?

I don't like that guy.

Her dad laughed. *We all don't like that guy.*

A few weeks later, Millie sat on a green plastic chair in her neighbours' shed. She remembered it was green because she tried thinking only green thoughts while she was on it. Grass. Trees. Frogs. Their garbage bin. Their couch. The stuff between her dad's teeth sometimes. The stone on that lady's ring. That beer can. Her pencil case.

Her dad was there, and all the man neighbours were there, and her mum was there, and all the woman neighbours were there. The man neighbours and her dad had scarves on and beers in their hands, and her dad had a beer cozy that had a map of Australia on one side and a lady in a bikini on the other side, and they all said very loud things about goals and tags and half-forwards, and wings and umps and squares, and they surrounded these words with other words you weren't usually allowed to say, but today, for some reason, you could say. Like *fucking* and *shit* and *Who's that arsehole*? and *Fuck, are you fucking kidding me, you bastard*? The woman neighbours and her mum floated in with plates of food, weaving in and out like slow dancing, and said, *See how he talks to me*? and *Do you want sauce, love?* and *Get yer hand off it!* Her dad was loud and her mum smiled a lot, and both of these ways of being were not usual. While the kids outside yelled, *You're it* and *You cheated!* and *You're not my best friend anymore*, Millie sat in her green chair and thought, *Celery. Cucumber. Avocado dip.*

And again, Millie felt like there were rules in her neighbours' shed, rules she didn't know but that everyone else knew, rules that were about how men, women, and children acted around one another; rules that gave men a spot in the shed in front of the telly, that gave women the spaces between them, that gave children the space outside.

Big men dressed in the same clothes as one another stood side by side on the screen, mouthing, *Australians all let us rejoice*. The camera swirled around the ground. It was so big it didn't seem real. *I'd die a happy man if I was there right now*, her dad said, above everyone else. Her dad and the man neighbours laughed together, but Millie could hear only his voice, those forbidden words, like skipping stones, skipping across the surface of everything else.

Can you die happy? she whispered to her gumboots.

karl the touch typist

Evie worked some afternoon shifts at the department store before she became ill. One night, over dinner, she said, *Did you ever dream of being locked in a department store?*

Of course, Karl said.

We should do it one night, she said. *We could hide in the men's change rooms while everyone locks up. No one ever checks them.* She grinned at him mischievously. *Men don't try things on in this town.*

They took turns to say what they would do once the event had been orchestrated.

Jump on the beds, she said.

Eat all the chocolate, he said.

Try on all the lipsticks.

You don't need to wear lipstick, love.

Type on all the fancy computers.

You don't know how to work a computer.

It doesn't have to be on.

I'd take off all the keyboard letters and make a love letter for you.

Oh, love, she said, holding his hand across the table. *But we're not vandals.*

Maybe we are? he said. *Maybe when we're locked in a department store together, we will be?* There seemed a promise of an alternative version of themselves in that department-store fantasy.

But they never did any of these things, because they said a lot but didn't do a lot, and they were both okay with that.

So when Karl the Touch Typist escaped from the nursing home, he walked straight to the department store and waited for it to open. He sat in the café and held his coffee with both hands. It steadied him, having something to hold like that. He watched people, with lives and futures and loves, and he felt like he was floating above it all, like all these feelings that people had were beyond any experience he could ever know. And then, at 4:30 p.m., he wandered into the men's change rooms, and waited.

It worked, just like Evie had said it would, so he stayed there every night, sneaking out of the change rooms after the lights went out and climbing into one of the display beds for as many hours as he dared. Every morning he walked the mile along the coast to the local campground, snuck into the showers, washed himself, then walked the mile back to the department store. In the afternoons, he sat in the department-store café, looking into his coffee cup and thinking, *Eat chocolate, jump on the beds, make a love letter for you.* And then, as the clock struck 4:30 p.m., Karl would begin the process all over again.

He was there almost three weeks, and had managed to carve out an existence for himself that was tolerable. No one had recognised him. No one seemed to be looking for him. There was the slight hiccup of Stan, a short, ferocious-looking man who didn't say a lot, and the security guard with whom Karl was familiar from Evie's time in the store. But it turned out Stan was the security guard for the entire town, that he only worked at the department store once or twice a week, and when he did, he mostly sat in the office in the back watching reruns of '80s television programs. Karl began to think he could live out the rest of his days here. That it would be a nice way to do that. He had everything he needed. He couldn't think of a single reason to leave.

And then Just Millie arrived, and things became more interesting, more complicated, more hopeful. On her first night, he stooped behind the racks of maternity wear and watched her look out the window to the deserted parking lot. He watched her wander back to the women's underwear section and it was then that he decided he needed to look after her.

On the second night Karl watched her from behind

Manny – he was working out how to say something without scaring her – when Stan came clattering toward them. Karl panicked and shoved Manny into Stan's path. He had only meant to distract Stan, to give Millie time to get away, but he ended up knocking Stan out for a few minutes. As Millie scampered off and Karl surveyed the scene – Stan face-first on the ground, Manny sprawled across his head – Karl thought, *Well, Stan is a bit of an idiot.*

Sneaking around the department store this time is a little trickier. People are after him. People who know what he looks like. There are posters of his face, for crying out loud. And he has Manny to consider.

What would Branson Spike do?

So he walks Manny to the bus station and hides him there, outside, behind the big Skip. He covers him with his purple jacket. *I'll be right back*, he says to Manny, patting him comfortingly on the shoulder. He visits the Two Dollar Shop and buys glasses and a new hat. And he walks into the department store, brazenly. His back straight, his eye contact challenging.

But no one seems to notice him, and this is annoying. He goes to all this trouble and no one notices. That he walks straight past the security guard, that Helen sits at the table next to him in the café, that the receptionist from the police station browses through magazines only metres from him. And not one of them spots him. They're not looking for him at all. If they see him, they don't care.

He doesn't matter.

So when he is locked in for the night, after he makes sure Stan isn't around, and after he has triple-checked that Millie is not hiding in the women's underwear section or behind the pot plant, Karl takes his screwdriver and hacks the dashes off every computer keyboard he can find. *See, Evie?* he says. *I am a vandal*. He lines all the dashes up against one another to spell out *I AM HERE* on the café counter. He finds some chalk in the kids' section and writes on the café menu board, *I AM HERE*. He pushes the tables together and arranges the salt and pepper shakers. *I AM HERE*.

He discovers the door to the department-store office unlocked so he wanders in and goes through all the drawers, searching for something, anything, that might reveal Millie's whereabouts. Nothing. Where could she be? Had they found her? What had they done to her? He sits on the desk and rubs his face with his hands. He considers the perfectly white wall. He uncaps his marker and writes, *Karl The Touch Typist Wuz 'Ere* in large, careful, rounded writing.

In the morning, he walks the half mile to the bus station to check on Manny. *You all right?* he says, lifting up the jacket. *Won't be forever*, he promises. *Just till we find Millie*. Manny is okay, if a little dewy in the morning air. *We just need a plan*.

Karl pokes his head around the corner of the bus station building. There are five bays with long parking spots for buses. One bus closes its door and rumbles to life. The faces of passengers line the windows. Some press their noses against the glass, others look straight ahead. The bus reverses and Karl stares at the faces in the windows, like head shots. He thinks, *Wanted. Missing.*

But then, on the back window of the bus, a sign, taped to the inside but facing out: *IN HERE MUM.*

Millie? he chokes. And then, with more urgency, as the bus takes off, chugging up the hill, *Millie!* He pulls the jacket off Manny and shakes him by the shoulders. *Manny,* he says. *Millie's on that bus.*

He throws Manny under his arm and rushes into the station.

Excuse me, he says, approaching the counter, out of breath. *Where's that bus going?*

The lady behind the counter doesn't look at him. *To Kal,* she says, staring at her computer screen.

Right. Is there another bus to Kal?

Sure is, the lady answers.

Oh, great! One tick

Leaves here same time tomorrow.

Karl sighs. He lays his forehead on the counter.

Excuse me, sir, the lady says.

He looks up at her. She is finally looking at him.

Don't do that, sir, she says, gently pushing him off the counter. She produces a cloth from underneath the counter and wipes the spot where his head was.

Karl stands on the footpath across from the bus station, the mannequin under one arm, trying to figure out what to do, when a car pulls up beside him. A very blond teenage boy leans out of the passenger window. *Did you miss the bus, sir?* he says. The boy's eyebrows lift so easily into concern on his face. Karl likes him immediately.

Yes, he says.

The boy nods in the direction of the mannequin.

You guys need a lift?

In the distance, Karl spies a police car coming down over the hill. *Yes,* he says quickly, turning his back and hunching his shoulders as if no one could possibly see through this careful disguise. He kneels down beside the window and looks through to the driver's side. Another blondie blinks back at him, a girl this time. The same easy face.

We're heading east, she says with a smile that would revive a dead person.

Oh, he says. *I need to go to Kalgoorlie.* Her perfect teenage legs glint and shine at him from under the steering wheel.

Uh, sir, says the blond boy. *Your, um. Your thing, sir.*

Oh. Karl realises Manny is head-butting the boy in the face. *Sorry about that. It's aliiive!* He jiggles the mannequin and makes a goofy face, but they don't appear to get the reference.

Meanwhile, the police car is only a couple hundred metres away, and Karl ducks.

Are you all right, sir? The boy leans out the car window, trying to get a look at Karl crouching in the gutter. Karl loves how this boy calls him *sir*, like he's in a suit shop.

Yes, thank you, he says, still crouching, peering around the car, watching the police drive by. *Just lost my footing*. Karl suddenly loves being old, that no one would ever expect him to lie. It's ageism, he supposes, assuming that the elderly are as innocent as children, but he doesn't mind. It seems a fair and just thing, a reward for managing to stay alive for so long. When the police have disappeared down the street, he stands again, dusts himself off, winks at the girl and smiles at the boy.

We're in love, the boy says. *And we need a licensed driver.*

Karl spots the learner tags on the windshield. *Right*, he says. *That's cool*, he says. *You know, I'm cool with that*. He watches their faces to see if *cool* is a word they use. They don't give much away.

The girl leans over the boy's lap. *We're happy to go up to Kal first*, she says.

Karl nods. He points in the direction of the backseat. *Got room?*

Karl sits in the middle of the backseat and tries not to think of the girl's shiny legs. Manny is strapped in on one side of him.

A box with a blender and a toaster on the other. He leans forward and rests his hands on the top corners of the front seats. The front windows are down, and the boy and the girl have their arms out the window, hands caterpillaring in the wind. These two have no idea What's Coming. There is so much for them to know, to find out. Does Karl remember finding out that he knew nothing? No. It was a gradual process, a kind of melting down that took place over years. He thinks of *The Wizard of Oz. I'm melting!*

The girl smiles at him in the rearview mirror. *Seat belt.*

Karl leans back in his seat, trying to be casual. Thinking of Branson Spike. *You know,* he says, *we didn't have seat belts when I was your age.* He clicks his seat belt into the buckle. *All this safety stuff. It's a bit much, don't you think?*

Wow, sir, the boy says, turning around to face Karl, looking at him with wide eyes, as if he's stumbled upon an ancient city. *No seat belts? You must be, like. You know.*

The *sir* is wearing thin. *You've probably never driven drunk, either,* Karl adds haughtily.

No, sir, says the boy. *Don't drink.*

He's gonna be a brain surgeon, the girl says.

Yeah, the boy says, shrugging sheepishly.

My baby has such a steady hand, she says.

The boy holds his hand sideways in front of his face. *I hope so,* he says. Karl is starting to dislike him.

Yep, Karl says, putting his arms around Manny and the

blender. *Used to drive drunk all the time. Cops expected it.* He can see Manny looking at him out of the corner of his eye, calling his bluff.

What did you do, sir? the boy asks.

What did I do?

For, like, a living.

That past tense. *I was, uh.* He searches for something impressive.

Who's that? the girl says, eyeing Manny in the rearview mirror, saving Karl from disappointing them. *Is that some weird kind of, you know, sex thing?* She whispers the word *sex*. *We won't judge you,* she says.

Yeah, we won't judge, says the boy, wiggling his eyebrows at Karl. *Whatever you're into.*

Oh, Karl wishes it was some weird kind of, you know, sex thing. *Yes,* he says before his brain catches up with his mouth. *Sex. And all that. Lots of it.*

Wow, the boy says, cocking his head to one side, looking at Manny as though he's trying to work out the logistics.

With grown-ups, Karl adds hastily. *Very old grown-ups.*

We like it, the girl says. *You know. IT.*

What's up with your hands? the boy says.

What's up with them? Karl says.

Yeah. What's happening there? Why you so twitchy? You on something?

Karl looks down at the seat beneath him. *On something?*

It's cool. Is that why you're headed to Kal? Looking to score?

In what? Karl feels very confused and takes a moment to gather himself. He cranes his neck around to look out the back window and watches the black tar of the road spear out from behind them as if a magician is pulling an endless ribbon out of a sleeve. He looks at the blender and the toaster beside him and thinks about how nice it would be to share appliances with somebody; how nice to start a whole new life with nothing but the capability to mix food and brown bread.

There was someone on that bus, Karl says. *I need to get to them.*

The girl ogles him curiously in the rearview mirror. *Are you in love with this person?*

Karl thinks about that. *In some way,* he says.

Oh, she says. *Old-people love. That is so cute.* She turns to the boy. *We really need to get him to that bus. We'll get you to that bus. You are too cute.*

Cute? Karl thinks. He doesn't know if it's a compliment or an insult.

Are you married, sir? the boy asks.

Yes. I mean, no. It's complicated.

Why? Where's your wife?

Karl looks down at his fingers. *I am here, Evie,* he types on his knees.

Port Cemetery, he says.

Oh, the boy says, and then, after a moment, *Meaning she's . . .*

In it, yes.

Oh. The boy turns to look at him. *I'm sorry, sir.*

You have such good manners, baby, the girl says, gazing at him, the car pulling to the left.

From the backseat, Karl points to the road. *Um.*

You do, the boy says, gazing back at her. *You have good manners, baby.*

She swerves the car to the side of the road and parks it. She grabs his face with both hands, looks him desperately in the eyes, and says, *Don't die. Don't you ever die.*

I won't, he says, putting his hands on her shoulders. *I promise.*

Say it, she says, squishing his face. *Say, "I'll never die."*

I'll never die.

He will die, Karl wants to say, as they begin to slobber all over each other with an urgency they must have learned from the films. They're grabbing at each other, pulling at clothes and hair and lips as if they want to turn each other's skin inside out. They're not going to stop anytime soon. They look set-in, the way country people talk about rain. *I guess I,* Karl says. *We'll just. Step out for some air.* They haven't heard him. Or, if they have, they don't care. The boy's taking his shirt off now. Do sixteen-year-olds normally have pectorals like that? *We'll just be.* Karl points outside. *I'll just let you.* He can't take his eyes off the boy's chest. It's unbelievable. Like something from the telly. *Have some.* Karl touches his own chest, where his pectorals might once have been. Were they ever there? *Alone time.*

Karl leans over Manny, opens the door, pushes Manny out, and falls out after him. He closes the door quietly. He doesn't know why he does this, like they're sleeping children, but he does it. He picks Manny up and hauls him over to a nearby tree. He leans Manny against it and stands next to him. Either side of the road is dotted with small gum trees, tufts of grass appearing sporadically out of the red dirt, like an adolescent moustache.

Show-offs, Karl says, pulling at the collar of his own shirt and peering in. He can feel Manny's eyes on him. *Don't look at me like that,* he says, leaning against the bark of the tree. *I'm sorry about the. You know. Sex thing.* He finds himself whispering *sex,* too. *I would never.* He shrugs. *I wouldn't even know where to start.* He folds his arms.

Karl can hear muffled noises coming from the car, rising in pitch. *What do they know about love, Manny?* The horn starts beeping, rhythmically, startling a bunch of pink-and-gray galahs into flight.

Karl falls asleep sitting against the tree, his arms wrapped around Manny's remaining leg. He wakes to the sound of slamming doors and giggling.

Sir? the boy calls.

Quick, Manny, Karl says with a rush of spontaneity. *Pretend you're dead.* He slumps to the ground. The gravel digs into the back of his neck. *Don't worry,* he assures Manny, tapping him on the foot. *It'll be fun. They'll love it.*

Through his eyelashes, Karl watches them walk toward him. The boy slaps her bum, and she jumps in the air and waggles her finger at him, mock-annoyed.

Sir? the boy says, standing over him. Karl can feel him blocking out the sunlight, casting a shadow over his body.

Karl feels a poke in the shoulder. *Sir,* the boy says again. *We're ready now.* The boy grabs his shoulders and shakes him. *You should get up now, sir.* Karl doesn't move.

Is he? the girl says, gasping a little.

Sir, the boy says, and slaps Karl across the face. *You can get up now.* Karl feels the boy's breath on his cheek.

The girl starts wailing. *You've killed him, you stupid bastard,* she shrieks. *I knew you'd kill somebody someday.* The boy says, *It wasn't me,* and she says, *We shouldn't have picked up somebody so old, I told you he was too old,* and Karl twitches a bit at this. *Shut up,* the boy says, *I'm trying to think, I can't think with all your yakking,* and she's hitting the boy now, flailing her arms at that chest, and the boy barely flinches – what is he, Superman? – and she says, *What are we going to do with the body?,* and the boy says, *We'll have to bury him,* and starts pulling at Karl's legs, and Karl is starting to feel really awkward now, so he opens his eyes and does a two-handed-wave at them, like the contestants sometimes do on *Millionaire. Surprise,* he says, but he's not very confident in his delivery, and the boy drops his legs and screams, and the girl screams, too. Has anyone ever screamed at him like that? He doesn't think so, so he smiles and pushes himself to his feet, wincing with the pain of having old bones. *Just jokes, see?* He spins around and does his best to do a little jig.

It is a tense drive from then on. Karl tries to make small talk, about family, weather, car makes. He reads out the signs they pass – *Kalgoorlie: one hundred, not far to go now. Give way. Cattle crossing ahead*. Pointing out lone birds, roadkill, changes in the scrub, trying to vary the pitch and tone of his voice to incite interest.

He tries a different approach. *Listen, how many Dead Things do you know?*

Excuse me? the girl says.

He clears his throat. *You know – has anyone in your life . . . passed away.*

Why are you asking us that? the boy says.

Are you going to kill us?

No! Of course not. It's just a question. When you get to my age, well. All the people you love have died.

The girl pulls up at the side of the road again and gets out of the car. *I'm pissing,* she says. *When I get back, no one better be pretending they're dead. Or I'll kill you.* She slams the door and disappears into the scrub.

The boy turns to Karl and says, *Way to go, old man.*

I wasn't born old, you know, Karl says. *Young man.* He leans forward. *Let's do something,* he whispers conspiratorially.

What are you talking about?

Steal something. Put beer in our water flasks.

What's a flask?

He thinks of *That Was Wack!* Of Branson Spike. *Knock over some letter boxes. Egg a house.*

We'd just have to clean it up.

Don't you want to flirt with danger?

Not really.

Karl thumps back in his seat.

It's over, old man. The boy raises both eyebrows at Karl.

What do you mean?

You know what I mean.

So Karl folds his arms. If that's the way he wants it.

Karl looks out the back window again. The road seems different now that they're stationary. It isn't a magic trick anymore. It's so bleak in its stasis. But then something moves over the horizon toward them. A bus. *A bus,* he says to Manny. *What?* the boy says. *The bus,* Karl says as it zooms past them, shaking the car. He leans forward over the gearstick and plants his palms on the dashboard. *Hey,* the boy says. Karl sees the outline of a white piece of paper in the back window of the bus. *It's her,* he says, turning to the boy. *It's her. It's definitely her. Follow that bus.*

What? the boy says.

It's getting away from them and Karl is desperate so he tries to climb into the front seat but the boy pushes him back and they grunt and groan at each other, but Karl can't win, he has no chance against that chest, those unbelievable pectorals, so he sinks back in his seat, and there's no sound but the sound of their breathing.

Just calm down, the boy starts to say, but Karl changes his mind, he can win, he will win, and he opens the back door and then the front door and tries to slide into the front seat but the boy pushes at him and Karl grabs at the steering wheel to lever himself but the boy tries to peel away Karl's fingertips, and it's unfair because he has all of his fingers and he hasn't lost anything, the boy doesn't know what it feels like to lose anything, to lose everything, he doesn't know, he doesn't know, so Karl releases his grip on the steering wheel, and this boy doesn't know, so Karl channels it all into his hands, anything he's ever lost, it's all in his fingertips now, the ones he has left, and he feels it all there, pulsing down the length of his fingers, *I AM HERE*, and he flicks him, he flicks the boy as hard as he can on the forehead.

Ow, Superboy says, rubbing his forehead and looking accusingly at Karl.

Sorry, Karl says, panting, already regretting the flicking incident, leaning into the side of the car, trying to catch his breath.

Seriously, man, that was not cool.

I said I'm sorry, Karl says. *Man.*

The girl appears next to Karl. *Well?* she says, hands on hips.

Well, what?

Well, she says, pointing up the road.

Karl walks forward, beyond the bonnet of the car, raises his hand over his eyes and looks toward the direction of Kalgoorlie. The bus has stopped up ahead.

It's right there, Karl says. *Wait,* he calls down the road, waving. *Thanks for the lift,* he says to the couple. *It was wack!* He grabs Manny from the backseat and slams the door. *I'm coming.*

As he shuffles down the road, he hears the girl say, *What the hell is wrong with you?*

He flicked me in the face, the boy answers.

God, you're pathetic, the girl says. *Mum was so right about you.*

Their voices drown out behind him. *Wait,* he says, shuffling as fast as is possible for him. *Wait for me.* He wishes he could break out into a run like he used to, wishes he could be boisterous and careless with his limbs. He focuses on the white square of paper on the back window. *Please don't go,* he whispers. The couple drive up alongside him and Karl's jacket is thrown out the passenger window. It hits Karl in the face. The couple speeds off, fishtailing in the gravel on the side of the bitumen, a cloud of dust settling over him. Karl removes the jacket from his face and watches the couple drive off into the oblivion of youth. He takes a deep breath and yells at the top of his lungs, *HE WILL DIE, YOU KNOW.*

millie bird

The bus driver is a woman, but she looks like she's wearing her dad's clothes: blue shorts, a collared short-sleeved shirt that's too big for her, socks pulled up to her knees, black lace-up shoes. She's very skinny, with spiky hair. Millie walks down the aisle, bringing the mannequin's leg with her.

The truth of
splendid
to go to the toilet?

She finds a seat behind the driver. There's a sticker on the dashboard that says, *Would you like to speak to the man in charge, or the woman who knows what's happening*? She watches the white dashes on the road. She loves how, if the bus moves fast enough, they join together in one long white line that splits the world in half.

Have you ever seen chicken come in a bucket? Millie says to the bus driver.

The bus driver doesn't answer for ages. She just sits there and drives as if Millie hasn't spoken at all. Millie's about to say it again when the bus driver says, *I done this for thirty years.* She's gazing out over the road and it's hard to tell if she's talking to herself or to Millie. *You reckon you wouldn't learn much, driving up and down the same patch over and over.* They pass a bright-green paddock with one gray, leafless tree sticking out of the middle of it. It looks like a person trying to attract attention. Millie waves at it.

On either side of the road, the ground is flat and wide, and completely white. The sun shines directly on it, and Millie has to shield her eyes from the glare. *Is that snow?* she asks.

The bus driver snorts. *You never seen the salt flats?*

Nope, Millie replies, wanting to lick the paddock of salt more than anything. Her forehead bumps softly on the window.

There was water there once, the bus driver continues. *Then the salt came up and* – she makes slurping noises – *sucked it all up. Killed off everything around it.*

Oh. There are swirls and shapes all over it, like giants have been finger-painting.

But then all sorts of things turn up that couldn't grow there before. Pretty beaut, eh? The salt glitters at Millie in the sunlight.

It's tough out there, though, the bus driver goes on. *All them hippies down our way goin' to find themselves in India or wherever. Hangin' upside down, eatin' lentils. It's nothin'. Walk in the park! Spend a night out here and you'll find yerself pretty quick.*

Millie can see herself in the reflection on the window. It seems strange to want to find yourself. Wouldn't you want to find somebody else? Aren't you the one thing you can be sure of? She puts her real hand on the glass, up against her reflection hand.

They drive past rows of gum trees, leaning out over the road and into the sky, like dancers posing. *Those trees there,* the bus driver says. *See how pink they are?* Millie nods. They make her think of the inside of her mouth. *Salmon gums. Always looks like the sun's setting on 'em.* Millie stares at them.

That yer granny back there?

Millie shrugs.

What's that on yer wrist? the bus driver says.

Millie looks down at the beer cozy. *It was my dad's. He died.*

The bus driver looks at Millie in the rearview mirror. *What did he go and die for?*

Dunno.

She nods. *Righto.* The bus starts to slow.

I'm Millie Bird.

Stella, love. The name's Stella. The bus driver yanks her collar. *These are my brother's clothes. His bus. He went and died too.*

Millie nods.

What about yer mum? Stella says.

Listen here, Toilet Brush, Agatha interrupts. She has made her way up the aisle and steadies herself by holding on to the back of Stella's seat. *Does the train still leave from Kalgoorlie?*

Stella squints at her in the mirror. *Nah,* she says.

No?

They got the flying cars now. They'll take you straight there. Fast, too.

Okay, Agatha says. *Okay, Toilet Brush. If you don't want to help, just say so.*

Hey, lady, I'm not the bloody info centre. I can drop you at the station. Work it out yerself.

Can't you just yell out the window to one of your relatives? "Hey, Mary! When's the train go?"

Stella flicks on the indicator and pulls the bus off the road, gravel skidding beneath the wheels. She brings the bus to a halt at a bus shelter. *Lake Cartwheel,* she announces. The door opens and a tall boy with earphones in his ears walks down the aisle of the bus and down the steps.

Stella turns her body so it faces the door, one arm resting on the top of her seat, the other draped over the steering wheel. *Not my problem,* Stella says to Agatha, but she doesn't look at her, and instead watches the passengers file onto the bus. A little boy with glasses and slicked-down hair takes big lunges up the stairs. *G'day, young Lawrence,* Stella says. *Hello, Stella,* Lawrence says without looking up. Stella knows all the new passengers by name – *Mrs. Cranley, Timbo, Vince, Felicity* – and they all know her name back.

The last man on is big and wide and wears a bright fluorescent vest. He has dirt on his face and arms and hands. *G'day, Stell,* he says. *Trent,* she says, flicking her head upward in recognition. He pauses at the top of the stairs and points a thumb in the direction that he came. *There's some bloke on his way,* he says. *Gonna be waitin' a while. He's about a hundred and seventy-five.* He grins. *Give or take.*

And then there's a surprise like balloons bursting, because Karl appears at the bottom of the steps. He has the mannequin tucked under his arm and is breathing heavily. Sweat drips down his face. Millie feels her heart in her chest as she jumps down the steps and wraps her arms around Karl's neck.

Just Millie, he says.

And then Agatha says, *Did you follow me, Gene Wilder?* She reaches into her handbag, pulls out an Anzac biscuit, and throws it at him.

agatha pantha

agatha and karl actually know each other (sort of)

Karl used to walk past her house, always wearing that purple suit. Sometimes he wore a long jacket, too, one that reached his toes. *Not enough hair!* she might yell from her Chair of Discernment. *Ridiculous suit! Annoying face! Trying to look like Gene Wilder!*

He stood there, once, for more than a few moments, and caressed her fence. She had initially been so flabbergasted that real words wouldn't form outside her head. *Gah!* she yelled. *Sah!* she tried. *What?* she said, eventually. She stood up, blood rushing to her head, and stuck her index finger out the window as far as it would go. *Stop molesting my fence!* She pushed her head through the window and pointed her finger at him. The man jumped, and looked toward her. *Shoo!* She yelled. *Yes, you! You're touching!*

He grabbed the top of her fence with both hands. *I'm sorry,* he shouted back, his hands tapping on her fence. *I didn't mean to – it's just that – I can help you with those weeds.*

Agatha pointed her finger down the street. *Walk!* she yelled. *Know how to do that?*

He did walk, but ran his finger along her fence as he did so. He was back the very next day, and the day after that, and the day after that. He would lean over her fence and rip out her weeds. She would lean through the window and try to hit him with day-old Anzacs. He bothered her, he bothered her very much. *You bother me!* she'd occasionally yell as he walked off down the street. She'd press her face against the window, her breath fogging up the glass. He never looked back, and this bothered Agatha even more. She didn't know why. *Why does he bother me so much!* she yelled, as she watched him scamper down the street, peeking into front yards. And then one day he stopped coming, suddenly, and she stood at the window from 12:51 p.m. to 1:32 p.m. for a week, dipping her fingers into a bowl of rock-hard Anzacs, waiting, and he didn't turn up, and it felt like vertigo.

karl the touch typist

He had hugged Millie and it felt like something he didn't deserve but wished he did. Surely he had once held his son like that. But the feeling seemed brand-new. And now the other woman is here, making his life more interesting, more complicated.

another thing karl knows about

AGATHA

He knew the woman's story, the whole town of Warwickvale did. Scott and Amy had driven past her house one day after they'd taken Karl grocery shopping.

Amy turned to his son and said, *I hope you don't expect me to barricade myself in our house if you cark it.*

Too right I do, Ames, his son said. *But if you go first, I'm throwing a party.*

Amy poked his son playfully in the ribs. *Slow down,* she said. *Let's have a peek.*

Nah, his son said. *Let's leave her alone.*

Come on, Amy said. *Sometimes you can see her looking out the window.*

Karl had never thought this woman's story to be relevant and had quarantined it to the realm of things Amy found interesting (the misfortunes of others, pigs small enough to be put in handbags, a man called Dr. Phil). But now that he was looking at this woman's house, he saw the story was very relevant. It was like looking at the inside of his guts in the form of a house. Dark and dying, it had waved its white flag long ago.

Ooh, there she is, Amy said.

The woman looked straight at them out of her window, her face cold and hard.

Creepy, Amy said. As they drove off, she added, *Shutting yourself in like that. Is that romantic, depressing, or just plain lunacy?*

All three, I reckon, his son said. *Whaddya think, Dad? She's a single lady. Want me to leave you on her doorstep?*

Karl didn't say anything. Everything about that house and that woman's face had made him feel less alone.

They stand outside the train station in Kalgoorlie, next to a war memorial, the statue of a soldier with gun at the ready looking out above their heads. Four-wheel-drives whizz past them, huge sprays of rusty red dotted and caked on their cars like art. The roofs of the pubs sweep across the sky in regal, commanding lines. On the bus on the way in, Karl had read the chalkboard outside one of the pubs. *Hot Topless Skimpies*, it read, which sounded to Karl like something you might catch in a saltwater lake. He stared at the sign for a few minutes as the bus idled at the traffic lights. The slow realisation of what it actually meant spread over his cheeks in hot red patches.

Back home on the southwest coast, the people have dazed eyes, blond edges, waterlogged strides. The people here are different: scratchy, like they've been sketched roughly on paper, like they are born of the very red dirt they scuff their feet in, made out of the salmon gums that line the streets. They yell outside the bakery, the supermarket, the pubs, and in the main thoroughfare, chopping at words as though throwing their sentences into a blender. Karl doesn't feel like he fits in here. Then again, Karl doesn't feel like he fits in back there, either.

The sky is between day and night, that deep blue it gets when it's shedding one for the other. Agatha storms toward Karl and Millie. She's difficult to make out in the deepening dark, but there's something about the way she walks that means he will never mistake her for anyone else. As though she is fighting with the air; as though the air is as thick as a sheet and she has to tear her way through it.

Well, it doesn't leave until tomorrow, she says, a cloud of dust surrounding her like a force field. *I bet that Stella woman knew it too! Never trust a woman skinnier than you! Write that down! What are we going to do? Typist! I'm not going to sit around here all night, gawking at you lot! It's seven thirty-seven at night! We don't have any money!*

Karl feels a rising sense of panic when he realises he is the only man there. Men have certain obligations in these circumstances, he knows. He can feel the eyes of all women on him. Not just the ones with him now, but generations of women, spanning centuries, countries, cultures. *Well,* he says, in what he hopes is a commanding voice, *We have to do something.* He points at the air with his index finger to punctuate the sentence. He begins to pace, hoping that the movement might jiggle the decision-making part of his brain. *Let's . . .*

Hide, Millie suggests.

Karl considers this. *That sounds pretty good.*

A friend of mine came to Kalgoorlie once! Agatha says. *Never came back! Don't know what happened to her! No one said for sure! But I know! She's in one of those brothels right now! Doing her business!* She takes a deep breath but then snaps her mouth shut. It appears something has caught her eye. She holds on to the fence of the war memorial and glares at it. *They Shall Grow Not Old,* she reads. *As We That Are Left Grow Old.*

Agatha seems unable to move. *As We That Are Left*, she repeats. She rests a hand gingerly on the base of her throat.

Millie puts her arms through the gap between the bars in the fence and looks up at Agatha. *What's a brothel?*

Agatha turns her back on the war memorial. Just as she says, *What are you two looking at?* a bus pulls off the road into the parking lot and stops next to them.

The bus door opens. It's Stella. *Seven o'clock*, Stella says.

Excuse me? Agatha says, peering into the bus, her stance thick and wide, planting her feet on the ground as if in a standoff.

The train, Grumble Bum. Leaves at seven in the morning.

Thought we weren't your problem, Agatha says.

I changed my mind, haven't I, Stella says.

millie bird

Stella's house makes a lot of sounds. The floor talks when Millie walks on it and it's like there are people wandering about in the ceiling and the walls, maybe trying to get in or out or maybe tap-dancing. Millie isn't to know. The whole house looks like the thrift store back home, so many things that don't match all piled together and forced to get along. Millie keeps finding new things she hasn't seen before, and she wonders if this is why Stella does it, to keep forgetting and discovering.

Millie has a bath and makes entire cities out of bubbles: houses and skyscrapers and driveways and trees and a cemetery and a supermarket and a school and a police station and a post office. She's in there for so long that the water goes cold, and Stella lifts her out of the bath, wraps her in a towel, and plonks her in front of a heater with red glowing bars across it.

And later Millie sits at the kitchen table with Karl and Agatha while Stella makes spaghetti for all of them. Manny is allowed in the kitchen too, but there aren't enough chairs for him so Karl props him up against the wall, close to the microwave. Millie smiles at Manny while she's slurping up spaghetti. When they've all finished their dinner, Stella makes cups of tea for everyone except Millie, who gets a big bowl of ice cream. Agatha and Karl sit in the lounge room – *We're ringing your mum in the morning,* Agatha says on her way out of the kitchen – and Millie stays in the kitchen with Stella and Manny.

Just be kind, her dad had said, and as far as Millie can tell, Stella knows what that means.

Millie watches Stella blow on her cup of tea, the steam rising up and making shapes, like the coffees did in the department store. What if everything breathed like this? Animals and people and grass and trees. Everyone and everything always always had curling lines of steam making patterns around them, and some people would have short, quick breaths from running or heart attacks, and others would have long, slow breaths from sleeping or watching telly. It'd be like watching music, if music looked like anything, and the world would always be filled with the music of breath.

Maybe when you let out your last breath, you let out everything, your memories and thoughts and things you wished you'd said and things you wished you didn't say and the pictures in your head of hot coffee steam and the last look on your dad's face and the feeling of mud between your fingers and the wind when you run down a hill and the colour of everything, ever.

I never been in, Stella says. *The cemetery's just down the road. I drive past it every night but I never been in. Know where he is. Straight down the path as you walk in. Turn right. On the first corner.* Stella sips her tea. *Errol. My little brother.*

Errol, Millie repeats.

Yep, Stella replies. *That's my brother. You know, I got home tonight and sat on me couch and thought of him. I know he would've looked after ya without even thinkin' about it. So I got back in me berloody bus. And now here we are.*

Millie spoons ice cream into her mouth. *Did you see him when he was a Dead Thing?* she asks.

Stella blows on her tea. *Yeah*, she says.

What did he look like?

She pauses. *You know when someone wears glasses all the time?*

Millie nods.

And then they take them off to clean them?

Yeah.

And their eyes look bigger, or smaller, or something.

Yep.

That's what it was like.

Were you sure it was him?

Well, I didn't do a berloody DNA test.

Do you know where he is now?

Other than in Kal Cemetery, you mean? Depends how you think about things. Some might reckon he's up there. Stella points up at the ceiling.

With Jimi Hendrix?

Who?

Jimi Hendrix.

The guitar bloke?

Millie shrugs. *Dad knew him.*

I reckon he's just in the ground. And he's not coming back as a beetle or whatever. Or floating around watching me sit on the loo. He's just dead. Done. You're alive and then you're dead, and that's it, that's the point.

Done?

Done. Stella studies Millie. *What do you think happens?*

I don't know.

There's your answer.

That's not an answer.

All I know for sure is that no one knows what's goin' on at the bottom of the sea, or in our brains, or when we die. That's okay, I reckon. Gives us something to think about. When we're driving buses or whatever.

Millie looks up at Stella, then to Manny, then back to Stella. She lowers her voice. *I think Dead Things turn into plastic and sometimes they get put in the shops.*

Stella nods. *Fair enough.* She stares at Millie. Like she's an X-ray. *Where's your mum, love?* she says, finally. *No funny buggers, now.*

Where's yours?

That sounds to me like funny buggers. She nods again. *Just up the road. We don't speak.*

Why not?

One of those things, I reckon.

Millie looks at her, and Stella sighs. *There's not much else to it, really. A lot of hot air.* She stands and starts placing the plates into the sink. *None of my family speak, you know. Like we can't. I'm sure you're supposed to be better than that.*

Millie clears her throat. *She's gone. Mum.*

Stella turns around and rests her back against the sink. Her hands drip soapy water all down her shorts. *Where, love?*

One of those things, I reckon.

Stella smiles.

Millie takes the piece of paper out of her pocket and unfolds it carefully. She smooths it out on the table. *It's my mum's itinerary,* she says, hoping she has the word right.

Stella pulls out her glasses from her pocket and holds the paper up to the light. She folds it back up and hands it to Millie. She takes off her glasses. Rubs her eyes. The hum of the fridge seems loud suddenly.

Stella stands at the sink and looks out the window. Her hands grip the sink so hard that her knuckles whiten. *Look,* she says, not looking at Millie. *Has it ever occurred to you that your mum doesn't want you to find her?*

Millie holds her stomach.

Stella turns and crosses her arms. *They're not yer grandparents, are they?*

Millie looks away. *They're helping me find Mum.*

Stella sits down in her chair and leans in close to Millie. *I'll take you home tomorrow, love,* she says. *It'll be fine. You'll see.*

Millie wakes in the middle of the night. She pulls a piece of paper out of her backpack, walks out of the bedroom and down the hallway, opens the front door, and sticks it to the door with Blu-Tack.

In Here Mum.

She still can't sleep, so she wanders around the house, picking up ornaments, touching faces on photos, sitting on couches, trying on hats. She makes shapes in the dust on the coffee table. She opens the back door and sits on the step.

The moon is big and it lights up a small, fenced-in backyard filled with old bunches of flowers wrapped in plastic and ribbon. The clothesline rises up out of it all and squeaks around in a slow circle in the breeze. The pile is higher than Millie's head. There's plastic wrapping and coloured ribbons in pinks and greens and reds and other bright colours, but all the flowers are brown and dead. She walks down the stairs and runs both hands up and down the pile, the backs of her hands on the way up, then her palms on the way down. It's like the pictures Millie has seen of the sideways view of Earth in books. A chunk cut out of the Earth.

Later, she would write in her Book Of Dead Things: *Number 30. Stella's pile of flowers.*

Her head detaches itself, and she's visiting her dad in the hospital. Millie had never seen so many flowers for one person. She lay on her back under his bed and watched all the visiting feet. Tiny feet, big feet, in-between feet. Sneakers, high heels, sandals. Red shoes, black shoes, green shoes.

When all the visiting feet had left, her dad said, *I wonder where Millie is.* He was breathing hard, like old people, and fat people, but he wasn't old, and he wasn't fat.

I don't know, her mum said. Her feet crossed and recrossed as she sat in the big armchair. *Probably out robbing a bank. Or preaching for world peace.*

Their words were huge and rounded, like they were winking at each other.

Her dad's hand dangled down by the side of the bed. She crawled toward his hand. She had never known it so white. The machines bleeped and blurped and binged. She slipped her hand into his and held it.

And now she clambers to the top of the pile of flowers, her legs sinking into the plastic and the dead flowers like it's quicksand. She thinks of the lakes made of salt and the trees made of fish and how people can hide from their own selves and how the world is a place like nothing Millie could ever have imagined.

She thinks of how Stella said that no one knows what happens at the bottom of the sea, and she wonders if Sea People live quiet lives down there, watching Sea Television and laughing at one another's Sea Jokes. Would they call the sky the ocean and the ocean the sky? Would their music travel through the air in bubbles? Millie wishes that all words and music and sound travelled in bubbles. That you had to pop each one to let the sound out. How silent and surprising the world would be. You would always get a fright when someone popped a bubble and a sound jumped out of it, ta-da! Except maybe more people would be hit by cars, and it would be harder to get your mum's attention from across the street. And what if a *HELP* bubble went sailing off into the sky, was popped by a jet plane, and no one could hear it over the roar of the engine?

The clothesline spins and spins and spins overhead, creaking like an old bed. She picks up the new flowers at the top of the pile. *Errol*, the card reads.

Millie writes, *Be Right Back Mum* in small letters on the bottom of the sign and walks out of the front yard and down the street holding Errol's bunch of flowers. When she finds the cemetery, it's lit up by the streetlights, and it's not like the one back home. It's flat, and there's no grass on the ground. Just red dirt as far as Millie can see. Large painted buckets filled with red and purple flowers. Giant gum trees lining the pathway and looming over the graves. She cranes her neck back to see the very tops of them. Her dad was always so high in the sky. She touches the bark of a tree as she walks past and thinks, *Don't trees need shade too?* The bark is still so hot from the daytime. The red dirt has stained the gravestones a light-pink colour. The graves are separated by signs into different religions, so that, Millie assumes, the heavens don't get mixed-up.

The thought occurs to her like a kick in the stomach: *Will I go to the same heaven as my dad?* And then, more panicked now, *Which heaven did he go to?* She never thought to ask.

There are no cars whooshing past, or planes whizzing, or birds singing, just the leaves on the trees sliding over one another, like the sound of someone wiping their feet on a welcome mat. It is the most perfect sound, a sound that is barely a sound at all, a Just Enough Sound so that she knows she is still here.

And then she sees it. First right, on the corner.

She kneels beside the grave, carefully placing the flowers in front of it. The red stones make imprints on her knees. Millie licks her fingers and rubs the red dirt out from the indentations on the gravestone.

Errol, Millie says. His name is sunken on there, like it's breathing him in.

The start date and the end date are always the important bits on the gravestones, written in big letters. The dash in between is always so small you can barely see it. Surely the dash should be big and bright and amazing, or not, depending on how you had lived. Surely the dash should show how this Dead Thing had lived.

Did Errol ever know that his life would be just a dash on a gravestone? That everything he did and all the food he ate and the car trips he took and the kisses he gave would all end up as a line on a rock? In a park with a whole lot of strangers?

Millie lies down flat on her back, the top of her head touching the base of the gravestone. She spreads her body out as far as it will go, reaching her arms out wide, stretching out her fingers so that they're as far away from one another as possible.

She looks up at the night sky through the break in the trees and can only think of one word, so she says it out loud.

Dad?

And suddenly she's certain she's the smallest thing that's ever been made, smaller than even the bits of gravel in her back, or the ants that crawl around her feet, because the world is so big, full of trees and stars and dying, and she thinks maybe a dash is most exactly what she is.

another fact millie knows for sure

When her dad was in the hospital, the words *Dad, are you becoming a Dead Thing*? wouldn't come out.

agatha pantha

9:06 p.m.: Sits in a foreign chair in a foreign room in a foreign house drinking tea out of a foreign cup at a foreign time slot, and tries not to think about it. *What's wrong with your hands?* Agatha yells at The Typist. The Typist puts his tea down on the coffee table and hides his hands under his armpits. *Nothing,* he says. *Why do they twitch like that?* she says. *They're not twitching,* he says. *They look like they're twitching,* she says. *They're not twitching,* he repeats. *They're typing. Typing?* she says. *Typing,* he confirms. *Why are they doing that?* she says. He shrugs. *You don't want to tell me?* she says. *Not really,* he says.

9:11: *This tea is terrible!* she whispers loudly to him.

9:13: *What's that?* he says. Her Age Book sticks out of the top of her handbag. *Your diary?* She pushes it back inside her handbag and zips it up. *What's what?* she says. *The thing you just put in your handbag,* he says. *I didn't put anything in my handbag,* she says. *Yes, you did,* he says. *No, I didn't,* she says.

9:16: *Your wife?* Agatha says. *Passed,* he says. *Ron, too,* she says. *Heart attack outside the pet shop. You?* He sits on his hands. *Cancer,* he says. Agatha nods.

9:17: *Why did you bother me at my house?* she says. *Maybe you're in love with me?* she adds. *I'm not in love with you,* The Typist says. *That's what someone who was in love with me would say!* Agatha says. *I don't even know you,* he says. *No,* she says. *You don't.*

9:18: But what she wanted to say was, *Why did you stop coming to my house?*

9:20: The Typist falls asleep, his head leaning back on the couch, his mouth wide open, snoring.

9:22: *They shall grow not old,* she whispers, *as we that are left grow old.*

9:23: Agatha Pantha allows herself to feel lonely.

karl the touch typist

Sometime between night and morning, Karl makes his way down the hallway to use the toilet, but stops when he overhears Stella talking in the kitchen.

Yeah, she's saying. *An abandoned child, yeah.*

Karl leans his back into the wall next to the kitchen doorway. The light from the kitchen stretches out across the hallway like the entrance to another, better world.

Don't know a whole lot, she continues. *Her mum's skipped town. Her dad's no longer with us. Some old folks are helping her out*. She pauses. *Yeah, look, I dunno. The woman's completely berko. The bloke's not much better. They're just . . . old, I guess.*

Karl presses his fingers together.

Great, she says. *Yeah. I'll bring 'em in tomorrow. And Bert*, she hesitates. *Sorry to be ringin' so early. Just couldn't sleep with the thought of it all*. She pauses again. *You're a good enough sort, Bert. Ta-ta.*

Karl's guts churn. He hears the sound of the phone being placed back in its cradle. The light clicks off and the other, better world disappears. Karl flattens himself against the wall, sucks in a breath, and shuts his eyes as hard as he can, with the logic of a child: *If I can't see you, you can't see me.*

When Karl opens his eyes, he can just make out Stella, at the end of the hallway, turning into her bedroom. He walks into the kitchen and stares at the phone. Stella's keys are on the kitchen table, lying there, cool, metallic, like an exotic insect.

He sneaks into Agatha's room. *Agatha*, he whispers as loudly as he dares, trying to shake her gently awake. Her snores are relentless. *Agatha*, he says again, a little louder.

What is it? she says, sitting up, pulling the blanket up under her chin. *Who are you? What do you want from me?* She gropes at her bedside table for her glasses.

Shh, Karl says, handing the glasses to her. *Please, Agatha.*

She puts on the glasses and stares at him. *Typist! You're not getting in here with me! I'll give you that news! It's 4:46 a.m.! This is when I sleep!*

Karl sits on the edge of her bed. He feels the warmth under his legs. *We need to go, Agatha. We need to go now.*

But when they turn on the light in Millie's room, she's gone.

Karl slings Manny under his arm and Agatha grabs Millie's backpack and they leave Stella's house as quietly as the floorboards allow them. Manny's leg sticks out the top of Millie's backpack, the plastic toes bouncing up and down behind Agatha's head. Karl leans Manny up against Stella's bus and puts a hand on Manny's shoulder. *Keep watch, Manny,* he says gravely.

He's plastic, Typist, Agatha hisses, and slides the backpack next to Manny.

Together, Karl and Agatha make their way down the street, calling for Millie, looking under cars, in front yards, and up trees.

They walk past the cemetery and hear voices. On the other side of the cemetery, with the help of some intermittent street-lights, Karl sees three men stumbling their way drunkenly toward them. The men laugh and swear. One of them attempts to climb a tree, another pees straight up into the air, the third throws a bottle against a gravestone. It smashes and the noise carries in the still night. Dogs in neighboring houses start to bark.

Oh no, Karl says.

What? Agatha says.

Karl points.

Oh no, Agatha says.

And there's Millie, not far from the drunken men, seated on the ground with her back against a gravestone.

They're headed straight for her, Karl says, leaning through the black iron bars of the gate.

I can't go in there, Agatha says quickly. *I don't . . .* She stops. *All those dead people,* she says quietly. *You can't make me.*

The drunks spot Millie. *Hey,* they say, and then, *Whaddya doin' out here in the dark? You're just a kid, aren't ya?* Millie stands, Karl's stomach lurches, another bottle crashes loudly, and Millie tries to walk away from them, but they surround her. And then, *You reckon you're Dora the Explorer or some shit?*

Agatha puts her hand in Karl's.

And it does something. Sends an electric current up his arm. His brain kick-starts as if it's been in a long slumber. Sleeping Beauty. Or whatever the man version of that is. There's got to be one, but he can't think straight. He's too busy thinking about her hand. Sticky with sweat, and rough. His hand feels soft in hers.

What ya doin' out here all by yerself, Dora?

Agatha squeezes Karl's hand.

Karl looks at her in his peripheral vision. That electric current. He turns to her. *We're taking the bus,* he whispers.

What do you mean, we're taking it? Agatha whispers back.

I mean, he says, handing her Stella's keys. *Start the bus. We're stealing it.* And he thinks he sees Agatha smile. Or maybe it's a twitch. He's not sure.

I don't – she starts to say, but Karl's already running, although it's more like a shuffle. The drunks wave their beers in the air at Millie. *Want summa me jungle juice, Dora?* one of them says, and Millie looks petrified. Karl doesn't know what he's going to do when he gets there, he thinks, *EvieEvieEvie*, she would know what to do, but he just has to get there, because Millie's just a child, she's justachild. *Hey*, he says as he approaches them, but they don't hear him, so he yells it, *Hey!* They all turn and Millie runs to him and hugs him around the legs. He puts a hand on her head and stands in front of her. *Hey*, he says again, quieter, steadying himself on his feet.

They could all be the same person, these three men. Blue jeans, work boots, hair spiked up at such odd angles that it surely can't be deliberate. As if they've hair-sprayed it in a wind tunnel. Their eyes follow Karl with a vagueness, like Karl is invisible and they're looking in the general direction of his voice. One wears a blue trucker's hat with a surf label on it, another has a T-shirt with *Breast Police* scrawled across it, the third wears a long-sleeved flannelette shirt. *It's Dora's grandpa!* Blue Hat says, and pushes Karl, and Karl says, *I don't want any trouble*, and Breast Police says, *Haven't you heard, you old fuck? This is the Kal Cemetery Creche*. Karl starts backing away, holding his hands up in the air like he's seen people do in the movies, and Blue Hat says, *We're just givin' Dora her milk, then we're gonna put her to bed*, and pushes Karl again, and Karl stumbles, and Karl says, *Do what you like to me, just don't hurt the little girl, she's just a child, just let her go*. They're red-eyed and swaying and surrounding them from every angle. They stink of alcohol and they don't care, Karl can see that clearly, they don't care about themselves or their lives and this makes them dangerous, and Karl says, *Go, Millie, go,* but she doesn't, she puts her hand in his and buries her face into his leg, and he closes his eyes and thinks, *Well, this is it.*

But then. A voice. *Too drunk!* Agatha appears behind the men and swings Manny's leg around as a weapon. She hits Flannelette square on the back of the head and he falls to the ground, hitting a gravestone on the way down. He is knocked clean out. She swings the leg wildly at the other two.

Hey, Blue Hat says.

Whoa, lady, Breast Police slurs. *We're just* – he looks like he's made of jelly as he falls into a tree trunk and hugs it, pushing his face into the bark – *having some fun.*

Yeah? Agatha says. *Yeah? Doesn't look like fun to me!* She swings at Blue Hat and misses.

Blue Hat puts his hands behind his head and twirls his crotch around and around in a circle. *You want summa this?* he says. *You just gotta ask, sweet cheeks.*

Agatha walks toward him and kicks him as hard as she can in the shins. *Hey,* he says, grabbing at his leg, hopping a few steps and then falling in the dust.

Trousers too tight! She swings Manny's leg at Breast Police and just misses a kneecap. *Not enough teeth!* Another swing that almost hits an elbow. *Bleak futures!*

You're crazy, lady, Blue Hat says. Agatha stands over him and kicks him again, in the bum this time. *Stop doing that,* he says, and stretches for her ankle, but misses and face-plants onto the ground.

Agatha stands on both of his hands. *I* – she says as he tries to wriggle free – *am not* – he lifts his head and tries to spit at her – *crazy!* She kicks dirt in his face.

C'mon, mate, Blue Hat slurs, crawling away from Agatha and trying to stand. *This is bullshit.*

Yeah, Breast Police agrees. *This is bullshit.*

I'll be writing to your mothers! Agatha says.

Whatdij ya say about me ma? Blue Hat says.

Mate, c'mon, Breast Police says.

Nah, nah, Blue Hat says. *Look, lady. We're gonna go get Nunnas and Scob and Fleety and we're gonna come back, and we're gonna finish this.* He points an unsteady finger at Agatha. And then vomits on his shirt. *Shit,* he says. *Shit.*

Don't worry, mate, Breast Police says.

But this isn't my shirt, man.

Don't worry. It'll come right out.

They sling their arms around each other's shoulders like old lovers and hobble off toward the exit, traversing the cemetery from side to side as if it's a ski hill, singing half sentences from a football theme song as they do so. *Up, up, to win the premiership flag.*

Millie wraps her arms around Agatha's waist. Agatha pats her awkwardly on the head. Karl wants to hug Agatha too, to rest his chin on her head and say, *Thank you,* to put a hand on

Millie's head and say, *You're okay,* but he doesn't. What would Branson Spike do? Instead he says, *You two get to the bus. You'll be safe there.* He feels strong and in charge all of a sudden. *I'll cover our tracks.* He nods in the direction of the unconscious Flannelette.

Agatha looks at him skeptically. *Well, don't plonk about for too long. You heard them. Flooty and Nunchuck and Scab are on their way.*

One minute, Karl says.

As Agatha and Millie wander out of the cemetery, Karl pulls out the marker he stole from the nursing home. He kneels down next to the gravestone, rolls up Flannelette's sleeve, and writes on his forearm, *Karl The Touch Typist Wuz 'Ere.* He pulls back, looks at his handiwork, and grins hugely. The sweat on Flannelette's forearm makes the ink run and the words look like the title of a horror movie.

Karl glances toward the road. It's starting to get light. They need to get going. He reaches into Flannelette's pockets and pulls out a wallet. Opens it up. He feels a buzz in his body, like this is the Karl he's been working toward his entire life.

He thinks, *I am Karl the Touch Typist, Present Tense.*

The sun is coming up. Karl feels invincible. He has made decisions, protected women – granted, with some help from said women – defaced public property, stolen money, resisted arrest. He can't stop smiling as he fusses over Manny in the front seat of the bus, buckling him in. Millie sits next to Manny, nursing his unattached leg.

You did a good job guarding the bus, Manny, Karl says, patting him on the head.

Yes, Millie says, pushing into Manny's side and leaning her head on him. *Good job, Manny.*

Yes, yes, yes, Agatha says. She sits in the driver's seat and riffles through her handbag. *The plastic man did a very good job.*

Are we stealing this bus? Millie says.

We're getting you to your mum, Millie, Karl says.

Are we going on the train?

Yes, Millie.

I don't have any money.

Karl feels the wad of cash pulsing in his pocket. *Just leave that part up to me.*

Millie looks out the window at Stella's house. *So we're stealing this bus?*

Borrowing it.

Like you borrowed those computer keys?

Yes. Exactly.

So we're stealing it.

Yes.

But it's Stella's bus.

Yes. It's not ours.

Stella's brother died.

I didn't know that.

I don't think we should steal the bus.

Sometimes grown-ups know best, Karl says.

Sometimes grown-ups don't know anything, Millie says. But before they can discuss just who does know best, Blue Hat appears in their headlights. *Hey,* he says, banging on the front window.

Close the door, Agatha, Karl says quietly.

I don't—

Hey, Blue Hat says again, kicking the tire. *Told ya we'd be back.*

Karl stands and sees Breast Police on one side of the bus, and another man he doesn't recognise on the other side. Breast Police has a cricket bat and grins menacingly at Karl through the glass. The men slap the sides of the bus with the palms of their hands. *Close the door, Agatha,* Karl says again, louder this time.

How do you—

Hey! Blue Hat stands at the bottom of the steps to the bus, in the doorway, brandishing a broken bottle, his eyes fierce, his nostrils flared. *Close the door, Agatha!* Karl shouts as Blue Hat puts his foot on the bottom step at the same time as Agatha finds the button and slams it down with her hand.

Blue Hat is half in and half out of the bus, and he squeezes one arm through the gap while using his shoulder to push against the closing door. He waves the broken bottle around, almost slashing Karl's hand as Karl tries to shove him out of the bus. *Stay back, Millie,* Karl says. Millie finds objects to throw at the man, a first-aid kit and some specs and a T-shirt and an apple core, and Blue Hat fends them off with his bottle like an amateur fencer. Karl tries to kick at him without getting too close. A window smashes at the back of the bus. Karl says, *Drive, just drive, Agatha!*

I haven't driven for seven years!

Work it out!

Okay, I don't – do I – is this—

You can do it, Agatha, Millie says.

The bus chokes and splutters and finally starts. *I did it! I did it!* Agatha says. *Now what do I do?*

Drive!

Oh! Yes!

And the bus starts moving, slowly, jerkily, and Blue Hat hops along next to them with one foot inside the bus and one hand clutching the edge of the door. Karl unbuckles Manny, holds him up high above his head, says, *This won't hurt a bit, Manny,* but he's lying, and goes to throw Manny in the direction of Blue Hat. Manny will save them again, Karl knows, knock the bottle out of Blue Hat's hand, dislodge his foot, crush his fingertips. *Say good-bye, Blue Hat,* Karl says, but just as he does, time seems to slow, the thumps on the side of the bus become like distant drumbeats on a faraway island, and it is in this moment that Karl realises that this man is just a drunk and angry boy, he's not a man at all. Pimples line his face and his eyes are filled with the kind of anger that doesn't know any other way. He is angry for a reason and the reason is not Karl. Karl recognises the struggle to Be A Man, and wants to say, *It's okay, I'm on your side*, and for a moment he thinks he might be able to negotiate with this drunk man, this drunk boy, so he begins to lower Manny, but then there's a flash and the drunk manboy has lunged and cut a gash in Karl's palm.

Karl, Millie says from behind him.

What? Agatha says and the bus swerves to miss a gutter.

It's okay, Karl says, though he doesn't know yet if it is okay and he feels weak at the knees at the thought of the blood gushing from his palm so he doesn't look. He is not going to try to understand the drunk manboy anymore. *You know, Drunk Manboy*, he thinks, *I have a lot to be angry about too*, and he summons all of his anger into his arms and feels like Superman, or the Incredible Hulk, or that sixteen-year-old boy from this morning, and holds Manny triumphantly over his head and throws him as hard as he can at the door.

But the bus rolls over a speed bump at the same time and Karl loses his footing. Manny is thrown straight up into the air. Karl falls backward onto his behind and Manny topples next to him. The bus is still moving slowly, but Blue Hat has to hop fast to keep up. Millie pushes on Blue Hat's foot with her foot and bites his shin and Blue Hat swears and takes a swipe at her and Karl says, *Get away from him, Millie*, and Agatha mounts the gutter and says, *Oh!* when she almost hits a tree on the verge.

Agatha finds the road again and Blue Hat falls and his foot comes loose.

Karl and Millie run to the side windows to watch him roll along the road behind them.

Everybody okay? Karl says. *Just Millie?*

I think so, Millie says, climbing onto the seat behind Agatha.

Karl picks up Manny from the floor and inspects him for injuries. *Agatha?*

Oh, I'm fine! Agatha says. *Just fine! Just suffering from post-traumatic stress disorder, but other than that! Is he gone?* The bus trundles down the street, passing small and dark brick houses. There are children in school uniforms, a man in a dressing gown picking up a paper, a lady walking her dog.

He's gone, Karl says. He sits in the seat opposite Millie, holding Manny on his lap.

Good, Agatha says. *Because it's 6:06 a.m.!* She points to her watch.

So? Karl says, examining his cut hand and feeling a bit lightheaded.

You! Captain Funeral! Agatha turns around to face Millie. *Take the wheel!*

I'm seven.

Exactly! When I was seven, I was driving semi-trailers across country!

You were not.

Just take the wheel! Agatha climbs out of the seat.

Agatha, Karl says. *What are you doing?* He jumps up and manages to grab the steering wheel before they veer off the road.

Agatha thumps her body down next to Millie and opens her handbag. She places an exercise book and a small mirror on her lap, and holds a ruler up to her face.

Karl watches her in the rearview mirror. *Agatha, what—*

Listen, Old Tricky Fingers! Agatha says. *I'm busy! I'm not taking calls at the moment!* She notes something in her exercise book.

millie bird

After some wrong turns and U-turns and arguments, they finally arrive at the Kalgoorlie train station. The air outside is sticky and difficult to breathe in as they wander onto the platform. The train is already there, gradually being loaded up with people and luggage. Tourists take photos of each other in front of the Indian Pacific logo on the side of the train. Men and women in uniform check tickets and direct passengers onto different parts of the train. Families hug and cry and laugh together.

Karl buys their tickets and they're directed to their cabin. It's small, with a couch seat that turns into a bed, a washbasin in the corner, and a big window with a curtain pulled across it.

This is it? Agatha says, and begins to unfold the bed. There's a commotion on the train platform near their window. A man's voice says, *I can't let you on without a ticket, miss. The train's about to leave.*

Oh fer Chrissakes, Derek, a woman's voice says. *I went to school with ya. I went out with yer berloody brother in seventh form for a bit. I used to come over to yer place for a roast on Sundays.*

We're on a strict time schedule, Stella, the man's voice says. *Can't help you. You know that. Train time and all.*

Millie yanks back the curtain. *Stella?* she says. Millie knocks on the window and jimmies it open. *Stella,* she calls.

Oh God, Karl says, and ducks.

All aboard, the man in uniform on the platform calls as he hops on the train.

Stella waves a hand at the man and runs up to their window.

I can see you, Karl, she says.

The train starts to move just as Karl stands. He wobbles on his feet.

Where are me keys? Stella says, walking alongside the train.

In the bus, Karl says sheepishly.

You better find her mum, Stella says.

He looks at Millie. *We're going to try,* he says.

You okay, love? Stella says.

Millie nods. *Yes.*

Promise?

Yes.

Okay. Stella stops walking and puts her hands in her pockets. The train starts to gather speed and Millie watches Stella get smaller and smaller on the platform. Millie looks at her beer cozy and says, *But I want you to come with us.* She can feel the tears coming and she can't help them, because Stella is kind and her dad is dead and her mum may as well be. Millie watches Stella until she can't see her anymore and it hurts, deep in her guts. All the grown-ups she knows keep taking bits of her guts away with them and never giving them back.

part three

karl the touch typist

When the train starts to move, Karl leaves the girls and Manny to settle into the cabin while he heads to the gents. He cleans his cut, pats his hand dry, and wraps toilet paper around the wound. He catches sight of himself in the mirror. It has always been strange, looking at himself in the mirror, and the exercise has only increased in strangeness the older he has become. He knows his face, and this is not it. How can you be inside a face for eighty-seven years and be surprised by the look of it every time? It suddenly occurs to him that everyone else knows his face better than he does. He doesn't even know his own facial expressions. He tries angry. Sad. Happy. Worried. Contemplative. Missing. Wanted. But he can only see tired. So tired.

I am never going to have sex again, he says. *Not with this face*. He closes his eyes, puckers his lips, and moves toward the mirror. He opens one eye, sees something like Death trying to kiss him, and recoils.

Right, he says. *That's that.* But Evie had loved him, and loved this face. He runs his good hand through his hair. He can barely feel the dying strands.

He was so jealous of that boy yesterday, the one with the chest like Charlton Heston in *Ben-Hur.* He wanted everything he had, that body, that girl, that car, that freedom, that way of thinking. That hair, that bloody hair. What he would give to have hair that moved so freely in the wind. But shouldn't that boy be jealous of Karl? Shouldn't he wonder what Karl had seen and done?

Shouldn't he look at Karl and think, *If only I get to lead a life like yours?*

When Karl returns to the cabin, Millie has made a new *IN HERE MUM* sign for the door, and Agatha lies spreadeagled on the bed, eyes closed, mouth wide open.

Millie puts a finger up to her lips: *Shh.* Karl nods. Millie motions for him to come closer. She's wearing her backpack. *Can I go explore?* she whispers.

Sure, Karl whispers back. *Just don't talk to strange men.*

You're a strange man.

Karl thinks about this. *Other ones.*

Millie closes the door behind her and Karl puts a pillow under Agatha's head. He sits upright next to her, his back against the wall, his hands in his lap. He stares out the window.

Red, green, blue. The earth, the scrub, the sky. Over and over and over again. The low-lying bush and the little trees that look like hunchbacks groping for the ground. And then the occasional big tree, reaching for the sun, rising out of the red earth.

Manny leans against the washbasin in the corner of the room. *Sleeping,* Karl whispers to him, nodding his head in the direction of Agatha. *She's had a big night.*

Agatha snorts and then shifts, turning over. He can feel her warmth next to him. He remembers Evie like this, lying next to him in bed. He closes the curtains.

another thing karl knows about

EVIE (PART TWO)

She had been like a dandelion, as if a single breath of his would cause her to fly off into the sky and never be seen again. She was so quiet, too, not just in the way she spoke, but in the way she conducted herself, as though she were always around sleeping people, tiptoeing everywhere, barely making footprints on the beach they walked along together in the early hours of most mornings.

Was she too quiet? Maybe. We're all too-something, he supposes.

And yet she was the most stable person he has ever known.

Every word felt measured out, like she'd poured her words into measuring cups and flattened out the tops of them before she upended them into the world. And there was so much room in her, for him, and for everybody else. She was always putting down her guns and raising her arms in the air, inviting a vulnerability that most couldn't.

Karl always felt as if he were thudding everywhere next to her, crunching leaves underfoot with such violence, sneezing as though he were trying to put a tear in the air. He did not like that his body had to make such an impact on things. But when he touched her, and she touched him back, she made him feel gentle, and those lines around her eyes, the ones that became deeper and longer and more plentiful, there was something in them that gave him clues that he was understood.

I am here, Evie, he whispers, as the tears fall down his face. When he opens his eyes, Agatha's sitting up with her face near his. Karl jumps.

Ron? What's the matter, Ron? she says. She's wearing her glasses and it's dark and they can't really see each other.

Agatha, Karl says, *I'm not—*

She puts her hand over his mouth. *Ron,* she says. She has both hands on his cheeks. She uses one thumb to brush away his tears. *I'm sorry,* she says.

Karl doesn't know what to say. *It's okay,* he says.

Are you crying because of me?

No, Agatha, he says. Their noses almost touching.

I'm sorry, Ron, she says, and leans in to kiss Karl.

Karl wants her to be Evie more than any other feeling he's ever had. He takes a big breath and closes his eyes, and he waits for her lips, but before anything can happen, Agatha's head falls into his chest, and she starts to snore.

He sighs and helps her back to her former sleeping position. Agatha lies there, her sensible shoes still strapped to her ankles, her head flopping back on the pillow, her mouth wide open, huge, erratic snores vibrating her nose and bouncing off the walls. There's a music to her snores, surely, in their rise and fall, an indication of how life works, in its ups and downs. He wants to graph the sound, and imagines mountains on a page, wide, curvy ones, rippled lines.

He opens the curtains a little and stares at Agatha lying next to him. It hits him that he never stares at anyone. He remembers staring as a child, though at the time he didn't realise that people could see what his eyes were doing. Why does it matter that people know he is looking at them? Why is everyone so afraid of being looked at? When did he stop looking people in the eye? There had to be a moment when he realised what it meant. What did it mean?

You seem to have no problems doing it, he whispers to Manny, who stares unblinkingly back at him from the corner of the cabin.

He remembers staring at Evie. Somehow, love made staring okay again. They lay in bed in those young days, rubbing noses and curling their feet around each other, and staring. He knew every bit of her, but he never stopped staring. There always seemed an angle to know, or a type of light reflected on her body, a crinkle, a fold.

another thing karl knows about

AGATHA ISN'T EVIE

That's for sure. He imagines Agatha standing in uniform at the head of a table, leaning over it, her fists digging into the table, pointing at maps, declaring which countries she's going to invade, men at her command. He likes this new version of woman-ness he sees in her, one that allows him not to actually be a man.

Karl is a man, he knows, insofar as he has the organ that identifies him as one, but he has never known how to walk or talk or look like one. Even now, at eighty-seven years old, he feels like a small boy taking a sneaky puff on his father's cigar, trying on his father's work shirt.

Agatha's nose wiggles and she smacks her lips. Her hands are folded across her stomach. He studies her fingers. They're big and thick, and he pictures them dumping loosely and heavily onto typewriter keys, like dropping a bag of clothes from seven stories high.

He lies down next to Agatha on the small bed, folding his arms across his body, listening to Agatha snore. Her back against his arm. Out the window, there are farmhouses in the distance, rusted-out cars and unidentifiable machines scattered around them as though they've fallen from the sky. Grass poking out of windows and through tires and out of boots like one of those men whose hair spills over their collar. Karl peeks under his shirt. Flexes his chest. Sighs. He rubs his neck. Rain dribbles down the windows. He can see where it is and isn't raining out on the horizon, patches of dark hovering over the desert like bruises, so heavy in the sky.

Agatha's exercise book rests on the bed next to her. He looks at the book, looks at her. Looks at the book again. *Age*, the cover says in spidery handwriting. In small, almost indecipherable letters, *Agatha Pantha's (HANDS OFF)* has been scrawled across the bottom. Keeping one eye on her, he picks it up, then flicks the pages over with his thumb. The handwriting inside is so angry, like it's trying to squash the paper. It's not a nice feeling, looking at this.

He puts the book back. He feels the rhythm of the train underneath his back, the movement of it, like rocking, like nostalgia.

millie bird

Millie sits on the bench seat in the common area of the carriage and rests the back of her head against the window. Across from her, a lady reads a book to a little girl. She's littler than Millie. The book doesn't have many words to it, and asks really easy questions. *What does a cow do?* says the mum, and prompts the little girl, *Moo,* and the little girl just mimics the mum, like an echo, and the mum congratulates the little girl. As if she invented cows. The little girl sits with her head up high, swinging her legs, and the mum leans in and kisses her on the head. Millie closes her eyes and wishes so much that it was her head, so when the mum says, *What does a horse do?*, Millie says, *Neigh!* in her best horse voice, she even lifts her head back like a horse does, and looks up at the mum, hoping for something, but the mum looks at Millie like she has done something wrong.

And suddenly Millie is filled with hatred for this tiny girl.

You know, she says, jumping off the seat and looking straight at her, *you could die today*. And she walks into the next carriage.

Sandwiches

What?

and curtains

read this

potatoes

Millie wanders into the restaurant carriage and slides into a booth. The vinyl seat sticks to the backs of her legs. She watches the world go by through the train window, and if she puts her hands around her eyes like goggles, the whole world is red and green and yellow streaks, moving so fast. There is something terrifying about that, but also something exciting. It is both things, and she thinks, *Everything is always both things*. She is sad to say good-bye to Stella but she is happy to go with Karl and Agatha. She is sad her dad died but she is happy his body isn't hurting anymore. She loves her mum but she hates her too. Can you love and hate the same person? If you love them more than you hate them, will they forgive you? Will they let you find them? She takes off her goggles, leans back in her seat, and surveys the length of everything out there, and it feels as if nothing will ever, ever end, or begin.

A lady wearing the Indian Pacific uniform walks down the carriage toward Millie. She has long blond hair and eyes that shine when she smiles. *Excuse me,* Millie says in her most polite voice. *When will we get to Melbourne? I need to be there in two days.*

The lady smiles sympathetically at Millie. *Oh, love,* she says. *I know it's a bit of a trek.* She reaches into her pocket. *Here,* she says, and hands Millie a Caramello Koala.

Millie squints at the Caramello Koala in her palm. She looks up at the lady. *I need to be there in two days,* she repeats.

The lady laughs. *I'll bring you a colouring book,* she says, and walks off.

Millie bites into the koala's legs just as a man's voice comes over the loudspeaker. *Good morning, everyone,* it says. *If you've just joined us at Kalgoorlie, welcome on board the Indian Pacific. We trust you'll enjoy your journey. I'll be using this PA system to not only make a few announcements along the way but to also give you a few facts about this glorious country of ours. We'll soon be traveling through the Nullarbor Plain. "Nullarbor" derives from Latin and means "no trees," but the plain is covered with bluebush and saltbush plants, hardy shrubs that are drought-resistant and salt-tolerant. The plain is the world's largest single piece of limestone, is twenty to twenty-five million years old, and is twice the size of England. It is also a former shallow seabed, and is mostly made up of seashells.*

Millie presses her face against the window. *So this is what the bottom of the sea looks like,* she says. She'll have to remember to tell Stella. She puts it in the part of her brain that remembers things for later.

At the next table, a boy about her age reads a comic. On the front is a picture of a cartoon man wearing a cape, his arm thrust high in front of him, the wind in his hair, a person tucked under his arm. A building burns beneath them. He has a wristband and it has lights and buttons all over it.

Millie looks down at her dad's beer cozy on her forearm. She imagines herself with a cape, flying down the aisles of the train, hovering over everyone, and saving them. Flying right out of this train and straight to Melbourne. Her mum would have to forgive her because she will have been so Good. She locks eyes with the boy over the top of the comic. He seems to be egging her on.

So Millie sneaks into the first-class carriage –

then I took the apple
was firstly understood as
how did that
Nova Scotia?

– and steals a white tablecloth. From her backpack, she pulls out her Funeral Pencil Case, writes *CF* on the tablecloth in thick black marker, and ties it around her neck. She takes off her gumboots and writes *C* on the right one and *F* on the left one. She writes *IN HERE MUM* on one forearm and *SORRY MUM* on the other. She gathers up all the menus in the restaurant carriage and, next to the *Welcome to the Indian Pacific* heading, writes in her very best writing, *You are all going to die*. Underneath, in bold letters, *IT'S OK*. She draws a happy face.

She watches a lady carefully apply lipstick on her lips, and then, when the lady's not looking, Millie reaches into her handbag and takes the lipstick. *Borrowing*, Millie says. She uses it to write her message on the bottom of windows, on the mirrors in the toilets and on the tabletops in the restaurant. No one seems to notice.

She walks down the aisles of the carriages, feeling her white cape billow out behind her, feeling like her gumboots have springs on the bottoms. People look at her. She smiles at them. Her smile feels as though it could provide all the world's electricity. She propels herself down the aisle, her arm up high in front of her body, her hand balled in a fist.

An old lady puts her hand on the seat next to her as if she is imagining the warm of someone there. Millie gets down on her knees and slides on the ground toward her.

You're going to die someday, she says.

The lady looks down at Millie. *I hope so, dear*, she says, patting Millie on the head.

A girl sits on the floor of the lounge carriage brushing the hair of a Barbie.

You're gonna die someday, Millie says, standing over her.

The girl doesn't look up. *YOU are*.

I know, Millie says.

A dad feeds a toddler while trying to stop two other boys from punching each other.

You're all going to die someday, Millie says, standing proudly, the beer cozy high above her head.

The dad tries to cover his kids' ears. *Rack off,* he says.

The mum, reading a magazine nearby, rolls her eyes. *She's just a kid, Gerard.*

So was Charles Manson once!

I'm not just a kid, Gerard, Millie whispers as she walks away.

There is a baby in a pram. Millie lets him grab her finger. She moves in close to his head. *You'll die too,* she whispers.

He smiles at her, farts, and smiles a little more.

That little kid's a bloody weirdo

I know

She finds a door with *Derek Fauntleroy: Head Conductor* written on it. She pushes the door ajar and sees a man sitting at a desk with his head in his hands and a phone up to his ear.

Dad I can't, I'm working

This is my real job

God, Dad

Why don't you ask Golden Boy

Well, it's the bloody truth

Don't hang up

Dad

Dad

Shit

Millie uses the lipstick to write on the window opposite his office. *IT'S OK.* The letters seem to fly along the line of the horizon.

Millie sits under one of the tables in the restaurant carriage. Every single person is sad and either showing it or hiding it, and some have been sad for too long, and some haven't been sad for long enough. And the thought of helping everyone is very, very exhausting. *Is this what a superhero is supposed to feel like?* she says, pressing her face into the chair cushion.

A boy pokes his head underneath the table and shimmies in next to her. It's the boy she saw before with the superhero comic. His hair is brown and his eyes seem to take up his whole face. He and Millie stare at each other.

I've been on this train thirty-seven times, he says to Millie eventually.

Good for you, she says.

I know everything about it. Ask me anything.

I'm busy.

You're a superhero, he says, pointing to her cape.

Yeah, she says.

So am I.

Which one are you?

He sighs, leans on his elbow, and rests his chin on his hand. *It's a secret.*

I'm Captain Funeral.

He sits up. *I'm Captain Everything.*

What do you do?

Uh, everything, he says. He rolls his eyes. *Duh.*

Oh.

What do you do?

Nothing yet.

Some sneakers and thongs and bare feet walk past.

Do you like feet? the boy says.

Millie considers this. *Mostly,* she answers.

My mum says never to touch anyone's feet. She says that after doorknobs, handrails, and hairy backs, they're the most disgusting thing.

There's more disgusting things.

Like what?

Boys.

Girls are more disgusting.

Poop, Millie says.

Poop on your face, maybe.

My grandma had warts all over her eyelids.

Maybe she was a witch.

You're gonna—

Die someday, I know.

How do you know?

Everybody knows.

You were eavesdropping!

No I wasn't.

Yes you were.

He sits back against the leg of the seat. *Want some of my muesli bar?*

Millie shrugs. *Okay.*

They chew loudly together. Millie eats the portion quickly. The boy watches her. He reaches into his pocket, pulls out some crackers, and hands them to Millie. She eats them gratefully.

Where are you going, anyway?

A trip.

The boy rolls his eyes again. *Obviously. Where?*

She takes a deep breath. *We're trying to find my mum. She forgot to pick me up. Then all her stuff was gone from the house. And before that, Dad was at the hospital. And then he died. And I think that's why she forgot to pick me up and why she wants to go far away and all I need to do is find her before she goes far away.*

Oh.

Is your mum nice? Millie says.

She's okay.

What kind of stuff does she do?

Mum stuff.

Like what?

Get me stuff. Pick me up from stuff. Make me stuff. That sort of thing.

My mum's taking me to Movie World, Millie says. *On the Gold Coast. You know, when we find her.*

Went there last year.

We'll probably go to Sea World after that.

The dolphin show there was okay, I guess.

My mum's in the dolphin show, Millie says.

I didn't see her.

You wouldn't know her.

Your mum isn't in the dolphin show.

We're probably going to outer space after that.

You can't go to outer space, the boy says, crossing his arms.

Who says?

Everybody says.

Mum knows a guy that can go to space.

An astronaut?

He's just rich.

Oh. You know rich people?

Some.

I know lots of rich people.

No you don't.

Yes I do. There's a girl at my school who buys lunch every day.

So? Millie says.

Every day.

Can she go to outer space?

Probably.

Where will she buy lunch?

She'll buy it beforehand, the boy says. *Obviously.*

What's your real name?

Not telling. What's your real name?

Millie Bird.

Mine's Jeremy.

Jeremy what?

No, Jeremy Jacobs.

I like your name.

Thanks. Yours is okay too.

Thanks.

They hear a voice from the other end of the carriage.

Excuse me, sir.

Jeremy's eyes widen. *That's Derek,* he whispers. *The head conductor.*

Derek walks past them. Millie can see only his feet. Black, shiny shoes. A straight, fast walk. *No breathing on the windows, sir,* he says.

Mum says he used to be a parking inspector, Jeremy says. *But,* he leans in closer to Millie, *he got fired. He used to fiddle with the parking meters so he could give more tickets.*

Millie crawls out from under the table to get a look at him. She can only see him from behind, but can tell it's the man who was on the phone. His shirt is tucked in and his trousers don't have any creases in them. He wipes down the tables and the seats and the walls and any surface there is. He seems to be in a race against himself. A child with Vegemite all over her face sits at one of the tables while her mum lines up at the food counter. Derek wipes her face with the cloth roughly, and she sits there stunned for a few moments, and then starts to cry. Derek passes the mother as he walks away from the screaming child. *No crying in the restaurant carriage,* he says.

Parking inspectors go to hell, Millie says, crawling back under the table.

What?

Dad said.

Oh.

The woman who gave Millie a Caramello Koala pokes her head under the table. *Found a friend, Jeremy?*

She's not a friend, Mum.

She kneels on the floor. *Girlfriend, then.*

Mum! Gross.

She smiles at Millie, and Millie smiles back. *She seems nice,* Jeremy's mum says.

Well. She's not.

He's not very nice either, Millie says.

Jeremy's mum laughs. *You two would make the perfect couple.*

Mum, Jeremy says, crossing his arms.

I'm on a break soon, darling, she says to Jeremy. *Why don't you come have dinner with me?*

He looks at her sideways. *Can we play Uno?*

Of course, darling, she says.

Black, shiny shoes stop next to Jeremy's mum. *Melissa,* a voice says. *FYI, you're not paid to sit on the floor.*

Okay, Derek, Jeremy's mum says. The black, shiny shoes walk away.

He's scary, Mum, Jeremy says. *I don't like him.*

Oh, darling, don't be too hard on him. He's just a little kid, really.

No he's not. He's a grown-up.

Darling. I mean, inside. She tickles his belly.

Millie puts her hands on her own belly. Jeremy's mum is so beautiful and smells like a mum so Millie says, *You're very beautiful and you smell like a mum,* and the woman's face softens and she puts a warm warm hand on Millie's leg and says, *Thank you, darling.* And Millie wants to curl up in her arms and stay there and never leave, but she doesn't do that at all because the lady isn't her mum and you can't really do that to mums who aren't yours. But you should be able to hug all the mums who aren't yours, because some people don't have mums and what are they supposed to do with all the hugs they have?

agatha pantha

2:02 p.m.: Agatha wakes with a start when an announcement is made over the loudspeaker. *Ladies and gentlemen, if you would kindly move your clocks forward an hour and a half. Throughout this journey, we'll be existing on what we call "Train Time." We'll keep you updated as to further adjustments.*

Agatha sits up. *Train time?* She moves all her watches forward.

3:32: Agatha gets out her Complaint Letters notepad and pen and starts writing: *Dear*— Her hand jolts as the carriage shakes, and the *r* streaks across the page. *Ack,* Agatha says, tearing off the sheet of paper and crumpling it. *Dear,* she writes again, and stops.

Agatha looks out the window. They're zipping through the bush. Everything always crackles and hisses at her in the Australian bush, the trees splayed out in the air like they're in agony. And that dirt, that deep-red dirt that gets under your fingernails, stains your clothes, and never seems to leave you.

She suddenly thinks of Ron's hair. Red hair like copper wire, flattened atop his head with a wave at the front and a perfect part on one side. She was fifteen when she met him; he, eighteen. It was a vulnerable and mysterious time. She remembers not often hearing her own voice. She remembers feeling so ridiculous just being alive. Her skin always felt watched. Eye contact was this dangerous thing. Her body was taking her to places she didn't want to go, to this strange address she had only heard of as womanhood. No one ever told her what to do once she got there. She just bumbled about and hoped no one noticed what was going on underneath her clothes.

She had seen Ron for the first time in the park near her grandmother's house. She was walking home from school and she knew she was thinking too hard about how to walk, that she was thinking too hard about how to move her arms, and that this must be obvious to everyone watching her.

What was the first thing he said to her?

Chuck us the ball, would ya? She thinks this is it.

The boys were playing cricket. She heard him, but she didn't look up. She felt her body tightening as she saw the ball out of the corner of her eye, rolling toward her feet. And that ball kept coming, rolling toward her like a snowball, growing bigger and bigger in her peripheral vision.

Chuck us the ball, would ya?

And then there was the look he gave her, under a hand that

was blocking the sun, and the way he sauntered over to her, and his voice, and the way he gestured, and the way he stood.

Can't you pick up a ball, he said, and smiled at her as he picked it up. It wasn't really a question. Agatha looked at the ground. *Okay then*, he said, and walked away. But there was a hesitation in his step that Agatha noticed, and kept, and felt, as she lay in her bed that night, eyes wide open, gazing up at the ceiling.

And later, when they were married and owned a house and lived an entire life together, he put his hand on the crown of her head after her mother died. It was just in passing, as he walked from the sink to his chair, but his hand on her head felt so heavy with love that it seemed to stop her head from falling forward onto her chest.

He made her a Bonox every night without her having to ask for it. He didn't gamble. Or smoke. He read the daily news out loud to her when she was sick. He ate her meatloaf, even when it was terrible. He didn't smile much, but he never complained.

Did this make him a good person?

Was he a good person? Was he a better person? Than her? Than most?

3:46: But there was this. Well into their marriage, Agatha saw Ron looking at another woman's bottom. It was what's-her-name from next door, Tallulah or Tiffany, some kind of name they probably put on handbags, and she had been pruning her rosebush in clothes that would make a prostitute blush. Her undergarments rose out of the top of her jeans as though they were trying to make their way to her neck. Like a dog yanking at its chain, trying to get to the food bowl. He was waiting in the car, and Agatha saw his face through the glass as she locked the door to the house. They had not had sex in years, but there was still something about this situation that shook Agatha. Something about her husband's face – blank to the untrained eye, but it was the slitting of the eyes that was different, the slight parting of the mouth – something about this bottom in the air, something about the space between his face and that bottom. Something about what Agatha wasn't.

She opened the car door and climbed in. When she sat down she felt her bottom spread out over the whole seat, right to the very edges. Handbag Name waved to them as they drove past, all red lips and curved lines. Ron's mouth was clamped shut, flat-lining under his nose, like a heart-rate monitor. *Beeeeeeeep,* his mouth seemed to say.

Beeeeeeeep, she says now, looking out the train window.

3:52: She looks at the sheet of paper in front of her. *Dear,* she says.

She wonders what her face looked like to her husband. She cannot recall ever looking at him with a soft face. She wonders if he ever felt love in his fingers and toes for her. There had been a lilt of impatience in her voice, always, hovering around her words. She never asked him selfless questions. If she poured orange juice for both of them, she would always take the bigger glass. She would walk through a door, knowing full well that he was following, and allow the door to close behind her. She didn't massage his crook neck, just let him crane it to one side and push his own fingers feebly into the muscle, feeling around for the source of pain like a mechanic. She saw his grimace but would continue spooning mashed potato into her mouth. His discomfort had seemed irrelevant to her, as though he were one of those orphan children in a war-torn country.

Was she testing him? Had the entire relationship been a challenge, a standoff? Just how much can you take, Ron?

How much are you willing to take? And why? Why, Ron, are you willing to take this?

4:01: She was a bad person to Ron. The sentence arrives in her head so loudly, it is as if she has yelled it. She was a bad person to Ron, purely because she could be, because it was easy, because he didn't stop her.

karl the touch typist

Karl sits in one of the booths in the Matilda Café, sharing a bottle of wine with Manny and watching the sun set over the desert. The train squeaks and creaks, and the sound of that, the gentle constancy of it, is comforting, like rain on a roof. A dust devil touches down on the horizon, and Karl watches with wide eyes as it twirls and twists and then disappears completely.

Karl unwraps the toilet paper from around his hand and examines it. He shows it to Manny, wiggling his eyebrows. *Shoulda seen the other guy.* Karl spreads Evie's typewriter keys on the table in front of him. *Forgot what, Manny?* he says, sighing. He shuffles the keys around. *Rift goo?* He turns to Manny. *Is there such a thing?*

An elderly couple walks into the carriage. They smile at Karl as they sit down in another booth. Karl nods at them politely. The woman opens her book and begins to read. The man winks at Karl. *Enjoying the train?*

Oh yes, Karl says. *Very much.*

Those trees, the man says, pointing out the window. *They're dead.* He nudges his wife. *They're dead, but they have new sprouts.* His wife doesn't react, so he looks to Karl for a response.

Well, I'll be, Karl says.

The man turns to his wife, who doesn't lift her eyes from her book. *I'll just go have a Bo Peep at what they've got,* he says.

He returns with two cups of tea. *Ow,* he says, placing them on the table. *Oh boy. Is that hot!* He blows on his hands and rubs them together dramatically. *Oh boy, they were hot.* His wife doesn't flinch and continues to read. *Those trees,* he says again, taking his seat and gesturing toward the window. *New sprouts!*

The other staff were nice, the woman says suddenly, as if her husband hasn't been talking at all, saying it with the confused urgency of someone who has just woken up from a dream.

What? the husband says.

The other staff were nice, she says, not raising her voice.

The other staff were nine! What?

Nice, she says, not taking her eyes from her book.

Oh, he says. *Nice.* He sips his tea while she reads her book.

Karl glances at her face. She appears so unmoved by this man, so beyond any kind of expression for him.

Why do they get to be alive? Karl whispers. He glances sideways at Manny. *I know, I know.* The table under his fingertips feels cool and hard as he types on it. *That's harsh. But . . .* He stares at the man, still shaking his head at the trees out the window, and the woman not in love with him in any way. *I loved Evie and she loved me. Shouldn't we get some kind of reward for that?*

Karl turns to Manny, who looks straight ahead at the couple. *Manny,* Karl says, flushing pink with embarrassment, *don't make it so obvious we're talking about them.* Karl turns Manny's face toward him. He holds Manny's upper arm while he does it and can feel the curve of Manny's muscle. *Manny,* he says. Karl unbuttons the top of Manny's shirt and looks in. *Wow,* he says. Karl lifts up the bottom of Manny's shirt. *Wow,* he says again, rubbing Manny's stomach.

Hello, sir, a voice says, and Karl jumps. A man in an Indian Pacific uniform stands at the end of Karl's table. A notepad hangs from a piece of string that dangles around his neck. A dishcloth is folded neatly over his belt. *I'm Derek. The head conductor.* He taps a forefinger on his name badge. He runs a finger softly over the part of his hair, and uses the heel of his hand to flatten his fringe to the side.

Hi, Derek the Head Conductor, Karl says. *I'm Karl the Touch Typist.*

Dining with us this evening, sir?

Sure am, sir, Karl replies. He puts an arm around Manny. *Me and my friend here, and the wife and grandkid.*

Sir, Derek says in a low voice, *we don't allow objects of sexual fantasy on the train.*

Objects of what now? Karl says, leaning forward.

What you do in your own time is none of our concern, but while you're on this train—

Sorry, objects of what?

I don't know what your caper is—

My caper?

But you must remove this sex doll from the dining carriage ASAP.

Karl slides his arm from Manny's shoulders. He looks at Manny apologetically. He puts his elbows on the table and links his hands together. *Manny is not one of those,* he says quietly.

Look, Derek says, holding out the notepad around his neck and scribbling on it, *I don't know what your type call them these days, but get it out of my sight. Understand?* He rips the sheet of paper off the notepad and places it forcefully on the table in front of Karl.

1 x SEXUAL MISCONDUCT, the note reads in capital letters. *SEXUAL* is underlined.

Before Karl can answer, Millie bounds into the carriage. *Karl,* she says, sliding in next to Manny. *Manny,* she says, and hugs him. Agatha is not far behind, and sits on the opposite side of the booth. Karl pockets the piece of paper.

That's a warning, Derek says. *Three of those and you're off the train. Sir.*

A warning for what? Millie says.

Excuse me, Agatha says to Derek, her eyes on his name badge. *What time do you make it?* She seems agitated.

Derek checks his watch. *Six thirty p.m.* He pauses. *Train Time.*

You know, Agatha says, tapping a finger on the table, *you can't just change the time and call it what you want.*

FYI, yes I can, Derek says. He leans back on his heels and folds his arms across his chest. *Think of this as my house. While you're in my house we use my time.*

What about Millie Time? Millie says.

Yeah, Karl says. *And Karl Time?*

No, Derek says. He places both hands on the table. *NO. Just Train Time.* And after an elongated look at each of them, he says, *MY HOUSE,* and turns, then walks down the aisle and out of the carriage.

Pleasant fellow, Karl mutters. *Who wants sangers?* He produces three sandwiches in a plastic bag from under the table.

Me! Millie says, raising her hand.

Karl gives one to Millie and one to Agatha.

Thank you, Millie says, and unwraps hers.

What time do you make it, Typist? Agatha says, snatching at the sandwich.

Karl looks at his forearm. *Freckle thirty, by my watch,* he says. *What time do you make it, Millie?*

Hair o'clock, she says, giggling.

Agatha still appears agitated.

All I know is that it's time for a drink, Agatha, Karl says in what he hopes is a sympathetic voice. *You can have Manny's,* he says. *Do you mind, Manny? He doesn't mind.* He fills up the second glass and pushes it toward her.

Agatha takes the glass, slams back the wine, and pushes it toward Karl. She wipes her arm across her mouth, and eyes Karl as though she's testing a bartender.

Karl laughs nervously and pours Agatha another drink. He sits up tall and says in his deepest voice, *So what did you get up to today, Millie? You look like you've been busy.* She's wearing some sort of homemade cape and has decorated her arms in letters and colours.

I met a boy, she replies.

Right, he says. *Do girls your age usually? Meet? Boys?*

He said he has something to show me, she says, chewing on her sandwich. *I'm very excited.*

Right, Karl says. *What about you, Agatha?*

She doesn't say a word, just throws back the second drink and pushes the glass toward him again.

Maybe some water for the next one? he says, his voice wavering a little.

Agatha taps her finger on the side of the glass.

Right. He hiccups. He puts his hand over his mouth. *Oops.*

Here's the dessert you ordered, a woman in an Indian Pacific uniform says, walking up to them and handing them a tub of yogurt each. She winks at Millie. Millie winks back.

But I didn't— Karl says.

The woman – Melissa, according to her badge – puts a hand on his shoulder and a finger up to her lips. His shoulder melts into the heat of her hand.

millie bird

Earth to Captain Funeral. Captain Everything to Captain Funeral. Over. Psst.

Millie looks under the table. Jeremy is down there. She slips off her seat and slides in next to him.

Hi, Captain Everything, she says.

Who's that? he says.

Who's who? Millie says.

That, he says, pointing to Manny.

Manny. He's a Dead Thing.

No he isn't. He knocks on Manny's leg.

He's plastic. He's our friend. He saved my life.

The boy stares at the mannequin. *You can't have a plastic man for a friend.*

Who says?

The Bible.

No it doesn't.

Does he have a, you know, thingy? He wiggles his index finger in the air.

I don't think so.

They both eye Manny's crotch uncertainly.

Have you ever seen a Dead Thing? Millie asks Jeremy.

Yeah. Of course. All the time.

Like what?

Like . . . I don't know. Some things.

Bet you haven't.

Bet I have.

Like what?

Millie pulls her Book Of Dead Things out of her backpack, opens it up, and hands it to him. *Like all of these things. Rambo. The Old Man. Spider. My dad. There's more.*

Your dad?

What do you think happens when you die?

Jeremy pulls a doughnut out of his pocket and chews thoughtfully on it. *A spaceship comes and takes you away.*

Where to?

Another planet, of course.

Which planet?

Pluto, maybe. Jupiter, too.

Who drives the spaceship?

God.

God drives the spaceship?

Of course.

But doesn't he have a lot of other things to do? Like help people, and run the universe, and all that?

He has sidekicks.

Like elves?

Kinda. They don't sing songs, though, if that's what you're thinking.

How do you know so much? Millie asks.

He shrugs. *You pick stuff up. Your mum's old.*

She's not my mum. I told you about my mum.

I was just testing you.

Want me to show you how to make Walking Poems? Millie asks.

Yeah, he says.

Jeremy and Millie crawl out from underneath the table, down the aisle, and into the next carriage without Agatha and Karl noticing.

Millie and Jeremy sit on the ground outside the toilet in the rear carriage.

Isn't it funny, Millie whispers to Jeremy, *to think that someone is going to the toilet right there?*

I guess.

There's someone with their pants down right there.

Yeah.

They're pooping or peeing right there.

I borrowed Mum's phone, he says suddenly, holding it up for Millie to see.

Millie takes it from him. *You stole it.*

I'll give it back, he says.

Millie stares at the phone. She feels Jeremy staring at her. She wants to ring her mum more than anything, but what if she doesn't answer? What if she does answer? What if she answers and she doesn't want to talk to Millie? What if she answers and doesn't want to be her mum anymore?

Can you stop being someone's mum if you want to?

Jeremy takes the phone back.

Hey, Millie says.

Tell me the number, he says.

Millie tells him, he types it in, presses the green button, and holds it up to her ear.

Millie takes a deep breath and holds the phone.

Ba-boom. Ba-boom. Ba-boom.

It rings and rings and rings. And rings and rings and rings. *Voice mail*, Millie says to Jeremy. *I'm sorry, Mum*, Millie starts to say, but her voice goes funny, and she starts crying, and the words won't come out anymore, because it's her mum's voice, and she just said *Mum* out loud, and she didn't realise how much those two things would make her body hurt.

Jeremy takes the phone from her and she doesn't look at him. She stops crying when he hands her an apple.

Thank you, Millie says, and puts it on the floor beside her.

I'm sorry for making you cry, Captain Funeral, Jeremy says.

It's okay, Captain Everything, she says, wiping her eyes with her beer cozy. *I've got a plan.*

I've got heaps of those.

Okay, then, what's your plan?

It's top-secret.

Millie rolls her eyes.

What's yours then? he asks.

You'll tell.

I will not.

You will!

I will not!

Okay, Millie says, moving in closer. *Promise?*

Promise, he replies, blinking solemnly.

You said you know everything.

Yup. Pretty much.

You know how that lady talks to everyone in the whole train sometimes?

The intercom?

Maybe.

It's called an intercom.

I need to find it.

What for?

She looks down at her beer cozy. *To do something good.*

You're gonna get in trouble.

She puts her face up close to his. He doesn't seem to know where to look. *I need your help, Captain Everything. Will you help me?*

He gulps. *Yes. Yes I will. Ca-Ca-Ca,* he stutters. Clears his throat. *Captain Funeral.*

karl the touch typist

What is love, Agatha Pantha? Karl announces, sloshing his wine around.

Love? she asks, pressing her nose against the window. *I can't see anything!*

Exactly. Exactly, Agatha Pantha. It's too dark!

Yes.

Her forehead bounces up and down on the glass of the window. *It's making me feel uneasy!*

Karl, his eyes closed, nods vigorously. He leans forward, unsteadily. *But it's worp it,* he proclaims, tapping his index finger on the table in front of Agatha and then raising it in the air as though appealing to a cricket umpire.

Agatha turns back to him. *What?*

It's worth it.

What is?

Love.

Worth what?

The struggle, the heartache, the turmoil.

I have no idea what you're talking about!

Karl sips his wine. *Hab you ever been in lub, Agatha Panfa?* he says softly, swaying a little.

What? I had a husband for most of my life! You know that!

Yes, but – Karl grabs Agatha's hand with his wineglass-less hand and looks her in the eye – *Did. You. Lub. Him. DID-YOU-LUB-HIM?*

Agatha snatches her hand away, downs the last of her wine, and plonks the glass on the table. She wipes her mouth with her sleeve. *I suppose so!*

You suppose so. Did you tell him?

Why would I? It was assumed!

Assumed? Assumed! Karl stands up and yells to the rest of the restaurant car as if he is delivering a public address. His wine splashes on the table as he flaps his arms around. *You assumed he knew you loved him?*

Agatha stands up, grabs the wine from him, and throws back the rest of it. *Yes!* she says defiantly, breathy with the activity.

They stare at each other for a few moments, both unsure of what the other will do. Eventually, they lower themselves to a seated position, as if they are playing mimes in a mirror.

Karl likes the vein that sprouts out of her neck and runs up to her earlobe when she yells. He has a sudden urge to lick it, to run his tongue along it and put her earlobe between his teeth. He wants to take off her glasses, kiss her face, press himself against her. He wants to see what is below that brown suit.

Did he lub you? Karl says eventually. He drags his fingers through the spilled wine on the table.

Agatha shrugs and stares into the darkness.

Karl makes love-heart shapes in the wine. *I'm sure he did.*

It didn't matter. It doesn't matter. It was never the point.

It's the only point, he says.

Agatha leans her head against the back of the chair.

Karl stares at her: her old, tired face, her old, tired lips, her old, tired eyes. He stands up and shuffles around Manny to the other side of the booth. He slides in next to her. He can smell her now, mothballs and juice, somehow. She won't look at him. He moves in closer, can feel her starchy suit on his arm, the heat of her body on his leg. Could he love this woman?

Could she love him?

He takes a deep breath, grabs her face, pulls her toward him, and kisses her.

He pulls back from Agatha, leaving her stunned and breathless, and stands. *We're only here because of sex, you know. And you're ashamed of it. You all are. You. And you. And you. Yes, you. Just intercourse her,* he says to the young couple in the next booth over. He looks to Manny for support. Karl's sure he sees Manny give a thumbs-up. *No,* Karl says. *Fuck,* he says. *Fuck each other,* he says to the couple.

We do, the man says.

The woman lets out a strangled sound and hits him on the bicep.

That's the spirit, Karl says. *Fuck*, he says again. The word feels amazing in Karl's mouth. *Fuck fuck fuckity fuck. Say it with me, Agatha.*

Agatha sits in the booth, not looking at him, holding on to the table as though it's the only thing keeping her upright.

There's other words too, you know, Karl says, on a roll now. *Pubic! Nipples! Pink bits!*

Get a hold of yourself, sir! Derek says, storming down the aisle, notepad flapping around his neck.

Two small children at the table behind them are wide-eyed.

Mum? one says.

Fuck, the other one adds.

The old woman who has been too engrossed in her book to look at her husband suddenly says, *Boobs*.

What? her husband says.

Yes, Karl says, pointing at her. *That's right*.

Hey, Derek stamps his foot. *You*. He walks closer to Karl and tries to shoo him with his hands. *You're – you're*. He spits as he talks. *I knew you were trouble*. He writes a note on his notepad, tears it off, and throws it at Karl. It swings through the air like it's conducting music. *Out! You're banned from the eating area*.

Karl smiles hugely. *Great*, he says. *That's fucking great*.

Agatha, who has been silent the entire time, stands and yells, *I think it's 9:23 p.m. but I'm not sure!*, and pushes past Karl.

Agatha, Karl says. He hoists Manny up to rest on his shoulder in the same way Branson Spike held his stereo, and follows her out of the carriage. But not before turning around to face his audience. *Thank you,* he says, and takes a bow.

What? the old man says to his wife.

The night is long for Karl. Agatha locks him out of the cabin. They are drunk and loud and he enjoys it. He feels Italian. Or Mediterranean. Foreign, anyway, as though they are in a faraway country, hurtling through mountainous terrain. He throws his arms around as though he is directing something, he uses dramatic language from films, he feels his face bending and moving in ways it never has.

She pushed him away and climbed past him, and he was amazed at himself, and at the moment, because everyone stared, so he trundled off after her, because that's what he was supposed to do, yes? Now he yells, *Agatha!* just for the benefit of the audience listening in on his drama (HIS drama!), and knocks on their cabin door, and there is so much silence, big and empty, like the desert and the sky, and he looks down at his hands, holds them up to the light and thinks, *You magnificent bastard.*

He knows Agatha doesn't want him, but it doesn't hurt in

the place it should, and in fact it doesn't hurt at all. THIS is real life! Heartbreak! He's had his heart broken! By a real woman! He kissed her, just like they do in the films – or perhaps just like people do in real life, he wouldn't know – he just took her head in his hands and kissed her! With everyone watching. They all looked at him as though he was someone who DID things, someone who may be questionable in spirit, and no one has ever looked at him like that before, and the thrill of not being linear, of grabbing a woman's face with both hands and kissing her. And everyone watching!

So he sits outside the cabin and talks and talks and talks, he tells her everything there is to know about him, his shoe size, his favorite teacher at primary school, his son, the time Evie kissed someone else, his phobia of low-flying objects, why he doesn't miss his fingers, the nursing home, his escape. Everything. And just as he is falling asleep, he whispers through the keyhole, *That's it, that's everything I have.*

He starts to fall asleep, his back against the door, his legs stretched out across the corridor, but then he remembers something else, and says, *Wait,* and puts his lips against the door. *I think I love you but I could never love you like I loved Evie.* But there is nothing from Agatha, nothing at all. He listens for something but there is nothing; he thinks he can hear her crying, but he can't be sure, and he falls asleep in an uncomfortable position, one arm around Manny, and dreams of voids and blackness, and it feels like nothing.

another thing karl knows (a little bit) about

CRYING

Karl can count on one hand the number of people who have cried in front of him. Evie. His mother. His uncle cried when Karl's mother died, and it was not like the crumpled-up, giving-in crying he had seen before. His uncle cried as though it was an activity, each tear pushed out with a violence that made Karl feel like he was doing it wrong.

Everyone knows that everyone else has a crying face, just as they all have an orgasm face, but they are on The List Of Faces No One Sees. Everyone knows everybody else masturbates and cries, and you speak to each other with this contract, you carry on conversations with this see-through wall between you: *I don't masturbate or cry, I don't masturbate or cry, I don't masturbate or cry, but because I really do, I know you do too, because we are all the same.*

He had seen Evie's Crying Face. Orgasm Face. Terrified Face. Death Face. Was that love, then? When you stopped pretending? When you were able to say to another person, *I masturbate. I cry. I'm scared. I die*?

agatha pantha

7:36 a.m.: Agatha wakes. Looks at her watch. Is that the time? The real time? Or Train Time? She begins conducting her Age Tests regardless.

7:38: She tries to use the window as a mirror, to stare in disbelief at her face, but her eyes keep focusing beyond the glass and on the landscape outside. The blue of the night is slowly making way for the warmth of the morning light; it's not night but it's not yet morning, and the air looks like it's made of honey. *Does this happen every morning*? Agatha says.

7:40: She can't stop looking at the honey light. *What important thing am I doing every morning that I miss this?*

7:42: She can feel Karl's body through the wall. Can hear him snoring out in the hallway. She lay in her bed last night, listening to him through the door but trying not to, holding her hands up to her ears but only halfheartedly, and she thought about him sitting next to her, his hand on the top of Millie's head, the way he held coffee cups, the way he sat with his legs crossed, always. Jiggling his top foot. And she thought about touching him, and being touched by him, and the thought was not unpleasant.

When had she last been kissed?

And then she thought about his question, if she had loved her husband, and she didn't think she knew.

7:53: *They're talking me into it,* she whispers, clutching at her throat.

7:54: *Karl looks at me in a way Ron never did,* she says.

7:55: She lies in bed and feels that she does not deserve anything good.

7:57: She opens the door. Karl is standing there, his fist raised like he's about to knock on the door.

Agatha, he says.

Karl, she says.

I was— Karl says, just as Agatha says, *Are you—*.

They both shake their heads shyly. *You go,* Karl says.

No, you, Agatha says.

A voice comes over the loudspeaker. *You're all going to die. It's okay.*

Karl and Agatha look at each other. *Millie,* they say together.

And then Derek walks down the hallway toward them. *You.* He points at Karl. *And you.* He points at Agatha. His face is in her face. She can smell his breath. Toothpaste and coffee. *Are.*

In. He puts his face right up to Karl's. *Very. Big. Trouble*. He looks at the mannequin. *You, too, FYI*.

8:06 a.m.: Agatha sits in a chair in Derek's office. The chair is similar to the ones she has at home. It's brown and creaks when she moves in it. She watches Derek pace the room from one wall to the other. It's a tiny space, so he can only take two steps and then has to stop to turn around. He breathes hard through his nose. His notepad flaps around his neck as he walks.

8:07: Agatha tries to think of names for the chair. She has her hands folded in her lap. Karl is seated next to her. He puts a tentative hand on her hands. Agatha bats him away. He yelps. She doesn't look at him. The Chair of Dislike.

Swearing, Derek says, and walks two steps. His hands are in fists by his side. He turns around. *Kissing*. Two steps, turns around. His steps are fast, purposeful, but contained, as if he's trying to get to a bus that's rounding the corner but doesn't want to let on that he's rushing. *Fraternizing with sex dolls*. Two steps, turns around. Nods toward the plastic man Karl calls Manny. Faces them with his arms crossed. *This is the Indian Pacific train. Not* Big Brother. *Understand?*

8:08: *Calm down, man*, Karl says. Derek stops midstep, closes his eyes, and shouts, *I am calm*. He breathes deep and massages his temples. *We're just living, Derek*, Karl says. *You should try it*. Derek says, *Don't YOLO me. MY house, remember?* Derek grabs the edge of the desk with both hands.

8:08.46: There is one small moment when Agatha feels something for Derek. Where she recognises hurt in another human being. But it doesn't last long.

8:09: Derek sits on the desk and crosses his legs. *Anything else you'd like to share?* Derek asks. Agatha shakes her head, *No.* She assumes Karl does the same, but she still won't look at him.

Derek pulls a phone out of his pocket. Agatha can see a thin film of sweat on his upper lip. She grimaces. The beads of sweat reveal something of himself and it seems weak to Agatha. She squirms at the betrayal of his body, at his inability to control emotion and body temperature. Chair of Disgust.

Derek thrusts the phone in front of them both. Agatha and Karl both move forward to look at the screen. It's a photo of the young flannelette-wearing drunk in Kalgoorlie. There, on the arm: *Karl The Touch Typist Wuz 'Ere.*

Oh, Karl says.

Agatha hits him on the arm. *Typist!*

Karl rubs his arm and doesn't look at her.

FYI, it's the mayor of Kalgoorlie's son, Derek says, looking at them with the kind of hateful glee usually reserved for cannibals lording over hard-won prey. *Ah*, Karl says. *He's a big man, the mayor of Kalgoorlie*, Derek says. Agatha hits Karl on the arm again. *Ow*, Karl says. *And, BTW, they've matched the tag to the Warwickvale nursing home and the department store nearby,*

Derek says. *Oh,* Karl says. *Ring any bells, Karl "the Touch Typist"?* Derek says Karl's name and title using his fingers to indicate air quotes. *I'm sure I'm not the only Karl the Touch Typist in the world,* Karl says. *I'm sure you are,* Derek says. *Well, aren't you about to shit yourself with happiness, Derek?* Karl asks. *I certainly am not,* Derek says.

8:10: *BTW, there's this.* Derek shows them a picture on his phone of Karl's face with *WANTED* across the bottom of it. Karl grins. *Ha!* Karl says. *Think this is funny, do you?* Derek says. *No,* Karl says, swallowing his grin. *I'll say again,* Derek says. *Anything you'd like to share? If you cooperate, the penalty might not be as severe.*

8:10.35: As Karl shakes his head *No,* Agatha can feel something bubbling inside of her. It's been bubbling inside of her for too long and she needs to stop it, so she answers the question with something that will stop the feeling, she can't betray a feeling, she doesn't want the sweat on her upper lip to show, so she says, *This man kidnapped me.*

8:11: Karl turns to look at Agatha, but she doesn't catch his eye. She looks at her knees as if they're interesting. They are, a little bit. *New Kninkle?* she thinks, scratching at her left knee through her stockings. The door bursts open. The blond Indian Pacific woman walks in holding Millie's hand. *Millie,* Karl says. *Thank God.* Agatha thinks, *Millie. Thank God,* but she doesn't say it. The woman says, *She's okay. She was with my boy.* Millie climbs onto Karl's lap. Agatha glances down at her interesting knees again. *Go easy, Derek,* the woman says from the doorway. *She's only a child, remember.* Derek watches her close the door behind her. *Oh, up your jumper, Mel,* he says after a few moments. He looks at Millie. *The devil child, more like it.* Millie leans her back into Karl's chest.

8:12: *Wanted,* Derek says, reading from the screen of his phone. *Assault. Robbery.* Agatha says, *Robbery?* Karl says, *Well?* as if the point could be argued.

Derek puts the phone back in his pocket. *And now kidnapping. Nail in the coffin, wouldn't you say? Who's LOLing now?* Karl asks, *What am I doing?* Millie asks, *Kidnapping?* Karl says, *No one's kidnapping anyone.* Agatha says, *Except for you!* Karl says, *Agatha, I know you're mad at me, but—* Agatha says, *Sir! Kindly cease with the familiarities!* holding up her hand to him. *That man on your phone there?* Karl says. *Agatha hit him on the head with a plastic leg. Just so you know.*

8:14: *You're going to hell,* Millie says. *What did you say?* Derek asks. *Dad said parking inspectors go to hell,* Millie says. *Your father's dead,* Agatha says. *I know that,* Millie says.

8:15: *You,* Derek says quietly, pointing at Agatha. *The yelling one. Don't lie to me now. If you do, you're going wherever he's going. And he's not going anywhere pleasant.* Agatha braces herself. *Have you, or have you not, been abducted by this man?* He gestures toward Karl.

8:15.28: Agatha can feel the little girl's eyes on her. She looks across at Millie. She's looking back at Agatha, calmly.

A child. A little girl. Agatha's suddenly sitting at the dinner table with her husband. *I don't want children*, she said. And his face, the gravity of it, the way it pulled down at her words, and her regret, the feeling in her body, later.

8:15.52: Chair of Deception.

8:16: *I have*, she says, looking directly at Derek. *Yes*.

millie bird

We're not that invisible, I guess, Millie says. Millie and Karl have been locked in Derek's office and Derek has taken Agatha away.

No, Karl says. *We're not.*

What's going to happen?

He kisses Millie on the forehead. *I don't know, Just Millie.*

Why's Agatha mad at you? she asks.

She's a woman.

Am I a woman?

Yes.

But I'm not mad at you.

Thank you.

Are you mad at me?

Of course not.

It's my fault.

No.

Are we going to find my mum?

Of course.

Do you mean that?

But before Karl can answer, the door is unlocked and Jeremy pokes his head inside. *Psst. Captain Funeral,* he says, checking the hallway behind him and then sliding inside. He stands with his hands on his hips. *Hello, sir,* he says to Karl, shaking his hand. *I'm Captain Everything, sir.* He looks at Millie. *Captain Everything is here.* He's drawn a black mask around his eyes and a moustache on his upper lip. He wears an Indian Pacific cloth napkin around his neck as a small cape.

What are you doing? Millie asks.

You're in trouble. I've come to rescue you.

Millie, Karl says, *who is this boy?*

I'm Captain Everything, sir, Jeremy says. *I told you. They're talking about you.*

Who? Karl asks.

All the train people. The police are coming to meet you at Kirk Station.

Millie and Karl look at each other.

Derek was like, I'm calling the bleeping police! And, Jeremy jumps a few feet to the left, *my mum was like, You should wait, Derek, and then,* he jumps back, *Derek was like, I'm bleeping doing it, Melissa, you bleeping try to stop me, and she did bleeping try to stop him, but he did it anyway, and Mum called him a bleeping face, and I was camouflaged so they didn't see me, so I stole the key to this room, and even if they did see me, I would have karate-kicked my way through them* – he does a kick in the air and chops with his hands – *because I can do all sorts of things like that.*

What's that on your face? Millie says.

He touches it with his fingertips and grins. *My disguise.*

I like your spirit, young man, Karl says. *And your moustache.*

Jeremy looks at them both with a grave face. *You have to leave right now.*

Are you serious? Karl asks.

I've never been more serious, sir.

Jeremy goes first. He looks out the door, right, then left, and turns back to wave them on. Karl goes next, holding Manny around the waist so that his chin rests on Karl's shoulder. Then Millie. Manny stares over Karl's shoulder at her as they walk through the carriages. *It's okay,* she mouths at him. She looks at Manny's plastic hair and her head detaches itself. Dad's hair when they are at the beach and Millie says, *Your hair looks like a pineapple,* Dad's hair on the tiles at the hairdresser's, Dad's hair in the morning, Dad's hair Dad's hair Dad's hair, and her stomach pulls, and her head reattaches itself, and they pass the farting baby, the angry man, the peaceful grandma, the girl who gets to have a mum. Millie holds the backpack on her front and feels the cape against her back, hanging there without moving, like the skin of a dead animal.

Jeremy leads them to a door that opens outside to the very

back of the train. The wind makes her cape alive again and it jumps around behind her, as if it's trying to get the best view, excited to be there, in the wind and fresh air. They look out at the desert. Millie has never seen so much sky.

What about Agatha? Millie asks.

Who cares? Karl says.

It's not kind, Millie says.

She's not kind.

Jeremy puts water bottles and muesli bars in Millie's bag.

Just go that way. He points, gazing up at Millie.

This is amazing, Karl says, holding Manny up. *See that, Manny? This is Australia.*

Here's a map, Jeremy says. *Mum helped me draw it when I told her I wanted to show everyone at school what I did for the holidays. And here's a compass. There's a pub here – The Great Australian Pub.* He points to a position on the map. *You can stay there for the night.* He looks behind him, then back at Millie. *Mum and I stay there when we're visiting Dad. Just follow the road south and you won't miss it.*

Where did you get all this stuff? Millie asks.

I'm Captain Everything.

Are you sure about this? Millie asks, feeling her own cape whipping about behind her.

Jeremy stands and looks Millie square in the face. His pen moustache twitches a little. *Yes, Captain Funeral.*

I feel like I'm in a movie, Karl says. *Will they make a movie about my life, Millie? Do you think Paul Newman could play me? Or that Branson Spike fellow?*

Millie looks over the edge of the train. The ground is running fast beneath them. *How are we going to get off?*

Yeah, Captain Everything, how are we going to get off? Karl asks.

Jeremy starts to say something, but Karl interjects. *Don't worry, Millie,* Karl says. *Manny and I'll jump off, then run to catch up with the train, then you jump off. I'll catch you, I promise.*

But sir, Jeremy says. *There's a—*

Karl puts a hand over Jeremy's mouth. *You've done enough for us, Captain Everything.* He takes a deep breath. He tucks Manny sideways under his braces so that his hands are free. *You believe in me, don't you, Millie?* Millie doesn't answer, so Karl takes that as some sort of an agreement and says, *I am going to do this. I am a very cool person.* He grips the railings, preparing for a run-up. *I am going to do this, I am going to do this—*

And the train comes to a very, very slow halt.

Karl releases his hold on the railings. He turns to Jeremy.

This is Roald Station, Jeremy says, looking up at Karl. *We have to pick up and drop off mail here. It always stops for a few minutes. Sorry, sir.*

Karl sighs and mutters to himself. There's a ladder off the back of the train, and Karl climbs down it. He does a jump off the bottom rung, and winces as he lands. Millie backs down the ladder. When she gets to halfway, she stops. Jeremy's looking down at her. She clambers back up the ladder.

What are you doing? Jeremy says. *You've gotta go. I order you, as another captain, to get off the train. I'm pulling rank. Get off the tr—*

Millie grabs him by the shoulders and kisses him on his fake moustache. His cheeks burn a fierce red, like her hair, like the earth out here. *Please tell Agatha where we are,* she says, and climbs back down the ladder.

Karl and Millie stand together on the train track. Millie salutes Jeremy. *Thank you, Captain Everything,* she says.

Good luck, he says, a lopsided grin on his face.

Millie stands on the track until the train starts up again and slowly moves farther and farther away. *I'll never forget you, Captain Funeral!* Jeremy yells, and Millie watches the train until it disappears, and there is no sound but the sizzling of the sun on her skin.

Karl hugs Manny to his chest. *Look at it all.* He sweeps his free hand through the air. *This is Australia. You know? Real Australia.*

Millie starts to walk in the direction that Jeremy pointed. *C'mon, Karl,* she says.

Look at this sky. Look at this dirt. Karl kicks it with his foot and it flies everywhere. *Look at this scrub. There could be dead bodies buried in every square inch of this place and we wouldn't know. The British exploded practice bombs out here, and no one even knew. Bombs, Millie. Back home I can't even scratch my behind without my neighbours wondering what sort of bum disease I have. But out here no one knows what I'm doing.* He holds Manny up over his head. *Did you hear that, Universe?* he says. He stops, takes a big breath, and screams at the top of his lungs, *NO ONE KNOWS WHAT I'M DOING OUT HERE!*

Millie is not listening. All she hears is the sound of her feet hitting the ground as she walks. Each footstep like this: Mum, Dad, Mum, Dad, Mum, Dad, Mum, Dad.

Karl is metres behind her, staring up at the sky, turning around in circles like Millie sometimes does when she wants to make herself dizzy. She is annoyed at him. They don't have time for this. *We need to hurry,* she calls behind her.

part four

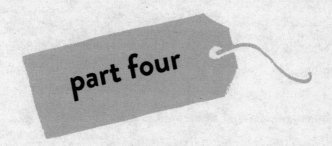

agatha pantha

10:37 a.m.: The blond woman helps Agatha off the train at Kirk Station. *Just sit tight, Agatha,* she says. *The train back to Perth will be passing by in the next few hours. They know to look for you.* She smiles reassuringly. *Make sure to remember to get off at Kalgoorlie. There's a bus connection there that'll take you back to the south coast. You'll be back in your own home sooner than you think. Take care, won't you?*

Agatha nods and watches her walk away. *Home,* Agatha says, bringing her handbag in close to her chest. *Yes.* She adjusts her glasses.

10:39: A man approaches her. *Excuse me,* he says. *Do you have the time?*

Agatha puts a hand over her watch. *Do I have it? Do I OWN time? No, I don't! I'd like to talk to the person who does, though! I don't know what the time is. I'm on Agatha Standard Time now!*

Whoa, lady, he says. *Sorry I asked.*

Yes! Agatha says. *You are!*

10:41: The train is still there and people are milling about, waiting to be told when they can reboard. A woman walks past Agatha. One of those uppity types, wearing her hair in a bun on top of her head, as though it were a topping. *You're not a dessert, lady,* Agatha says, leaning forward. A man walks past wearing a pink jumper. *Jumper too pink,* she says a little louder. *Walking too wide,* she says, raising the volume a little more. She holds on to the edge of the bench with both hands. *Clouds shouldn't be doing that!* she yells, coming to stand. *Unreasonable nose! Serial-killer haircut! Sunglasses too big! Too many children! Eyes too close together!*

She's interrupted by a young boy running up to her. He has a black moustache drawn on his face. *You dropped this, miss,* he says, handing her the Age Book. She takes it, and then he runs away, his neckerchief catching the wind. She watches as he jumps and kicks at the air and then disappears onto the train.

Not a real moustache, she says. She opens the book and runs her eyes over her careful measurements of Cheek Elasticity. Arm Wobblage. Distance From Nipples To Waist. Number Of Times I've Almost Kissed Karl.

What? she says.

In handwriting she doesn't recognise, it continues. Snore Graph. Smiling Moments. Number Of Times Karl Has Wanted To Kiss Me. My Favorite Agatha Faces. Buses I've Attempted To Steal. She turns the page. Boozy Men I've Beaten Up. She laughs at this and keeps turning the pages. Number Of Insults I've Yelled. Dead Things I've Seen. Distance I've Traveled By Bus/Train/Foot. People I've Loved.

After the last one there's a big question mark.

A map is stuck onto the next page. Someone else has written, *Hello. You Are Here,* with a red cross and a drawing of a car. *They Are Here.* Another red cross and another drawing, this time of a building with *The Great Australian Pub* scrawled along the top of it. A black arrow from one red cross to the other. *Yours sincerely, Captain Everything.*

The book shakes in her hands.

10:54: She stands in front of the mirror in the train-station toilets. *They shall grow not old,* she says. She pinches her cheeks. *As we that are left grow old.*

Forearms too spotty! she yells suddenly. She unbuttons her jacket and tosses it on the ground. *Man hands!* she yells, holding her hands up in front of her. She kicks her shoes off into the wall. *Fat feet!* She unbuttons her blouse and drops it on the ground. *Boobs too long!* She unzips her skirt and pushes it down from her waist, wiggling it over her hips to the ground. *Belly button too high up!* And she stands there, in her bra, undies, stockings, her glasses still firmly on her face, looking at herself in the mirror, breathing heavily from the effort of looking at herself like this. *Nostrils flare when speaking!* She links her hands together in front of her, resigning herself to something, trying to lend some sort of sophistication and dignity to a situation that has neither. *Too old*, she says. She takes off her glasses and rests them on the sink.

She puts her palm on her face, against her cheek, and leans into it. *Too old*, she says, looking into her eyes. It occurs to her that Ron's face will never age again. She will never get to see what he looks like as a really old man. It doesn't seem fair somehow, that she has to show the world what she looks like as an old person, and he doesn't. Like he's got away with something.

She's hating herself, her body, and she's crying now, tears that dribble down her face so pathetically, and she is an old old old sad sad sad woman and she hates herself, she hates herself so very much; more than anything else, this is what she feels the most.

And then a toilet flushes and a woman walks out of the stall.

The woman walks straight to the mirror and washes her hands in the basin. She's skinny and muscular and has a long, thin nose that draws attention to itself. Agatha stops herself from yelling it, and stands there in her underwear, unsure of what to do. There's an awkward silence as the woman washes her hands.

Then. *Where you headed?* the woman says.

Um. The southwest coast, Agatha says, feeling her body around her so hugely.

Perth for us, the woman replies, smiling at Agatha and then pulling at the skin around her eyes. *Just trying to get away*. She pokes her tongue out at herself in the mirror. *You know how it is.* She straightens her shirt, winks at Agatha, and walks out.

11:12: Dressed again, Agatha stands near the train station café counter, gazing longingly at all the fried food, feeling her stomach grumble. She stands a few metres away from the counter.

The man behind the counter looks back at her. *You all right?*

Yes! she says, but doesn't move.

D'ya want something?

Yes!

He sighs. *What is it, then?*

One of those! She points to a spring roll. *And one of those!* She points to a meat pie.

The man behind the counter puts them both in a brown paper bag. He slides it along the counter toward her. He nods at it. *That'll be six twenty-five, thanks.*

Agatha is very, very hungry. She thinks about grabbing it and running. People do that, don't they? She has never wanted anything more. But then her mouth says, *I can't.*

You can't what?

I don't . . . She sighs.

He grabs the bag. *Not a charity shop, lady.*

I've got it, a voice says behind Agatha. She turns around to see the woman from the toilets waving a twenty-dollar bill in the air. She smiles at Agatha and breezes up to the counter. *I've got it.*

Just trying to run a business.

Grow a heart.

Just gimme the money. He grabs the note and dumps her change on the counter. He holds up the bag and shakes it, looking at Agatha. *Yer lucky day, eh?*

The woman snatches the bag from him and walks off. She motions for Agatha to follow. *I'm Karen,* she says, and puts the bag down on a table where a man sits. *This is Simon,* Karen says, brushing a hand affectionately across his shoulder.

Simon is noticeably younger than Karen. He has strong, dark features. *Son?* Agatha thinks. Simon smacks Karen playfully on the bum. *No,* Agatha thinks.

Hey, Simon says to Agatha with a wave and a smile. There are chunks of pastry in the gaps between his teeth. Karen pulls up a chair and pats the table gently.

Agatha takes a seat and watches the bag, as if waiting to see what it might do next.

You got a name? Karen asks.

Yes, Agatha says.

Karen smiles. *The quiet type, I see. Well, go on. Eat up.*

What do you want from me? Agatha says.

Ha, Karen says. *What do I want from a woman who can't pay for a meat pie? Who yells at herself in her underwear? Just eat yer pie, lady.*

Did someone say underwear? Simon says. He flicks the band of Karen's trousers.

Karen nudges him with her shoulder. *Jesus, Sime,* Karen says, stroking his cheek. *You got a whole lot of shit in yer teeth.* The two of them stifle giggles. *Go get yerself cleaned up, would ya?*

Simon stands. *Your wish is my command.* He grins, bows, and walks away.

Agatha fishes the pie out of the bag and places it on top. She grabs some cutlery out of the stainless-steel holder in the middle of the table, cuts the pie into small squares, and begins to eat it, one square at a time. She feels Karen's eyes watching her.

Want to talk about what happened in the loo? Karen asks.

No, Agatha says.

Can I tell you a secret, then? Karen asks, leaning in closer.

No, Agatha says with her mouth full.

Karen laughs. She leans farther forward in her chair. She glances behind her, then turns back to Agatha. *I've done something terrible,* she whispers. *I'm trying to, you know, get all that karma shit realigned. I dunno if I believe in that, but.* She winks. *Just to be on the safe side. Good?*

Agatha nods. *Thank you,* she says. And then, *You haven't killed anyone, have you?*

No! Of course not. Karen shifts in her seat.

Drugs?

No.

Guns?

No.

You're a sex worker, aren't you?

No!

How bad?

Really, pretty bad.

Out of ten?

Eight.

Agatha swallows and looks at Karen.

And a half. Karen wrings her hands. *Ten. Definitely ten. It's ten. I'm . . . I'm . . .* She puts her elbows on the table and interlocks her fingers. She looks Agatha in the eye. *Not a good person.*

Agatha picks up her spring roll and takes a bite of it from the side of her mouth. She watches Karen as she chews. Agatha swallows, wipes her mouth with a napkin. *I'm, um . . .* Agatha clears her throat, and says, loudly and clearly, *I'm not a good person either.*

Karen lets out a shaky noise, as though Agatha's words have pulled this sound out of her mouth. She shoots her hand across the table and grabs Agatha's. *Do you think anyone is?* She squeezes Agatha's hand.

Agatha looks at the hand on top of her own. She can see Age settling like Glad Wrap over the surface of this woman's hand, and she doesn't feel happy about another woman experiencing the ravages of Age, like she normally might, but she doesn't feel sad about it either, as she does about her own body; she only feels connected to this woman, like she is Agatha, and Agatha is her, that they're the same.

Well? Karen says. *Do you think anyone is good?*

Ron. She thinks of Ron. And then Millie's face appears in her head and hangs there, so strong and still. And Karl? Is he good?

I'm Agatha, Agatha says, because she doesn't know how to answer the question.

Simon wanders back toward them. *I peed on the urinal cake,* he says. *It was pretty awesome.* He bares his teeth at Karen. *All gone?*

Karen reaches for his hand. *All better, hon,* Karen says. Agatha looks at their hands fondling each other like it's the only thing in the room. She can't imagine having someone around with whom she'd be so familiar. *Look, Sime,* Karen says, checking her watch. *Would you go fill up the car? We better get going.*

Yes, Mum. He winks.

Simon walks off and Karen turns to Agatha. *I left my husband yesterday. Simon left his wife.*

Agatha stares at her.

I got kids. Not too little. But not too old, either. We didn't tell anyone. We just left. Karen stretches her arms up over her head and back down again. *God, it feels so good to get that out. Hope you don't mind.*

I do, Agatha says.

Karen laughs. *Fair enough. Anyway. I just want to be with Simon. I love my kids. But I love my life. I want one. A life, that is. The kids'll understand one day.*

Probably not, Agatha says.

Karen nods. *Well, I sure hope you're wrong.*

Agatha thinks of Millie's mum. Of how she left Millie. Agatha feels her body flushing with anger. It's rising up her body, is blotchy on her skin. She wants to see Millie's mum, to say: *Who do you think you are? She's just a child.* And she wants to say it to Karen now, *Who do you think you are?* But instead Agatha says, *It's a ten.*

Karen slumps back in her seat. They sit in silence for a few moments. The cash register pings and fridges open and close and people around them have inaudible conversations. *Look, can we give you a lift anywhere?* Karen asks finally. *We're heading pretty much the same way. We'd be happy to have the company.*

No, says Agatha tightly. *I'll be taking the train back. Thank you.*

Agatha sits at the table in the service station and looks at her Age Book. People I've Loved. That question mark. That look from Millie's mum through her window so many months ago appears in her thoughts. *How do you get old without letting sadness become everything?* She thinks of the moments after Ron died, how she walked down the street and up her pathway and into her house, and the pressure she felt, the feeling as though her body were imploding. She thinks of the spare room in her house. What if, when she walked in that door after seeing her husband dead, a child, their child, was sitting in the spare room, in their room, and Agatha had to sit down on the bed, their bed – her bed? Would it have been a her? She had sometimes allowed herself to imagine it would be. And she'd had to say – what? What would she have said? *Your father is dead.* How do you tell a child, your child, that this is how life works? That you live just to die? That as long as you're alive, people you know, people you love, will die? That, really, the best thing to do is to never, ever care about anyone?

Agatha, Karen's calling to her from the line-up to pay for petrol. She looks harried. *Sorry, love, do you drive? Would you mind just scooching the car away from the gas pumps? God knows where Simon's got to. The keys should be in there. Sorry to be a pain.*

Agatha stands to look outside. There's about six or seven cars lined up, waiting their turn. One of them beeps their horn every now and then. The man behind the counter is having trouble with the computer system. Agatha looks back at Karen. If Agatha narrows her eyes into slits, Karen looks a little bit like Millie's mum. *How do you tell your child that this is how life works?*

You have to find a way, Agatha says, slinging her handbag over her shoulder.

Sorry? Karen says as Agatha walks toward the automatic doors.

I said, I can drive, Agatha says.

Oh, thanks, love. Karen smiles. *Sime's probably found something else to pee on.*

Probably, Agatha says. She stops when she reaches the doors and turns to Karen. *Look.* The door opens behind her and Agatha can feel the heat on her back. *I'm really very sorry.*

Karen waves her apology away. *No harm done, love. The pie hardly cost a thing.*

No, Agatha says to herself as she walks out to the car. *Not for that.*

Agatha opens the door and slides in. The keys are in the ignition. She cups them in her palm. They make a twinkling sound. She starts the car. She suddenly sees her face on a poster like Karl's. *Wanted.* And presses down on the accelerator.

The thing is, she doesn't stop. She thinks of that hand-drawn car following the black arrow toward The Great Australian Pub and she doesn't stop.

Well, she says to nobody. *This is most definitely a ten.*

12:17: And then she's driving on the highway. She, Agatha Pantha, is driving a car on the highway in the middle of the desert. She doesn't go faster than sixty kilometres an hour, but she's driving. *I'm driving,* she says out the window. *I'm driving!* she yells to a council worker smoking by the side of the road. *No shit, lady!* he calls back. *I'm driving!* she yells to a woman whose car appears to have broken down. *Fuck you!* the woman shouts. *I'm driving!* she yells to the sky, to the birds, and nothing yells back, it's just wind in her face and the sound of that, the sound of rushing, rushing wind.

Good job, birds! she yells out the window. *This road is particularly smooth!* She's holding on to the steering wheel with both hands and grinning at everything. *Boisterous letter box! Perfect signage! Nice spots, cows! Good-looking trees! That cloud is smiling at me! Nice blue, sky!*

Agatha goes to adjust her glasses and they're not there. She sees them, in her mind's eye, on the sink in the service-station bathroom. She tries not to blink, and opens her eyes wider and wider, letting the cool air onto her eyeballs.

She sees a sign by the side of the road. *Oh!* she says, and screeches the car to a halt in front of it. *The Great Australian Pub*, it says, and points down a long straight dirt road that looks unending. She consults the map.

Agatha gulps. Finds the blinker. Puts it on. *Nice sound, blinker,* she whispers. And turns left.

karl the touch typist

Well, we're going to die, Millie, Karl says. They've been heading south through the desert for most of the day. The sun is still strong and hot overhead and their water is running low.

I've been trying to tell you, Millie says.

No, I mean sooner rather than later. Is that what you wanted, Agatha Pantha? he says up to the sky. *Murderer.* His voice doesn't echo, just disappears into the flatness of the surrounds. *I'm so. Thirsty.*

He holds Manny in front of him and looks deep into his eyes. *Right, Manny? You understand. I hate this place! Australia – what kind of name is that? It's so dry. It's all the same. And it never ends, Manny.* He kicks at the dirt. *I hate this dirt. It's dirt. Who likes dirt? No one. That's who. I hate this sky. I hate this scrub. How are you supposed to live out here?* He kneels down on the ground, using Manny for support. *THERE'S NOTHING OUT HERE,* he yells, and buries his head into Manny's chest.

Hurry up, Millie says.

Karl stands and continues to walk. *We're not going to get to Melbourne by tomorrow, Millie.*

Yes we are.

We'll never make it.

We're going to make it.

It's impossible.

You don't know everything, Millie says, stopping suddenly. *Is that the pub over there?* she says, pointing.

He squints in the direction of Millie's gesture. *Don't toy with me, Millie. I'm very thirsty. I think I'm getting dehydrated. You know what that means? It's one of the first stages of death.*

There's a pub right there, she says, holding out the map. *The one that Captain Everything told us about.*

Well, I can't see anything. Karl puts a hand on Millie's forehead, checking her temperature. *Oh God,* he says. *The heat's getting to you. It's okay, Millie. We'll be okay.* He tries to lift her up to carry her, but she struggles against him.

I'm fine. Millie pushes away from him.

Save your energy, Millie, Karl says.

Millie walks on ahead of him. *I said, I'm fine.*

Wait, Karl says. There's a rumbling sound in the distance. *What's that?* A white car roars along a dirt road half a mile away, dust spraying behind it as though it's waterskiing in a red lake. *A car,* Karl says. *It's a car, Millie. People.*

The car starts to slow and then stops. Dust settles over the landscape, is drawn back into it, as though it's breathing out and breathing in. It's then that Karl realises he's looking at a building. *Is that . . .* Karl closes his eyes and then opens them again. It's still there. *Millie, it's a pub,* he calls after her. Karl holds Manny up and kisses him on the lips. *We're saved.*

Karl has never been happier to see a building. It's brown, wooden, and has a chunky gaudiness that makes it look like a plaything, as if some giant kid has gathered together some old bits and bobs and superglued them together. The large rounded lettering on the sign attached to the roof reads, *The Great Australian Pub.*

This is the place, Millie says, and disappears inside, though not before writing *IN HERE MUM* in the dirt with her fingers.

Karl has heard about the men who frequent these types of places. All leathery and quick to fight; thick hands and eyes permanently squinted from the sun. Their sentences a few nouns and verbs bookended by swearwords.

He expects this to be a saloon moment. He'll walk in and everyone will turn around to look, the music will stop, a glass will break somewhere, inexplicably (who will play him in a movie? He's just remembered that Paul Newman is dead. Is anyone he knows still alive?), and, with a new burst of confidence, he will walk in with Man Shoulders, you know, pushed back, a proud chest, A Man Stride; these kinds of men can sniff out an imposter, but he is A Man, he has Faced Death and defeated it! He has cheated death! He is A Man! Everybody! A Man! See this Man! He will walk over to the bar in two or three steps, pull out a barstool, and sit his Man Bum down, slam his Man Fist on the bar, and order – no, not order, *demand* – a double something-or-other (what would Paul Newman drink?) and the entire pub would be looking at him, and he would lean in to the bartender and say – in a low, rumbly kind of voice, because someone who has power does not need to speak in a loud voice – *Make that a triple.* Would there be a collective gasp? Maybe. But he wouldn't hear it, because he would be too busy Being A Man. And then the other Men would rejoice in his presence, shake his hand or high-five him or whatever it is they do, and they would talk about Man Things, like Tools and Agriculture and Centrefolds.

But when he opens the door he realises he will not make the bar in three steps.

Karl, why are you taking such big steps? Millie whispers.

What? Karl whispers back. *Does it look stupid?*

Yes, she says.

He walks to the bar in normal-sized steps. License plates from all over Australia line one wall, like some kind of graveyard for dead registrations. There are five big-screen tellys scattered around the pub, and they all play the same AFL game on them. The ceiling is low. The air is dense. Dust swirls in the small patches of sunlight.

There are two men sitting at the bar, chatting, and they barely notice him. The bartender is polishing glasses and nods in his direction. Karl nods back. *He knows,* he thinks. *He knows I'm A Man.* He pulls out a barstool. It scrapes loudly across the floor. He looks up at the barman. *Sorry,* he apologizes, doing something with his face that he doesn't normally do. Something very feminine, he can feel that much.

He hates himself already.

Karl leans Manny against the bar. The barman raises his eyebrows. Karl goes to sit down on the barstool, but he's flustered with all the attention, with this pressure to Be A Man, and he misses the stool completely and falls backward onto his bum, and Manny comes crashing down on top of him, the noise from it all combining and echoing throughout the pub.

The worst thing is not this, however. The worst thing is the noise that Karl makes, which involuntarily escapes his mouth like a volcano releasing toxic gas that's been building up for hundreds of years. A noise only Very Old Men make when pushed to the end of their physical tether: *Ugggggghhhh.* It's the worst noise he's ever made, he's not even sure he could do it again, and he hears it as if he's standing outside of his own body.

He lies on the ground for a few moments, reflecting on that small but satisfying moment in his life when these men thought he was One Of Them. He lets Manny's nose rest on his, closes his eyes, and takes a deep breath.

You 'right, mate? a voice says from above.

Yeah, need a hand, mate? another voice says.

And suddenly, he's sitting at a bar with two men (Men!) and they're slapping him on the back and laughing and ordering him a drink and asking, *What's your story?* And Karl cannot wipe the smile from his face.

millie bird

Millie sits with her back against Karl's stool. She fiddles with the hem on Manny's trousers, who has been positioned so that his back leans on the bar. The men say things about the footy and Karl tries to join in. *Yes,* she hears Karl say. *That young man should not have been replaced by that other young man.*

Millie reaches into her backpack for some food, but her hands fall on a folded piece of paper, nestled in there among the muesli bars. *Captain Funeral,* it says. She opens it.

Dear Captain Funeral,

On the day you left the train, we had a missed call from your mum's phone. Someone left a message. It wasn't your mum though. I listened to it sixteen times to make sure I wrote it down right. I've put it in a speech bubble so that you know it's not me talking.

Mills love it's Aunty Judy. Where are you love? We're looking for you. Your mum she's well she's not right love. She's taken off. I sent Uncle Leith out west to get you but you weren't there. He went all that way. Where are you love? Just tell a policeman and stay where you are we'll come get you. Okay love? Okay?

Sorry for not telling you. I was afraid of making you sad. You can borrow my mum, sometimes, if you like.

Yours sincerely,
Captain Everything
Superhero
Indian Pacific

Millie folds the letter and puts it back in the bag. She holds on to her stomach.

And then, *Hi*, she hears.

Millie leans forward and looks around Manny's leg. There's a girl sitting cross-legged against one of the other stools. She's about Millie's age, with straight black hair tied back in a pony-tail. She has a box of matches in front of her. She lights one and watches it burn.

Hi, Millie says back, eyeing the flame.

Who's that? the girl asks, after the flame dies.

That's Karl, Millie says.

No, the girl says, *not him.* She points at Manny with the burned match. *Him.*

Oh, Millie says. She clears her throat. *Manny. He's dead.*

The girl raises an eyebrow. *He's plastic.*

Yes, Millie says. *Dead bodies turn into plastic. And they use them in shops to sell clothes.* She looks at her fingers. *Is what I think.*

The girl looks at her for a long time. *You're weird,* she says finally.

YOU'RE weird, Millie says.

When my uncle died, my dad burned him. The girl lights another match. *Then we threw him into the ocean.*

I'm sorry for your loss, Millie says quietly.

Dead bodies stink, so then you have to burn them, the girl says, and looks at Millie. *Is what I know.*

Depends on how you think about things, Millie says uncertainly.

No, it doesn't. The girl crawls over to Millie and stares at her. She lights a match and holds it up between them. The flame makes shadows dance all over her face. *Let's burn him,* she says, grinning. *If he's dead anyway.*

Millie feels a weight in her stomach. She watches the flame until it burns out. She looks at Karl behind her, who's laughing and telling a story in a much deeper voice than she has ever heard from him before. She looks back at Manny.

What are you afraid of? the girl says, cocking her head at Millie.

Nothing, Millie says. *I'm not afraid of anything.* But it isn't true because she is afraid of everything and she feels that deeply in her stomach.

the night before the first day of waiting

After her dad died, people in the town acted like they loved her. *Yes, Millie*, they said. *You poor love*, they said. *Here's a lolly*, they said. But she knew it was because her dad was dead and they were:

1. either glad their dad wasn't dead but were imagining it but couldn't imagine it, or
2. their dad was dead too.

So the ladies at the health-food shop gave her all the glass jars they had, and the man at the hardware shop gave her as many tealight candles as she wanted, and she asked her mum while she stared at the wall in the bedroom, *When was Dad born*? But her mum didn't answer so Millie asked the lady at the library, who was surely the oldest person alive, and they worked it out by looking through all the old school photos in the archives, and they found one of her dad, his face leaner and brighter and clearer, but her dad for sure, and after it went dark she crept past her mum, who was on the couch in her underwear watching telly without the lights on. It was a hot, sticky night, and the cricket was on, but her mum didn't like the cricket, so Millie could tell her mum wasn't watching it, but her dad liked the cricket so maybe that's why she was watching it. The glass jars were clinking around in Millie's backpack, but her mum didn't move, she hadn't moved the entire day, except when Millie brought her a bowl of grapes from the fridge and put it next to her, and she had patted Millie on the head, but when Millie walked past in the dark, all the grapes were still there.

So Millie snuck out to the tree in the vacant lot. She climbed up and down the tree, attaching a glass jar with a burning tealight to every single branch. When she had finished that, she positioned some tealights on the ground in front of the tree to spell out *DAD*. Beneath that, she lined up the remaining tealights in a long line. It was the longest dash she had ever made.

Millie lit all the candles and sat back on the grass. She lay on her front and made a pillow with her hands to rest her chin. The grass cracked beneath her, spiking her skin. It had been such a dry, hot summer. The candles in the tree gently swayed and those on the ground flickered. There were stars in the sky and now it looked like there were stars in the tree and on the ground, as if Millie had made a starry night sky out of the whole world. She stood up and strolled around her sky, wondering if her dad was doing the same, all the way up there.

A gust of wind blew through the street, like it did those months ago when she held Spider in her hands. She heard the glass jars clink against the tree, she watched as some of the tealight candles on the ground toppled over, and she stumbled backward as she saw the grass catch fire. It started small but then it was big and then it was huge and then the whole lot was on fire. Millie stood there. She watched it all happen, she watched the night sky disappear. She backed away to the footpath. The heat hurt her skin, embers shot out, glass jars cracked and burst. So she ran, she just ran. She found a tree farther down the street and climbed it right to the top. The street woke up and people appeared and there were buckets of water and hoses and the fire engines came and Millie watched it all from the top of her secret spot and no one knew she was there. When it was light again Millie went home because you always went home, didn't you? The police were there holding her bag and her mum looked at Millie like her mum was only a drawing and Millie's guts hurt and she didn't know how to say sorry about it because it was the worst thing she'd ever done.

Well? the black-haired girl is saying. It happens so quickly, the girl lights a match, it burns so brightly, and she holds it up to

Manny's shirt, and Millie tries to say no but it's too late and the girl lights Manny's shirt on fire.

Millie stands up and steps back, and the fire creeps up his shirt, *ba-boom ba-boom ba-boom*, the flames climb higher, and it's the tree, but then she runs at him, she doesn't know how to put out a fire, she waves at it, and blows at it, and she can feel the fire hot near her skin, and does she say, *Dad?* She doesn't remember. But it's her dad, IT'S HER DAD, and she watches the fire and curls up in a ball, *SORRYMUMSORRYMUMSORRY-MUM.*

karl the touch typist

Millie's on the floor, coughing. She looks up at Karl and he feels his heart rip to shreds. Is there anything worse than seeing fear in a child's eyes? Manny is on fire, ON FIRE, and the bartender hoses him down, and it's out. There's another little girl – where the hell did she come from? Why are there so many little girls all of a sudden? – and she holds some matches, but Karl's brain doesn't make the connection yet, and he kneels down next to Millie, she coughs and cries, and he puts a hand on her cheek, and then looks over at the little girl and says, *What did you do?* He knows he's not supposed to shout at little girls, especially ones he doesn't know, but it just happens, and she starts to cry too, but he doesn't care, and then one of the men says, *Wait a minute, mate, don't you yell at my daughter,* and Karl knows the *mate* is being used ironically in this instance, and he wants to use it back in this way – has he ever used it in this way? Has he ever used it at all? So he stands up and walks over to the man, and Karl is taller than him, that's got to be something, doesn't it? And he says, *Well, mate* – he puts the extra emphasis on *mate*, and it feels amazing out of his mouth, he will be doing it again, if he lives through this – and then he says, *if your daughter wasn't such a criminal, then I wouldn't have to.*

And Scotty or Jonesy or Crusher or whatever, the man he was drinking and laughing with moments ago, has his hands around Karl's neck, and Karl pulls at the hands and chokes, but manages to lift a wobbly knee into the man's stomach. The man doubles over and a barstool clatters to the ground and Karl puts his hands to his own neck – he never knew what it felt like to be strangled, and he is grateful for the experience – he says, *Sorry, mate*. ScottyJonesyCrusher looks up at him, and growls at him – growls at him? Yes, he definitely growls – and lunges at Karl, and Karl somehow guesses the right way to move, and they stumble gracelessly around the pub and Karl feels as if he dodges every lunge, hurdles chairs and small children, uses tables as shields, but really, if he's honest with himself, Scotty JonesyCrusher is a bit on the chubby side so he's easy to outrun. Then, in what Karl can only call a moment of distraction – surely every Great Man has one? – he forgets to dodge, and ScottyJonesyCrusherFatty grabs his shirt and pulls Karl into him, and they slap each other a bit, elbows clunking, palms flailing as if they're both trying to dig their way out of being buried alive.

A white foam squirts from above them somewhere, it covers them both, and they peel themselves away from each other, cough and splutter, cough and splutter. Karl reels backward and wipes the foam out of his eyes with his hands. The cut on his palm has reopened during the scuffle. Blood weeps from it and Karl feels a little woozy but then he looks up, and, through the film of foam and red dirt and sweat, there is Agatha Pantha. Hair wild and unkempt, breathing heavily, holding a fire extinguisher with the raw animalism of someone in a ruthless war, presenting the extinguisher to them both as if it were the bloodied head of someone they knew, someone on their side, as if they were next.

She looks so goddamn incredible that Karl cannot look away.

What have you done? Agatha demands.

And with everything that's been going on, he's forgotten about Millie, how could he forget about Millie? He points to the other little girl, cowering under a table in the far corner and still crying, and says, *Ask her*. Millie's still lying on the ground against the bar, her tiny body, her tiny body, and he thinks of Evie, her tiny body, *I will always be here, Evie,* but ScottyJonesyCrusher Fatty says, *Now, wait a minute, mate,* and runs at Karl again, crouching down, grabbing him around the waist and pushing him into a wall. Agatha puts the fire extinguisher on them again. With as much poise as he can muster, Karl stands, wipes his face clean with his sleeve, and says, *I'm not your mate, mate.*

Oh, shut up! Agatha yells. *Everybody shut up! You!* She points at the bartender. *Get me some cold water!* The bartender blinks at her. *Well?*

The bartender hops on the spot, fumbles behind the bar, and hands her two large bottles of water.

Take them, Agatha says to Karl, so he does what she says, giving the bartender a tight smile.

Agatha grunts as she leans down and hoists Millie up over her shoulder. *Everything hurts,* Millie says between coughs.

I know, Agatha says, walking toward the entrance of the pub. Karl shuffles ahead of them and pushes the door open with his side. Agatha doesn't look at him as she passes him by.

Karl follows her out into the parking lot and stops when she opens a car door. *Whose is this?*

Agatha doesn't seem to hear him, or if she does, she ignores him. She lays Millie on the backseat and turns to Karl. *Water,* she says flatly, holding out her hand and snapping her fingers. Karl hands her a bottle and she snatches at it. He watches through the driver's-side window as Agatha presses the bottle to Millie's lips. *Drink, Millie,* she says. *It'll make you feel much better.*

Millie takes the water, sips at it, and closes her eyes.

Karl remembers the fear in her eyes and feels a surge of protectiveness. *You'll be okay, Just Millie.*

Agatha closes the car door and starts hitting Karl.

Hey, Karl says, shielding himself.

You should have been watching her!

You can talk.

Agatha picks up a branch from the ground and comes at him, branch raised, ready to strike.

Hey, Karl says, hiding behind a tree. *Just hang on. You need to stop. Stop right now. You are HORRIBLE. Do you hear me? You are the rudest person I've ever met. I bet your husband died on purpose.*

Karl is shocked at himself. *Shit. Shit shit shit shit. Agatha. I didn't mean it like that, it came out wrong—*

Agatha begins to yell. Not words, just sound; it seems to start deep in her belly and she screams it. Karl puts his hands over his ears because it's so loud, but there's nothing to echo off, so it is swallowed up and fades out into the sky.

Agatha stamps her way over to Karl. She stands in front of him, close. He can feel her breath on his neck. They stand there, looking at each other, square in the face. Karl has no idea what she is going to do, he shakes with the thought; she is always mad, but he's never seen her like this, he does not know what she is capable of. She throws the branch over his head, and she grabs the back of his neck with both hands, and he almost screams, but she covers his lips with her lips, and she kisses him.

It's not a long kiss. It's short and harsh and dry, but it's still a kiss. Agatha jerks her head back and crosses her arms, glaring at him. Karl stares at her, mouth wide open.

So! Agatha yells. She turns on her heel and stomps back to the car.

Agatha drives them down a long dirt road. Karl watches the dirt spread out behind them as if the car is pushing out rocket clouds, propelling itself along the ground. He twists in his seat and looks back at Millie. She's sound asleep, lying on her side, with Manny's newly melted arm around her waist.

The world is too difficult for Millie, and he doesn't know how to tell her this. He wants to strap her to his back and show her beautiful things. He wants to stroll next to her while she walks on the tops of brick walls, and he wants to point out how there is music to everything if you just close your eyes and watch the notes in your brain. He wants her to know how satisfying it is to put a book that you've just read back on the shelf, and words, he wants to show her beautiful words, how much beauty there can be on a page. And he wants to show her everything good, and he never, ever wants her to see anything bad.

He turns back to face the front. *Where did you get the car?* he asks.

Agatha doesn't answer.

He pushes the door lock up, down, up, down. He thinks about The Kiss. It is the sexiest thing that has ever happened to him. Beer and dirt and fighting and a woman grabbing his neck and kissing him on the lips, in front of everybody. And the way she holds the steering wheel, like she is HOLDING IT, like someone who knows how to HOLD THINGS, and the way she watches the road with those steely eyes, as though she is ready for anything, a kangaroo or a snake or Armageddon. And the way she doesn't squeal when she hits rabbits, and the way she does up her buttons right to her neck, like no one, not ever, is getting in there.

Agatha looks over at him and he winks at her.

What's wrong with your eye?

Nothing, Karl says. He stares out the window, feeling the gentle rumble of the car against his legs. *There's really nothing out here, is there?* He presses his face against the window.

Agatha doesn't answer straightaway. Keeps her eyes on the road and her hands tight on the steering wheel. But then: *Everything's out here,* she replies.

millie bird

When Millie wakes, the car has stopped and it's dark and the doors are opening and closing.

She'll be
SLAM
We'll just
Not more than
SLAM
Okay?

Karl opens the back door and puts a towel over Millie's legs.

Are we in Melbourne? Millie says.

No, Millie, Karl says.

Karl hugs her and it feels like her dad is hugging her and she whispers, *Did I dream him?*, and Karl says, *Who?*, and Millie says, *Did I make him up?*, because she's sure she did, but Karl says, *No, Millie*, and then, *We'll be right back, Just Millie*, and he closes the door and it's so dark and she says, *Am I dead?* But there's no answer because they're gone already and everyone's always leaving and her question just hangs in the dark in front of her, like a skeleton in a horror house, and she sits up and watches them walk away, and then she hugs Manny into her and squeezes her eyes shut.

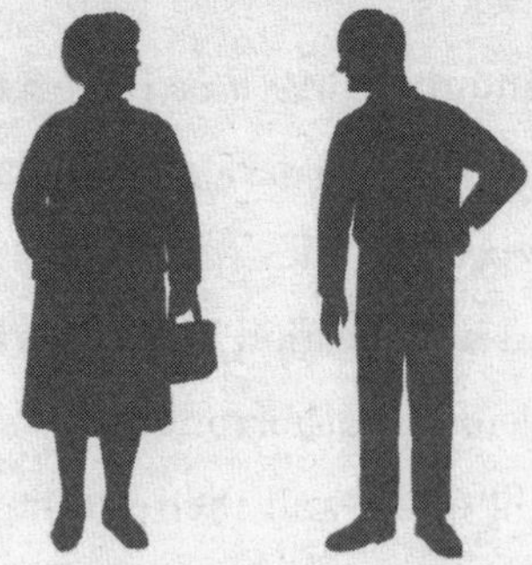

agatha & karl

Morning(ish) Agatha Standard Time: The sun is coming up. That moment when it's not night and it's not day. Agatha's not missing it this morning. They hear the ocean smashing into the cliffs. They stand in the shrubs, a few hundred metres away from the car, facing each other.

Karl puts a hand on Agatha's cheek. The feeling is not unpleasant. *Your cheek is so soft!* he yells suddenly.

Agatha smiles. *Your hand feels nice!* she yells back.

I'm going to put my other hand on your other cheek! Karl yells.

I'd like that!

Karl moves in closer, and holds Agatha's face in his hands. He can't really see her, because it's still dark and his eyes are terrible, but he can feel the heat of her and he loves her skin on his hands. *You smell good!* he yells.

She yells back, *I think you should take off your shirt!*

He steps back and undoes the buttons on his shirt. *You should take off your jacket!* he yells, throwing his shirt to the side.

Agatha undoes the buttons on her jacket and drops it on top of his shirt. *Skinny arms!* she yells at him.

Yes! he says, looking down at them. He looks back up at her. *Smooth neck!*

Undershirt! she yells.

He pulls his undershirt up over his head and throws it to the side with the other clothes. His hair is spiky on top of his head. *Blouse!*

I can see your ribs! she yells as she unbuttons her blouse. *Shoes!*

I can see your bra strap! he yells while stooping down and untying his shoelaces. *Shoes!*

Relatively inoffensive chest! Socks!

I want to rub your feet! Stockings!

I'd like to put my head on your chest! Trousers!

Strong calves! Skirt!

And then they're both standing in their underwear. They look shocked to see each other. The light warms up around them. They're both becoming more than blurry silhouettes to each other.

Karl stands in front of Agatha, wearing nothing but his boxer shorts. He is so skinny, hair growing across his chest in fits and bursts. Skin droops from his arms, around his nipples, and around his elbows in sad U-shapes, like someone is pinching them downward. She moves toward him, until she's so close she can see the hairs on his chest shifting and moving with every breath she exhales.

Agatha lets Karl look at her. She is all clumps and bulges and rolls, and there's just so much flesh there that he wants to push his face into all of it. She wears a bra that means business, one that you could probably attach to trucks to tow them out of trouble if you were in a bind. Her stomach bulges out over her slip, and there's fat sneaking out the sides of her bra.

With a bit of difficulty, she sits on the ground, her legs out in front of her. Karl, with a similar amount of difficulty, does the same. They lean in toward each other, their faces hovering, so close. They both notice more wrinkles on the other's face. Agatha notices more ear hair than she first thought. Karl notices a hair growing out of Agatha's chin. They close their eyes, and kiss.

And then they do IT, because even old people call it IT.

It's not classy, or something you'd want to see close-ups of. Nothing works the way it should, and they get red dirt up their noses and have to take a break to clear them, and Agatha keeps her bra on because it has been a big day of new things and you've got to stop somewhere, and they have to work out which parts of their bodies still work, and those that don't; they have to spend a long time working each other out. *Is this okay?* Karl says, and *Is this okay?* Agatha says, and it is too slow, and too fast, and they never get it quite right, it is not good, but it is warm and thrilling, in its way, and Karl makes as many Very Old Man noises as he pleases, and Agatha is quiet for the first time in a very long time, and Karl says, *Aren't we lucky to have hands?*, because he just loves the feeling of grabbing her stomach, and Agatha nods, because she loves the feeling of being grabbed, and Karl sits up suddenly, the typewriter letters from Evie falling into place in his mind, and says, *GO FOR IT,* and Agatha says, *I AM,* and Karl says, *No, I mean that's what—* and he almost says Evie's name, and wouldn't that be a big mistake, so he lies down and says, *Forget it,* and Agatha seems to. As the sun rises and warms and yellows, they know they should be playing mah-jongg and sitting in chairs and making tea and writing letters to grandchildren, they should not be having sex in the desert, but they are, and it makes them feel like movie stars, because surely only movie stars do things like have sex on a cliff as the sun rises, and Karl thinks, *I could play me in a movie, I am better than Paul Newman, he is dead and I'm alive, I'M ALIVE,* and their skin, it feels amazing against the fresh air, there is beauty in the entitlement they feel, they have lived long and deserve this moment, and everything flaps and flies and wobbles and jiggles and sags, and it's like flying, sort of, and Agatha can't stop holding her arms up to feel the air on them, it is such a true feeling, and Karl can't stop looking at her, and they look each other in the eye for a long time, and Agatha has never felt this good in her body before, she has never felt like it was right to be in it, and she does not speak, she cannot speak.

And later, after they've done IT, they sit against each other, feeling the cold dirt on their skin, holding each other up, watching the sun prepare to start a new day. Agatha says, *I loved him, you know. Ron.*

I know, Karl replies, as he writes, *Karl And Agatha Wuz 'Ere* in the dirt around them.

millie bird

Millie wakes up. Pinches herself. She's not dead. She looks at Manny. He is all melted. She runs her fingers over his face. His shirt is stuck to his body. She holds her beer cozy in front of her and stares at it. Traces her finger around the edges of Australia. She wonders where she is right now, and imagines a pulsing red light blinking at her on the beer cozy, and a neon sign: *You Are Here*. She gets out of the car and walks around it. *Karl?* she says, looking under it. She climbs onto the roof. *Agatha?* she says.

The sun is starting to light things up. They're parked near a huge cliff. She stands at the cliff edge, and feels the wind so strong against her clothes, rippling them like water. Her cape flies out behind her, and she sticks her arms out in front of her, like she's preparing to fly. The drop to the ocean is so far below. There is so much space out here. The sound of the waves against the cliff and the rocks is deafening.

She's surprised to see a man on the edge of the cliff, about fifty metres away. He's facing away from her and hits golf balls into the water. She watches him for a few minutes. Watches him swing far up behind his shoulder, and follow through, watches the ball move so far, so high, and then drop, all the way through that space, and into the ocean. She wonders what it would feel like to be that ball; she imagines flying through the air, her cape billowing out, and then dropping, dropping, so fast, losing her stomach, and plunging into the ocean.

She walks up next to him. *You're gonna die, you know,* she says.

Shit! He jumps, turning toward her, his golf club raised. *Bloody hell, love.* He scans the area behind her. *You just crash-land your alien ship or something?*

No. How long till Melbourne?

Where's Mum and Dad?

How many kilometres? Exactly?

Oh, jeez, love. Ages. I dunno – about fifteen hundred k's?

Will you take me there? I have something very important to do there today.

Nah, love, he says. *Goin' the other way.*

Okay, she says, sighing, turning, walking away, because she is SO SICK of grown-ups and their promises and the fact that they never do anything for you, and she decides that she is most definitely going to do every single little thing on her own, because she is the only one she can trust, and she knows that whatever she says in her head she will do, and that words people say can go either way, they can be true or they can be false, she is sickofit sickofit SICKOFIT. She knows Karl and Agatha have gone off somewhere and left her, she knows her mum doesn't want to be found, but she doesn't care, she is Captain Funeral, and she is the boss of herself.

You orright, love?
Where's Mum and Dad?
They're dead
You wouldn't know
You're just an adult

She opens the car door and climbs onto Manny, kissing him softly on the forehead, like her dad used to do to her, and she drags him out of the car and toward the edge of the cliff. His body makes lines in the ground, and red dust sparkles in the morning light. She is going to fly him to Melbourne, she will do it, she will do it right now, because no one else is going to do it, no one else is going to help her; she is going to have to be strong, she will hold him under one arm, and she will jump, and she'll fly up in the air like the golf ball, but she'll keep going, and Karl and Agatha and her mum will be sorry, they will be very, very sorry, and they will all say, *SORRYMILLIESORRYMILLIE-SORRYMILLIE, WE ARE SO SORRY, MILLIE.*

agatha & karl & millie

Karl and Agatha return to the car like teenagers. Karl actually slaps Agatha on the bum. And she actually giggles. They are caked in red dirt. Their hair sticks out at odd angles. The air shakes between them when they look at each other, and Agatha feels like women would be jealous of her, and really, that's all she's ever wanted.

But then.

Millie? Karl says when he reaches the door. He turns around. *Millie?* he shouts.

Agatha puts her face against the car window. *Millie?* she breathes into the glass. *Millie!* she yells in the other direction.

They run around the car in circles, checking underneath it and on top of it. They both keep saying, *Millie* as if it's the final word in a magic spell. She's nowhere to be seen, and it's so flat out here. Agatha turns around and around on the spot, scanning the landscape, willing Millie's shape to appear in front of her. Agatha looks toward the cliff and has to lean onto the bonnet of the car for support because the thought has arrived in her mind with a knee-collapsing suddenness: *That's it, out there, that's where she is, that's the only place.* The unsurvivableness of out there is what makes her knees buckle.

Karl spots a man, a golf club resting on his shoulder, walking toward them with a relaxed gait that seems disrespectful. *Excuse me,* Karl says and runs over to him. *Have you seen a little girl?* He holds his hand out to his side to indicate her height. In the wind, all Agatha can hear the man say is, *Melbourne* and *odd* and *draggin' somethin' toward them cliffs.*

She watches Karl grab the man's collar and say, *Why didn't you stop her?* and the man push Karl in the chest and say, *Hands off, mate.* So Agatha takes a big breath and walks toward the cliff edge.

Agatha walks as fast as her fear will let her. She can hear the men yelling at each other behind her and she is tired of yelling, so very tired of loud noises coming from people's mouths, especially her own, and the ocean is so enormous in front of her, it is so endless; even when it looks like it ends, she knows it doesn't. She stops a couple of metres from the edge, kneels down, and lies on her stomach. She pulls herself forward, feeling the gravel scraping her legs. She grunts with the effort. She grabs the edge with both hands and peers over it.

Millie, she calls, but it's lost in the wind. She says it over and over again, as if trying to wake Millie from a deep sleep.

Agatha scans the ocean for any signs of her, but there are none, and she has killed her, she has killed this tiny girl, and it is her fault, it is her fault, and she buries her face in the dirt and sobs.

But. *Agatha?*

Agatha shoots her head up, looks toward the voice, there is something there, but without her glasses she can't make anything out properly. *Millie?*

Agatha, someone replies faintly, and it has to be Millie's voice, so Agatha crawls along the cliff edge toward the voice. And then she sees her, clutching that plastic man, standing on a small ledge jutting out from under the cliff edge like a sulky bottom lip.

Millie, Agatha doesn't know what else to say. What do you say? How do you ever know what to say?

Millie looks up at her. She's crying. Agatha has never seen her look so wild. *Rack off, Agatha,* she says. *I don't need you. I'm fine on my own.*

I'm sorry, Millie, Agatha says, crawling closer. The ledge looks unstable, like it could break off at any moment.

No you're not.

Don't move, Agatha says. She looks behind her for Karl's help but he's still arguing with the stranger.

You're not the boss of me, Agatha Pantha, Millie says, turning away from her.

No, Agatha says. *I'm not.*

You'll just leave me.

Agatha looks toward the car again, wishing Karl would come, wishing for his help. The drop to the ocean is making her dizzy. Forcing herself to look down, Agatha says, *That's true. I will one day. That's what life is, Millie.* The air is crisp and cold and the noise of the ocean is so overpowering. *But while we're both alive, wouldn't it be nice to be friends?*

I'm doing it, Agatha, Millie says. *And you can't stop me. No one can.*

No, Millie, Agatha says, and she doesn't even think, her body just does; she will think later, is that what it feels like to have a child? To do without thinking? To be so outside of your own body and so inside of theirs? She slides herself down onto the ledge, scraping her legs and arms, but she doesn't feel it, because she's trying to keep her eye on Millie, trying to grab her, just to get to her, but Agatha is so far away, she will never reach her, she's on her hands and knees and she tries to yell out to her, but the words won't come, her throat feels like it's closing, and she watches helplessly as Millie hugs that stupid plastic man to her and takes a step toward the ocean, and Agatha shuts her eyes and stops breathing altogether and hopes you can die from making yourself stop breathing because there's nothing else left to do.

But after a few long seconds of holding her breath, she feels a warmth next to her. Agatha opens her eyes, and Millie is there, standing right next to her, looking down at the ocean. Agatha follows her gaze and it's that plastic man, falling,

falling, falling. Millie's cape is tied around his neck and for a moment it looks like he's flying. He hits the ocean with a tiny splash and then bobs to the surface.

Agatha sits up and takes a deep breath, one that inhales and doesn't just breathe; one that takes in all the atoms from this moment and keeps them in her lungs.

Millie wipes her eyes with her sleeve and sits down next to Agatha. *What does abandoned mean?*

There's a smattering of peaks in the ocean like a classroom of children raising their hands. Agatha pauses. Every thought, every breath, every movement feels so important in this landscape. Words seem to count more. *Left behind*, she replies.

Lost?

Sort of. Without looking at Millie, Agatha reaches for her hand and holds it really, really tight.

When Karl finds them, his shirt is ripped and his hair is all mussed up. He helps them climb up the ledge and hugs them both. Agatha relays the fate of his plastic companion. Karl feigns indifference. Millie informs him that they can share Manny's leg and this seems an agreeable thing to Karl. They all pile into the car and drive away from the Bight, feeling the presence of one another amid the drama of the landscape. Agatha listens to the quiet. Millie puts her hand on her reflection hand in the window. And Karl smiles because he's written, *WE ARE HERE* in the dust on the bonnet.

things that millie, karl, and agatha can't know for sure

Ten years from now, Agatha will sit at Karl's hospital bed and watch his life end in front of her. Millie will be in a different country and will miss it, but she will return for the funeral. In her eulogy, she will say, *Karl is my best friend*, and she will use the present tense on purpose. Agatha will die three months later, and it will be Millie who finds her, dead in her armchair, and Millie will believe she looks happy-sad. Millie will die, too, eventually, like everything does, leaving behind an ex-husband and two grown children. It will be an accident, it will be quick, and her last thought will not be a thought at all: *What will I* –

But they don't know any of this yet.

Because for now, Millie, Karl, and Agatha drive back the way they came.

acknowledgements

I know Mum believed moments of thanks between human beings to be one of the most important things. She taught me to write ridiculously thoughtful thank-you notes to everyone for everything they ever did for me. I didn't understand it then – less time to spend on staring/dancing to Bananarama/writing obvious Roald Dahl nonsense poetry knock-offs, as far as I was concerned. But as you get older, things your mum once said can have such a ring of inevitability about them that you're not sure how you ever thought differently.

But how do you thank a bunch of people who made you who you are, who made you better, who gave you and your work worth? You just tell them, I guess.

I wrote *Lost & Found* as part of a PhD at Curtin University in Western Australia, so thanks must firstly go to Curtin and its inhabitants. They gave me a scholarship, a space to write, and a heap of mentors and friends who I plan to bug for my whole entire life, whether they like it or not. I was an unknown, wanting to make space in her life to write a novel, and Curtin University gave me the social, cultural, and financial permission to do that. I'm so grateful.

More specifically, thanks to my two supervisors, David Whish-Wilson and Ann McGuire. Dave was such a calming presence, pushing me to "cut the cute" in *Lost & Found*, and having faith in my ability when I didn't. Most of our supervision meetings often descended into dissections of the AFL, and I now deem that to be a vital part in my creative process. Ann didn't run away when I cried my story to her upon our first meeting, but instead gave me a whole bunch of tissues and made me feel like it was her project too. Special mention must also go to Julienne van Loon, who – although not directly involved – seemed to always have time for me if I needed it.

So many people read *Lost & Found* in its various forms while I was writing it, and then said all sorts of helpful stuff: Jeremy Hoare, who knows the story better than I do, and who is my Ideas Man; Mark Russell, who showed me where all the commas are supposed to go, and said in his polite way, "No one would fit in a ceiling vent, ever"; George Poulakis, who showed me where the commas are supposed to go when I forgot them again; Sam Carmody, who is my other (equally as important) Ideas Man, plus Therapist, plus Food Quality Control Manager; Sarah Hart, who read an early draft when she had more important things going on; Julia Lörsch, my emotional barometer, who cried reading parts of it; Elizabeth Tan, who gave me such thoughtful notes; James Stables, who spent most of the time reminding me that his tax dollars were going toward its creation; the girls from Beaufort Street Books – Jane Seaton, Geraldine Blake, and Anna Hueppauff – who read it so enthusiastically; Adam Brenner, who told me he thought people would actually buy it; my dad, Ken Davis, who read every draft with an urgency only a proud parent could pull off. He dutifully called it a "masterpiece" and gave me a two-page list of reasons as to why I should take out the swearing; his partner, Lorraine Jennings, whose eagle eye prevented me from making embarrassing errors; my older brother, Rhett Davis, who read many drafts of it, quickly and without fuss, and always gave me important insights; my younger brother, Ben Davis, who read it on his iPad in Romania, and didn't seem to have much to say about it.

Thank you also to those involved in the Curtin workshops, who helped me with early decision-making: Eva Bujalka, Steven Finch, Maureen Gibbons, Simone Hughes, Laura King, Kerstin Kugler, Kandace Maverick, Paul McLaughlan, Max Noakes, Ian Nicholls, Rosemary Stevens, Marcia Van Zeller, and Yvette Walker. I feel very lucky to have been at Curtin University during this time, surrounded by such exciting talent.

Is it too much like an Oscar speech to name the teachers who have helped me find out writing was something I wanted to do? Probably, but I'm doing it. To Barb Tobin, who I still want to impress. I showed her a poem when I was nine and she pointed to a line in it and told me I'd written a metaphor. I remember what it was but it was pretty average, to be honest, so let's pretend I don't. Mr. Robertson, who was so encouraging of me in primary school, and Ms. McCarthy, who gave me my first B in high school English, and consequently taught me not to get complacent. I still think about that B and get a little pissed. At university, Francesca Rendle-Short taught me about experimental writing, and Felicity Packard taught me to be sparing with my prose. And Jen Webb, while I was not taught by her, has always been so supportive of me and my work.

To the cafés in various states and countries that put up with me skulking about their spaces for hours and hours while I sipped at an endless pot of tea. Seriously, I spent ages in those places and barely spent a cent and they seemed to be cool with it. A particular thank-you to the girls at 50mL in Leederville. Your chai and warm hospitality was (and continues to be) so appreciated.

To Sarah Rigby and all at Hutchinson for taking a chance on an Australian writer they'd never heard of with such warmth and enthusiasm, and for giving *Lost & Found* a home in the UK.

Thanks to Craig Silvey, who took time out of his much more important life to give me some encouragement, and who pointed me in the direction of Benython Oldfield from Zeitgeist Media Group Literary Agency, whom I must also thank, as well as his European counterpart, Sharon Galant, and their North

American co-agent from Foundry Literary & Media Agency, Stéphanie Abou. Thank you all for general awesomeness, and for helping Millie, Karl, and Agatha find their way in the big, wide world.

I decided I'd like to make a book trailer for *Lost & Found* and mentioned it to a few talented people I know. They were pretty enthusiastic about it and three weeks later – without any prodding from me – it was done. I didn't expect that to happen. Thank you to my glorious sister-in-law, Tara Coady, for her art, patience, and careful video production; to musical wunderkind Bensen Thomas for making me a whole song; to the brilliant Matilda Griffiths for being the most perfect Millie Bird; and to the too-wonderful-for-words Todd Griffiths for his late-night audio-production efforts and permission to borrow his daughter's voice, even though she had to say "poop."

I really, really need to thank the ladies at Beaufort Street Books and Torquay Books. They let me work at their shops, and give me a pretty mental amount of support. My two bosses – Jane Seaton and Rosemary Featherston – work so hard for this industry for little glory and they make me feel proud to be a part of it. Let's be kind to booksellers and make sure they stick around.

There are people who have shared their grief with me and who aren't scared when I share mine, and I believe this to be a wonderful thing. I reckon grief can be lighter if there is sharing and listening. I've done this with strangers and acquaintances and customers and friends and family members, but I must thank particularly Jodi Ladhams, Jeremy Hoare, and Anna Hueppauff, whose intimate grief I have been privy to, and whose strength I am in awe of. This book is for Ruby, Cedric, Elli, and Kaiser, too. I'd also like to thank Chris Donahoe, whose emotional support during the early stages of this project (and my own grief) was so important.

Thanks, also, to my grandparents, Ken and Lorna Davis, and Ted and Jean Newton, for your stories and time and care. In your different ways you helped me understand that old people weren't always old. A particular thank-you to Nanna Jean, who is still plugging away at ninety years of age, even though she thinks my name is Judy, and that I'm forty-five.

And then there are the people who are just there, all the time, even when they're not. I'm lookin' at YOU, family, particularly: Mum, Dad, Rhett, and Ben. I am who I am, and do what I do, because of all of you.

But mostly, of course, to Mum: thank you.

This thing (writing a book, being alive) doesn't feel quite right without you.

relearning the world

an article by brooke davis

The first dead body I saw was my mother's. This wasn't as dramatic as it sounds – I was at the place where you expected to see dead bodies, and I knew it was going to happen – but it was dramatic enough for me. It was a small room, her coffin propped up in the middle, flowers strategically placed in all corners of the room. Her eyes were closed, white satin framing her body and climbing her skin. I remember thinking her wrinkles were missing. Someone else's makeup and her shirt buttoned right up to her neck and her downturned lips (I'd never seen her lips do that). Her body devoid of all the lumps and folds and lines I'd known. The mood lighting too; how it all formed some sort of grotesque retail display.

That word: *grief*. It is a word I never needed, until I did, and then it wasn't enough. Like Millie, and a lot of Western children I suspect, my Very First Dead Thing was Bree, our family dog. I was away at the time and never saw her body. I have never felt connected to that undulation in the ground beyond Nan's lemon tree. There was Francesca, a loud and toothy friend I had when we lived in America. We were back in Australia when my parents led me into my room and closed the door behind them. "Her heart stopped," Mum said, and cried. I waited till they left the room and cried too. I don't know where I learned to be ashamed to cry. In my journal, I wrote, "When someone dies, it feels like you have pins and needles." I have no idea what this means, and I doubt I did then either, but I do remember trying to manufacture sadness; I do remember the guilt for not feeling enough. I was nine, I already had a new best friend, and Francesca had become this vague blob in my head that didn't mean anything anymore.

I read Katherine Paterson's *Bridge to Terabithia* over and over again, and cried every time Leslie died. I'm not sure why I so enthusiastically subjected myself to this feeling. As I grew older, I cried watching the news of people dying in faraway places. Three of my grandparents died, in that inevitable way the elderly must. I cried at their funerals, and at other times, behind doors and under covers, but I was crying for them, and not for me; crying at old age, at the way life is, at how things don't stay the same.

There was distance, always, between me and all this grief:

by species, geography, age, comprehension; by medium of representation.

But then, on January 27, 2006, my mum on the front page of the newspaper for all the wrong reasons: "Freak Gate Crush Death" in capitals. Letters so thick, so black; death so close it could have been me.

Grief is a word that has been forced on me, but one that I have chosen to bring closer to me. Professor Robert Neimeyer, with a nod to Freud, says that, for most of the twentieth century in Western culture, bereavement was understood "as a process of 'letting go' of one's attachment to the deceased person, 'moving on' with one's life, and gradually 'recovering' from the depression occasioned by the loss so as to permit a return to 'normal' behavior." Here, grief is an experience that you endure, and then it ends. As the literature on loss grew, he says, "this modern conceptualization of grief was gradually expanded to detail . . . both 'complicated' and 'uncomplicated' bereavement, and the presumed stages through which it would be 'resolved.'" These stages, or stage models as they are commonly referred to in the literature – this idea that grief could be universally experienced as unfolding in a specific sequence of phases – was popularized in the 1970s by Elisabeth Kübler-Ross's work on death and dying. She described Denial and Isolation, Anger, Bargaining, Depression, and Acceptance as the emotions one experienced when diagnosed with a terminal illness. Models like this "began to dominate the Western cultural perspective on bereavement" because, Neimeyer says, they were "associated with recovery" from grief, or closure on grief, offering "an apparently authoritative road map through the turbulent emotional terrain" of grief.

It makes sense to me, to want to classify grief in this neat way, because don't we like order? Isn't that why we get so much pleasure out of narrative? But as we move further into the twenty-first century, we start to see a backlash against this neat compartmentalization of the experience of grief; the emergence of a "new wave," one that embraces the disorder of grief. Pat Jalland, author of *Australian Ways of Death: Changing Ways of Grieving in Twentieth-Century Australia*, says that psychologists have "modified this early theoretical 'stage' model," arguing that "the final stage of 'acceptance' of death had often been interpreted too rigidly to mean 'closure' or detachment from the dead person." The philosopher Thomas Attig, another contributor to this "new wave," says, "Grieving is nearly always complicated—'nearly' because sometimes we grieve moderately for someone who was not particularly close . . . nearly 'always' because, ordinarily, grieving involves nothing less than relearning the world of our experience."

"Relearning the world" began for me at the Ho Chi Minh City Airport in Vietnam, when my dad's voice said over the phone, "Now, you're going to get some very bad news here, so you have to prepare yourself." And then the blur that followed: the lady at the check-in counter who said, so very bluntly,

"What is the matter with you?" And my discovery that, despite all my best efforts and expectations, I couldn't say, "I just found out my mum died," without crying. The man sitting next to me on the plane who said, "Have a cold, do you?" The CNN ad that kept appearing on the screen: "By the time this plane lands, the world will be a different place." The little boy who gave his mum hell on the plane ride, and how much it startled me to realise that from now on I would notice mothers and their children. The circle of family that I fell into when I arrived at Melbourne Airport; how seeing them made it suddenly very real. The front page of the newspaper with a picture of my mum's car and that horrifying white sheet next to it. Waking up that first morning without Mum and having to remember, again. The physicality of it, how my body was very much involved in this, how it was not just something of the mind. Having breakfast every morning with my brothers on the verandah of my mother's house, taking time to share our dreams or nightmares, to cry, to laugh, to be silent together; I believe this is what saved me. Writing messages to Mum in the sand at the beach with my brothers on her birthday. We wrote them in really big letters, out of some sort of hope or instinct. How I constantly felt like someone else was speaking out of my mouth. How we didn't know who to ask about getting rid of the pollen stains on the carpet. Finding a loving, adjective-heavy letter from me in among Mum's things; the great, sobbing relief and the words I said: "She knew." How the funeral came and went, and the flowers stopped coming, the casseroles stopped appearing, and no one visited anymore, and the quietness of it all was so loud.

Later, I would come across a line from Yeats in an Irish museum that would remind me of these early moments: "All changed, changed utterly: A terrible beauty is born."

In the beginning, my grief made the world a television screen. It came upon me suddenly, this feeling that I was outside of everything and looking in; that I was somehow invisible to the people in the television. It gave me the most curious feeling of infallibility, and utter vulnerability. The glass eventually – shattered? Smashed? Broke? There was nothing that dramatic, that clear; nothing that metaphorically neat. It was more like a fading away; a barely perceptible slinking back onto the other side of the screen.

There were other things to notice: things I could do, and couldn't do. There wasn't anyone who specifically informed me of these social limitations, it was just instinct. I wasn't supposed to cry in the middle of the supermarket. I wasn't supposed to say that my mum had *died* or was *dead*; I had to use phrases like *passed away* or *gone*. It seemed incredibly at odds with the way my mum's death was so brutally and succinctly worded in the newspaper – "Freak Gate Crush Death" – as if there were different rules for the words you say and the words you write. I wasn't supposed to enjoy driving around in the car Mum died in. I love, and still love, how close she was when I drove it. I wasn't supposed to request a copy of the autopsy report and pore over it. I wasn't supposed to ask to talk to the police about what happened. When the police officer showed me the statement from the man who had tried to save my mum, and photos of the scene of the accident, he said, with a kind of wide-eyed breathlessness, "I haven't included the other photos." I realised two things at this point: that photos of my mum, dead, existed somewhere; and that this man was frightened I would ask to see them. I could see all these Not-Supposed-Tos on the faces of people around me; people who were overwhelmingly kind and supportive, but who told me with a flicker of their eyes that there were things I simply could not do.

Part of my own process of "relearning the world" was writing my own grief. Tammy Clewell, in "*Consolation Refused: Virginia Woolf, the Great War, and Modernist Mourning*," says this is something that Virginia Woolf did in much of her writing. "Her textual practice of endless mourning," Clewell writes, "compels us to refuse consolation, sustain grief, and accept the responsibility of the difficult task of remembering." Clewell also posits that it is precisely this "persistent attachment to the lost object" that represents this approach to grief "not as a debilitating form of melancholia, but as a creative and productive engagement with the past." Woolf, Clewell says, recognised that her "novels might step in and provide a kind of shared mourning practice . . . for a culture bereft of viable expressions of grief . . . by creating a social space and shared language for grief."

What does this all mean for me, as a grieving person, writing a novel about grief? That I am "allowed" to keep my mum close and "sustain grief"? That this may even help my creative practice? (Is this the "terrible beauty" that Yeats was talking about?) That I can use the writing of a novel as a space to grieve at a time when social expectations make these spaces difficult to find? Perhaps, but there is something more to this than just my own grief. Louise DeSalvo says:

> *Woolf needed an audience to listen to the testimony she made about her life, to witness and validate the meaning she had made of her experience, to let her know that she was not alone. Only with an audience, Woolf believed, can we transcend the limits of the self, can we understand our life's true meaning. As Maya Angelou has said, through writing, the "I" becomes "we."*

As I wrote *Lost & Found*, I became increasingly aware that it was, like Clewell says, "creating a social space and shared language for grief." Not, of course, in the way Clewell intends when referring to Woolf – as a revolutionary figure in the field of grief in Western culture – but in a much smaller way that is about me, and the connections I am able to make with other people. In social settings, a person will begin a conversation with the ritual question, "What is your novel about?" and end up relaying long, sometimes teary, stories about their own experiences of grief. We begin as two "I's," and then become "we." It seems we want to speak grief, but we don't know how. Or perhaps we don't know when. In writing this novel, I've come to realise how speakable grief really is; that, perhaps, all I needed to do was speak it in the first place.

Nearing the end of his memoir, *A Grief Observed*, C. S. Lewis talks about the endlessness of the grief he felt at the death of his wife:

> *I thought I could describe a state; make a map of sorrow. Sorrow, however, turns out to be not a state but a process. It needs not a map but a history, and if I don't stop writing that history at some quite arbitrary point, there's no reason why I should ever stop. There is something new to be chronicled every day.*

Grief is not neat like a narrative arc. It does not end; it is not "resolved." It does not follow a checklist of emotions from beginning to end. It is not one thing, or the other thing; it is lots of things. And to say that binaries and stage models are reductive approaches to the grief process is not new; there is, in fact, an entire body of theory devoted to this way of thinking. But the process of grief is new to me, and it is new to me every day. Every day I learn something about grief, from myself, from my writing, from others, from everything around me.

As I drive my mum's car around Perth, "relearning the

world of [my] experience," I will move back and forth and up and down and over and sideways through different stages of grief for as long as I'm allowed to be here. I am beginning to understand that grief is now, simply, a part of everything I do, everything I say, everything I write. Everything I am.

This is a shortened version of a longer article by the author published in 2012 by TEXT: Journal of Writing and Writing Courses. *The article in its entirety – as well as more comprehensive bibliographic information – can be found here: www.textjournal.com.au/oct12/davis.htm*

bibliography

Attig, Thomas. "Relearning the World: Making and Finding Meanings." In *Meaning Reconstruction & the Experience of Loss*, edited by Robert A. Neimeyer. Washington, DC: American Psychological Association, 2002.

Clewell, Tammy. *Mourning, Modernism, Postmodernism*. London: Palgrave Macmillan, 2009.

———. "Consolation Refused: Virginia Woolf, the Great War, and Modernist Mourning." *Modern Fiction Studies* 50:1, 2004.

DeSalvo, Louise. *Writing as a Way of Healing: How Telling Stories Transforms Our Lives*. London: The Women's Press Ltd., 1999.

Hagman, George. "Beyond Decathexis: Toward a New Psychoanalytic Understanding and Treatment of Mourning." In *Meaning Reconstruction & the Experience of Loss*, edited by Robert A. Neimeyer. Washington, DC: American Psychological Association, 2002.

Jalland, Pat. *Changing Ways of Death in Twentieth-Century Australia:*

War, Medicine and the Funeral Business. Sydney: UNSW Press, 2006.

Kübler-Ross, Elisabeth. *On Death and Dying*. New York: Scribner, 2003.

Lewis, C. S. *A Grief Observed*. London: Faber and Faber, 1966.

Neimeyer, Robert A., ed. *Meaning Reconstruction & the Experience of Loss*. Washington, DC: American Psychological Association, 2002.

Paterson, Katherine. *Bridge to Terabithia*. New York: Harper Trophy, 1987.